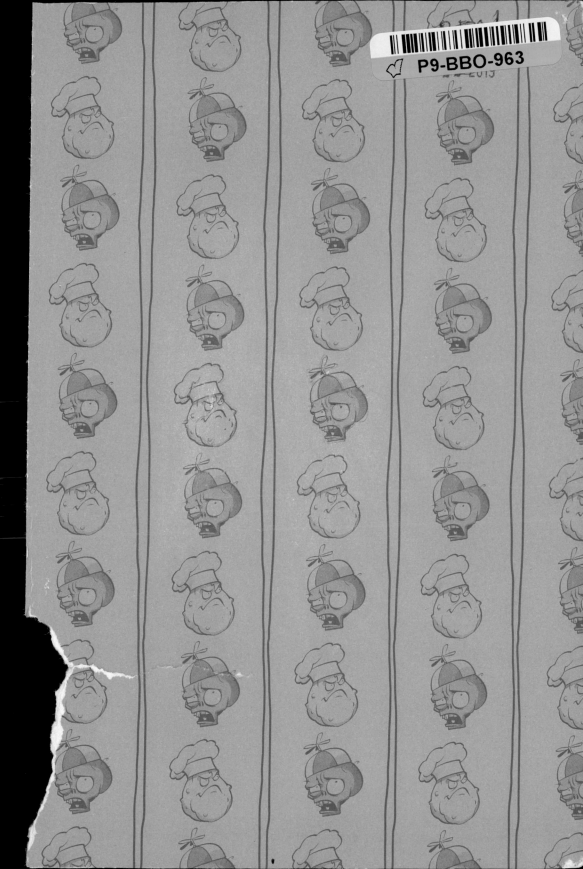

PLANTS VS. ZOMBIES™

LAWN OF DOOM

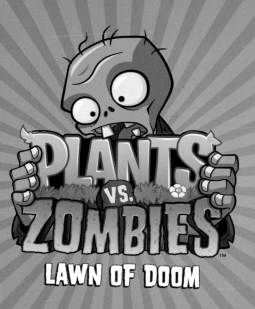

Written by **PAUL TOBIN**

Art by **RON CHAN**

Colors by **MATT J. RAINWATER**

Letters by **STEVE DUTRO**

Cover by **RON CHAN**

DARK HORSE BOOKS

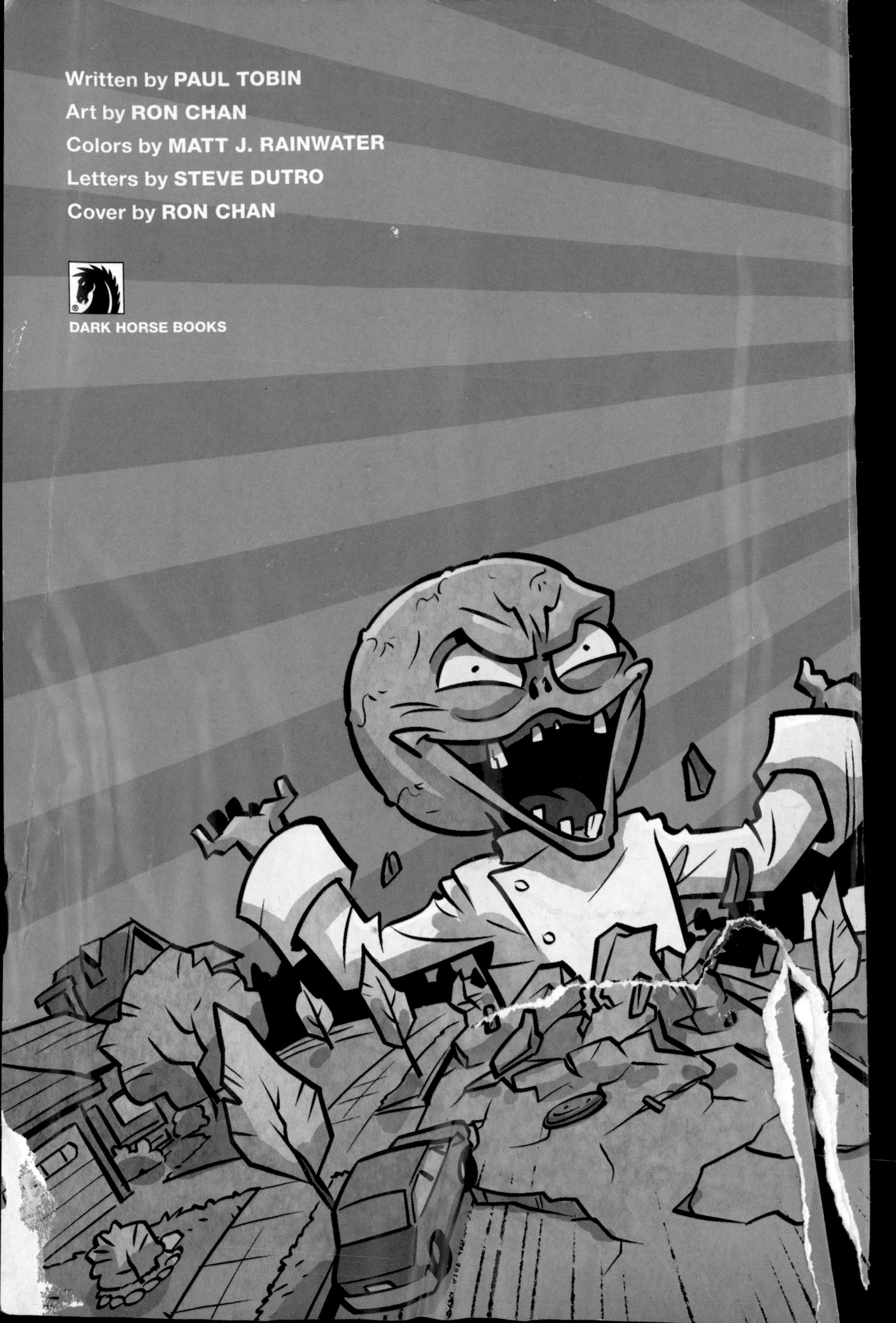

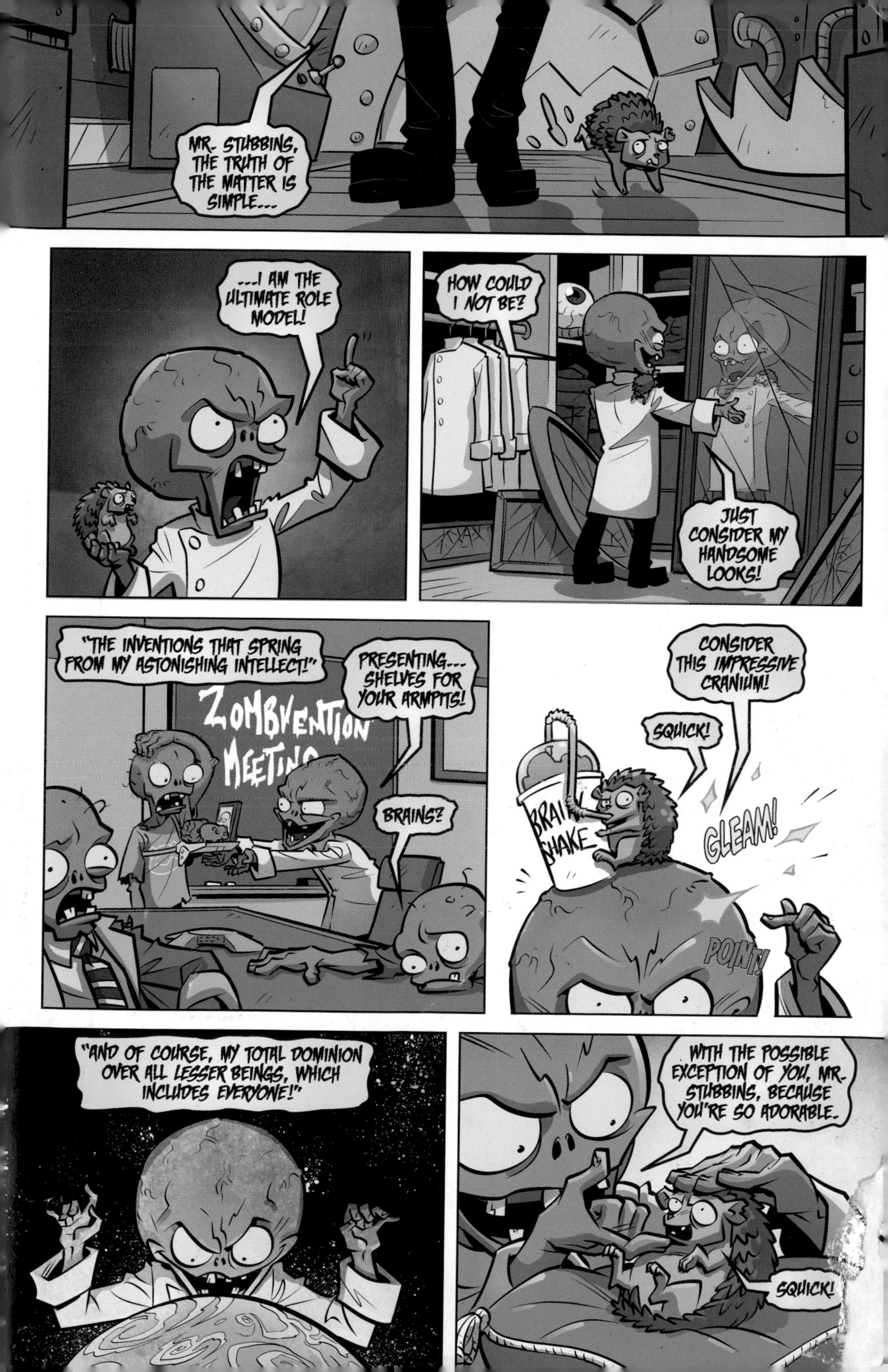
MR. STUBBINS, THE TRUTH OF THE MATTER IS SIMPLE...
...I AM THE ULTIMATE ROLE MODEL!
HOW COULD I NOT BE?
JUST CONSIDER MY HANDSOME LOOKS!
"THE INVENTIONS THAT SPRING FROM MY ASTONISHING INTELLECT!"
ZOMBVENTION MEETING
PRESENTING... SHELVES FOR YOUR ARMPITS!
BRAINS?
CONSIDER THIS IMPRESSIVE CRANIUM!
SQUICK!
BRAIN SHAKE
GLEAM!
POINT!
"AND OF COURSE, MY TOTAL DOMINION OVER ALL LESSER BEINGS, WHICH INCLUDES EVERYONE!"
WITH THE POSSIBLE EXCEPTION OF YOU, MR. STUBBINS, BECAUSE YOU'RE SO ADORABLE.
SQUICK!

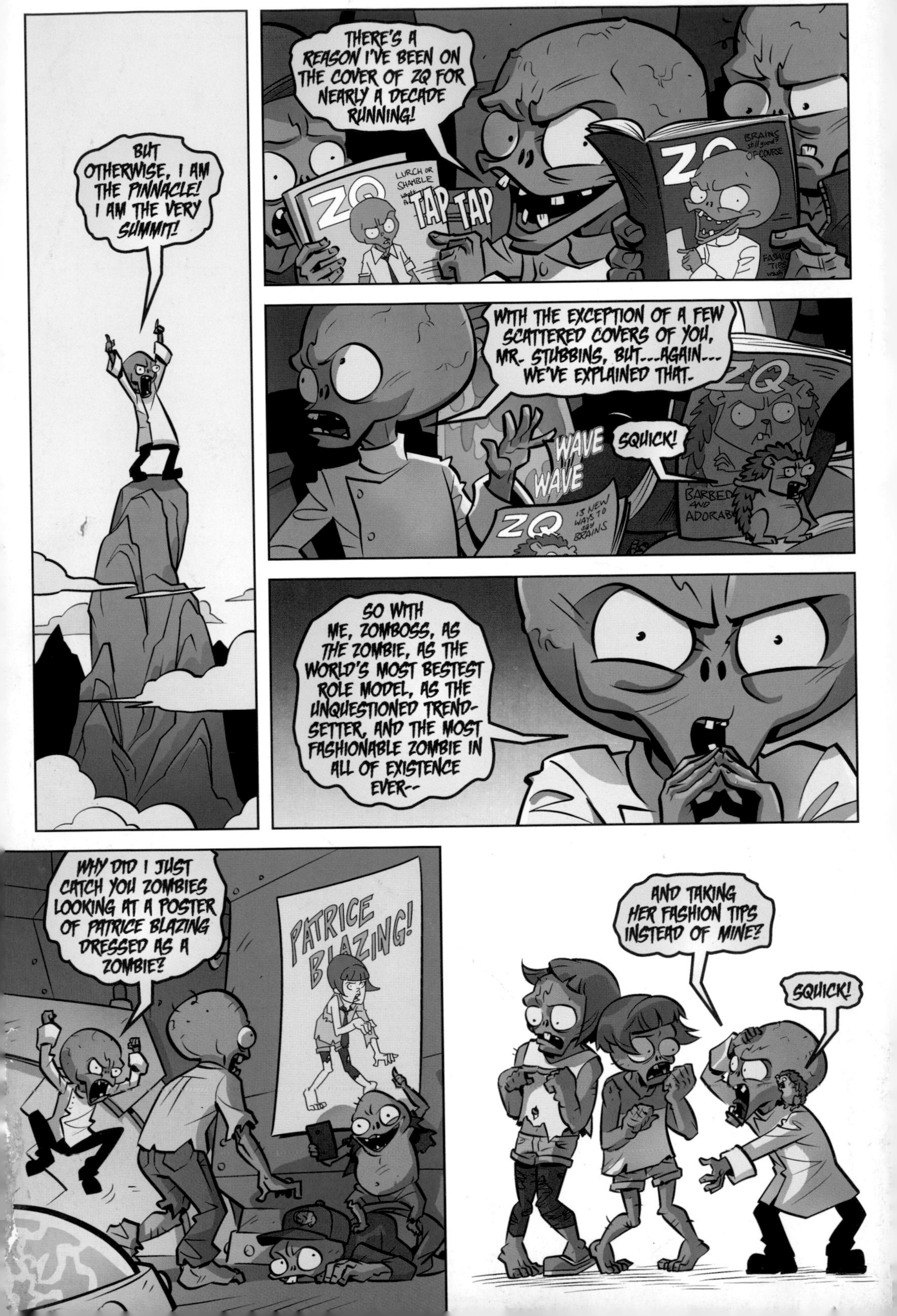
THERE'S A REASON I'VE BEEN ON THE COVER OF ZQ FOR NEARLY A DECADE RUNNING!
ZQ
LURCH OR SHAMBLE
TAP TAP
ZQ
BRAINS still good? OF COURSE
WITH THE EXCEPTION OF A FEW SCATTERED COVERS OF YOU, MR. STUBBINS, BUT...AGAIN... WE'VE EXPLAINED THAT.
WAVE WAVE
SQUICK!
ZQ
ZQ
13 NEW WAYS TO say BRAINS
BUT OTHERWISE, I AM THE PINNACLE! I AM THE VERY SUMMIT!
SO WITH ME, ZOMBOSS, AS THE ZOMBIE, AS THE WORLD'S MOST BESTEST ROLE MODEL, AS THE UNQUESTIONED TREND-SETTER, AND THE MOST FASHIONABLE ZOMBIE IN ALL OF EXISTENCE EVER--
WHY DID I JUST CATCH YOU ZOMBIES LOOKING AT A POSTER OF PATRICE BLAZING DRESSED AS A ZOMBIE?
PATRICE BLAZING!
AND TAKING HER FASHION TIPS INSTEAD OF MINE?
SQUICK!

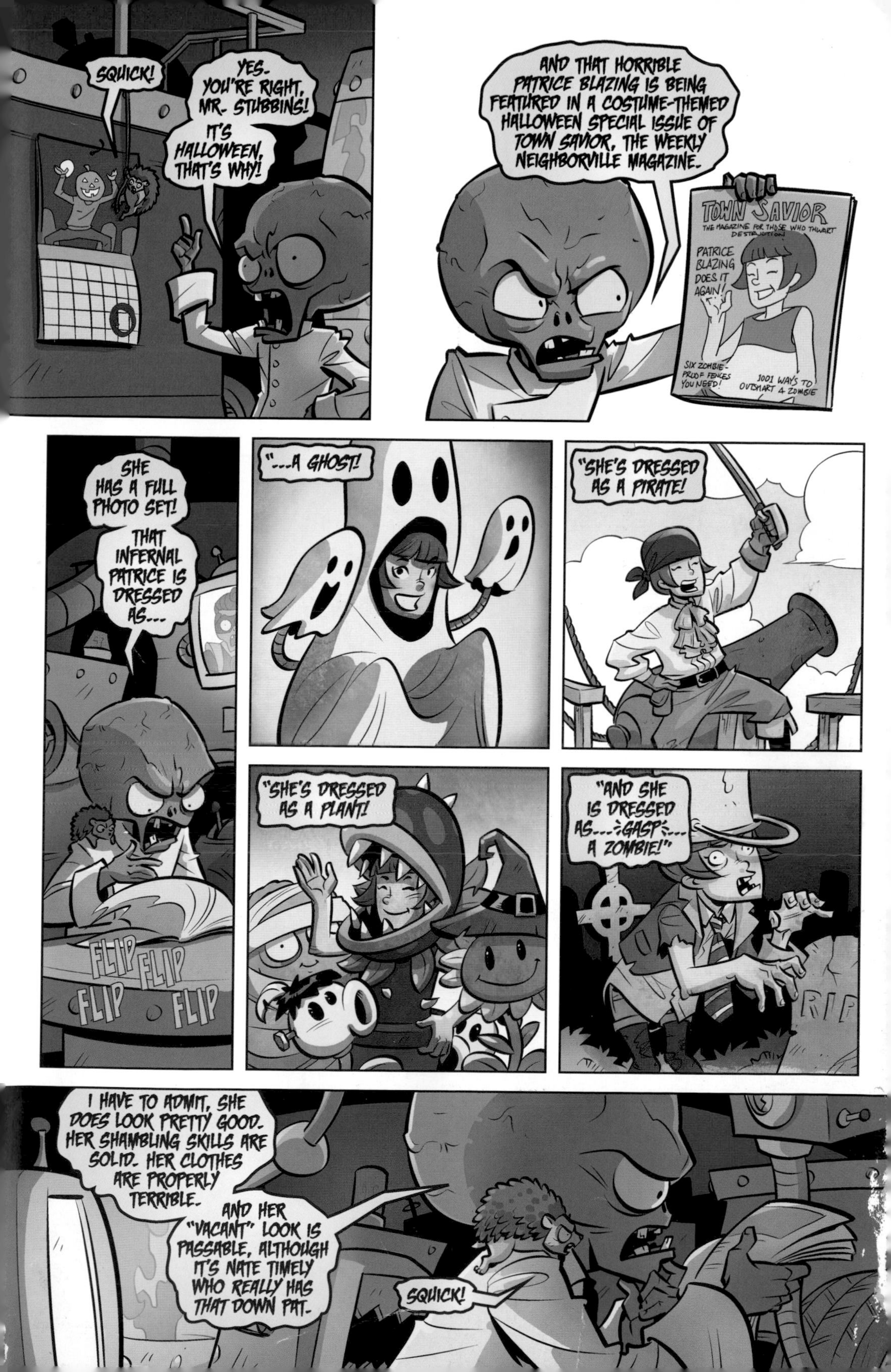
SQUICK!
YES. YOU'RE RIGHT, MR. STUBBINS!
IT'S HALLOWEEN, THAT'S WHY!
AND THAT HORRIBLE PATRICE BLAZING IS BEING FEATURED IN A COSTUME-THEMED HALLOWEEN SPECIAL ISSUE OF TOWN SAVIOR, THE WEEKLY NEIGHBORVILLE MAGAZINE.
TOWN SAVIOR
THE MAGAZINE FOR THOSE WHO THWART DESTRUCTION!
PATRICE BLAZING DOES IT AGAIN!
SIX ZOMBIE-PROOF FENCES YOU NEED!
1001 WAYS TO OUTSMART A ZOMBIE
SHE HAS A FULL PHOTO SET!
THAT INFERNAL PATRICE IS DRESSED AS...
FLIP FLIP FLIP FLIP
"...A GHOST!
"SHE'S DRESSED AS A PIRATE!
"SHE'S DRESSED AS A PLANT!
"AND SHE IS DRESSED AS... GASP... A ZOMBIE!"
RIP
I HAVE TO ADMIT, SHE DOES LOOK PRETTY GOOD. HER SHAMBLING SKILLS ARE SOLID. HER CLOTHES ARE PROPERLY TERRIBLE.
AND HER "VACANT" LOOK IS PASSABLE, ALTHOUGH IT'S NATE TIMELY WHO REALLY HAS THAT DOWN PAT.
SQUICK!

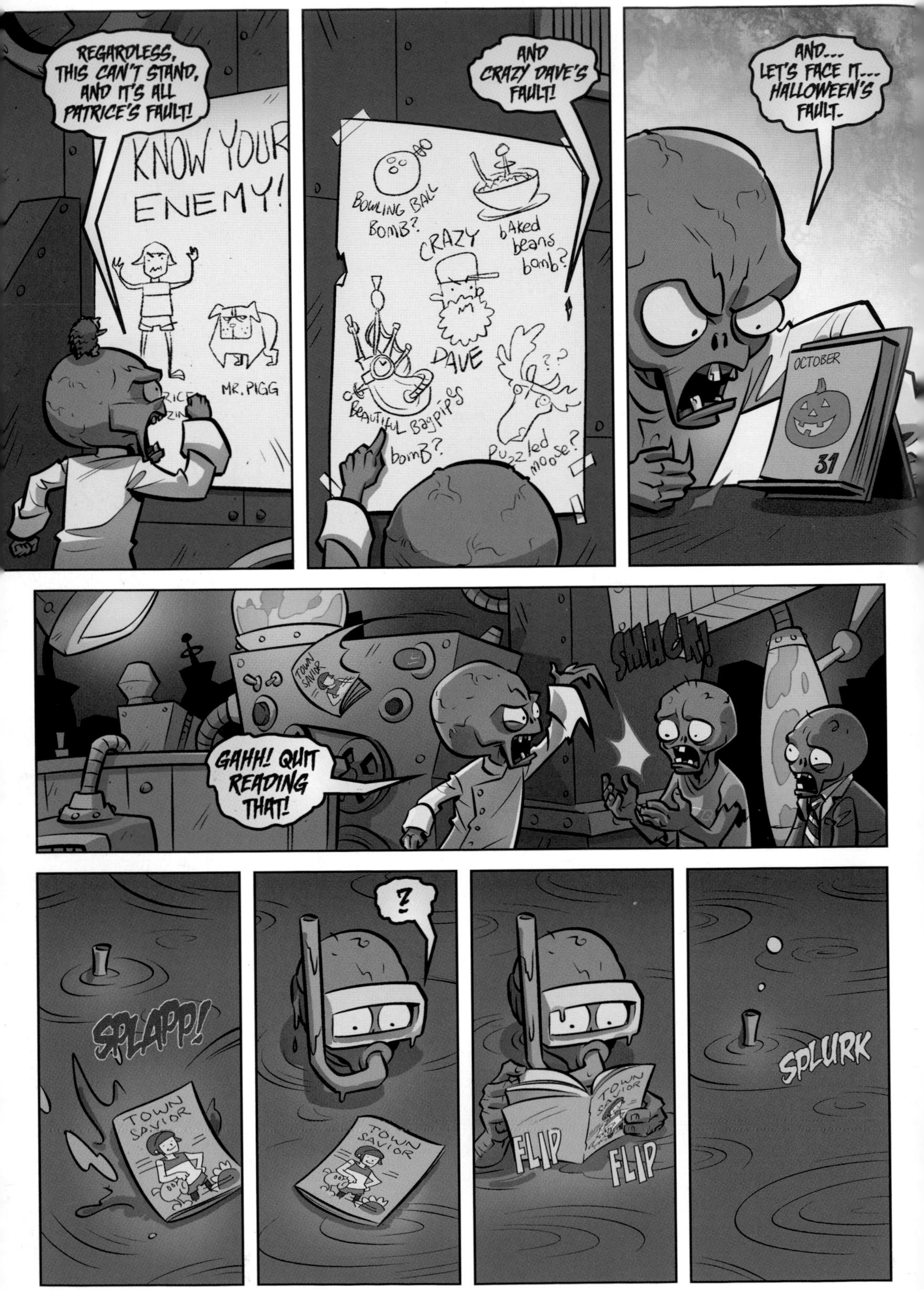
REGARDLESS, THIS CAN'T STAND, AND IT'S ALL PATRICE'S FAULT!
KNOW YOUR ENEMY!
MR. PIGG
AND CRAZY DAVE'S FAULT!
BOWLING BALL BOMB?
baked beans bomb?
CRAZY DAVE
BEAUTIFUL Bagpipes bomB?
Puzzled moose?
AND... LET'S FACE IT... HALLOWEEN'S FAULT.
OCTOBER
31
TOWN SAVIOR
SMACK!
GAHH! QUIT READING THAT!
SPLAPP!
TOWN SAVIOR
TOWN SAVIOR
?
TOWN SAVIOR
FLIP
FLIP
SPLURK

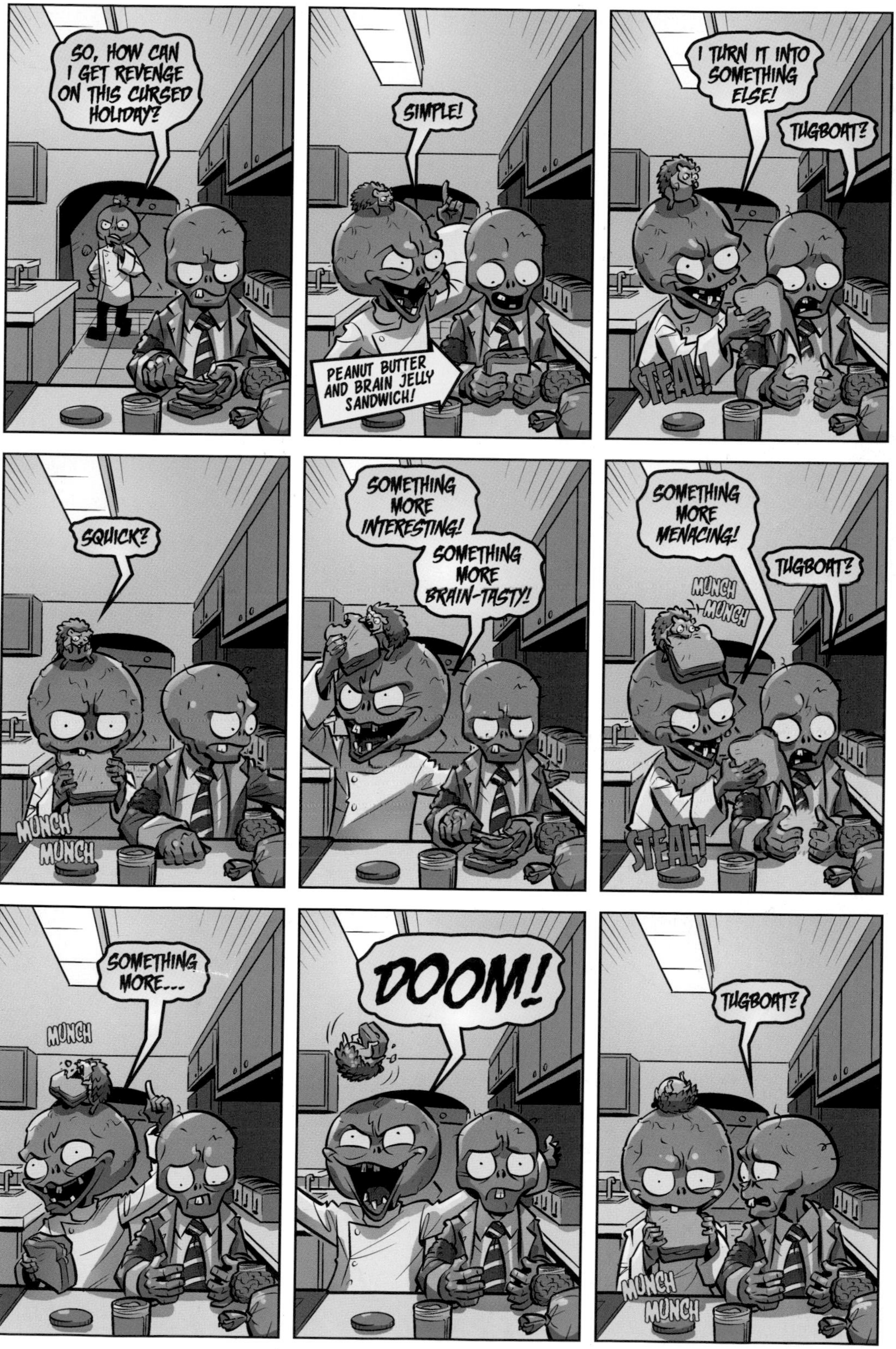
SO, HOW CAN I GET REVENGE ON THIS CURSED HOLIDAY?
SIMPLE!
PEANUT BUTTER AND BRAIN JELLY SANDWICH!
I TURN IT INTO SOMETHING ELSE!
TUGBOAT?
STEAL!
SQUICK?
MUNCH MUNCH
SOMETHING MORE INTERESTING!
SOMETHING MORE BRAIN-TASTY!
SOMETHING MORE MENACING!
MUNCH MUNCH
TUGBOAT?
STEAL!
SOMETHING MORE...
MUNCH
DOOM!
TUGBOAT?
MUNCH MUNCH

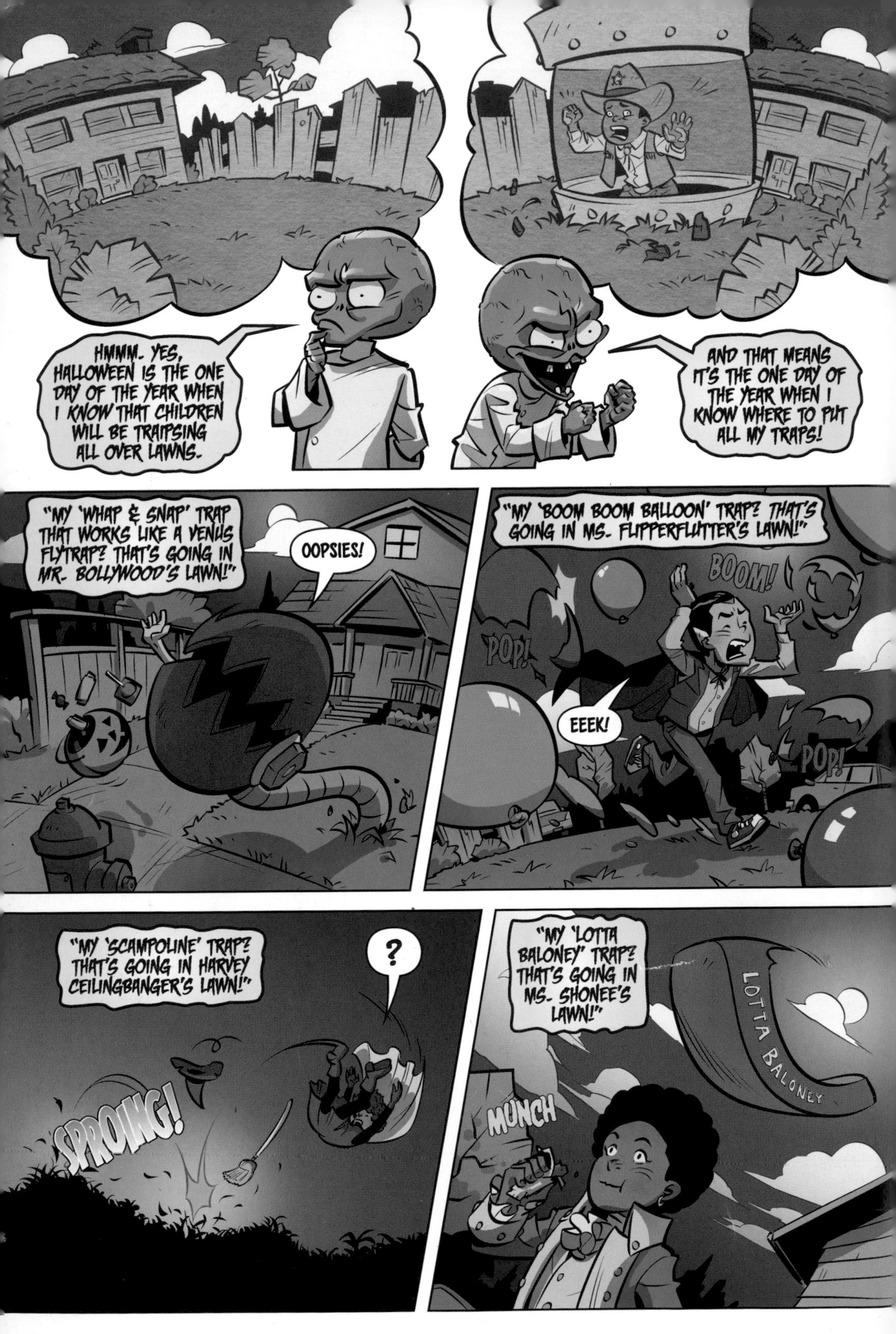
HMMM. YES, HALLOWEEN IS THE ONE DAY OF THE YEAR WHEN I KNOW THAT CHILDREN WILL BE TRAIPSING ALL OVER LAWNS.
AND THAT MEANS IT'S THE ONE DAY OF THE YEAR WHEN I KNOW WHERE TO PUT ALL MY TRAPS!
"MY 'WHAP & SNAP' TRAP THAT WORKS LIKE A VENUS FLYTRAP? THAT'S GOING IN MR. BOLLYWOOD'S LAWN!"
OOPSIES!
"MY 'BOOM BOOM BALLOON' TRAP? THAT'S GOING IN MS. FLIPPERFLUTTER'S LAWN!"
BOOM!
POP!
EEEK!
POP!
"MY 'SCAMPOLINE' TRAP? THAT'S GOING IN HARVEY CEILINGBANGER'S LAWN!"
?
SPROING!
"MY 'LOTTA BALONEY' TRAP? THAT'S GOING IN MS. SHONEE'S LAWN!"
LOTTA BALONEY
MUNCH

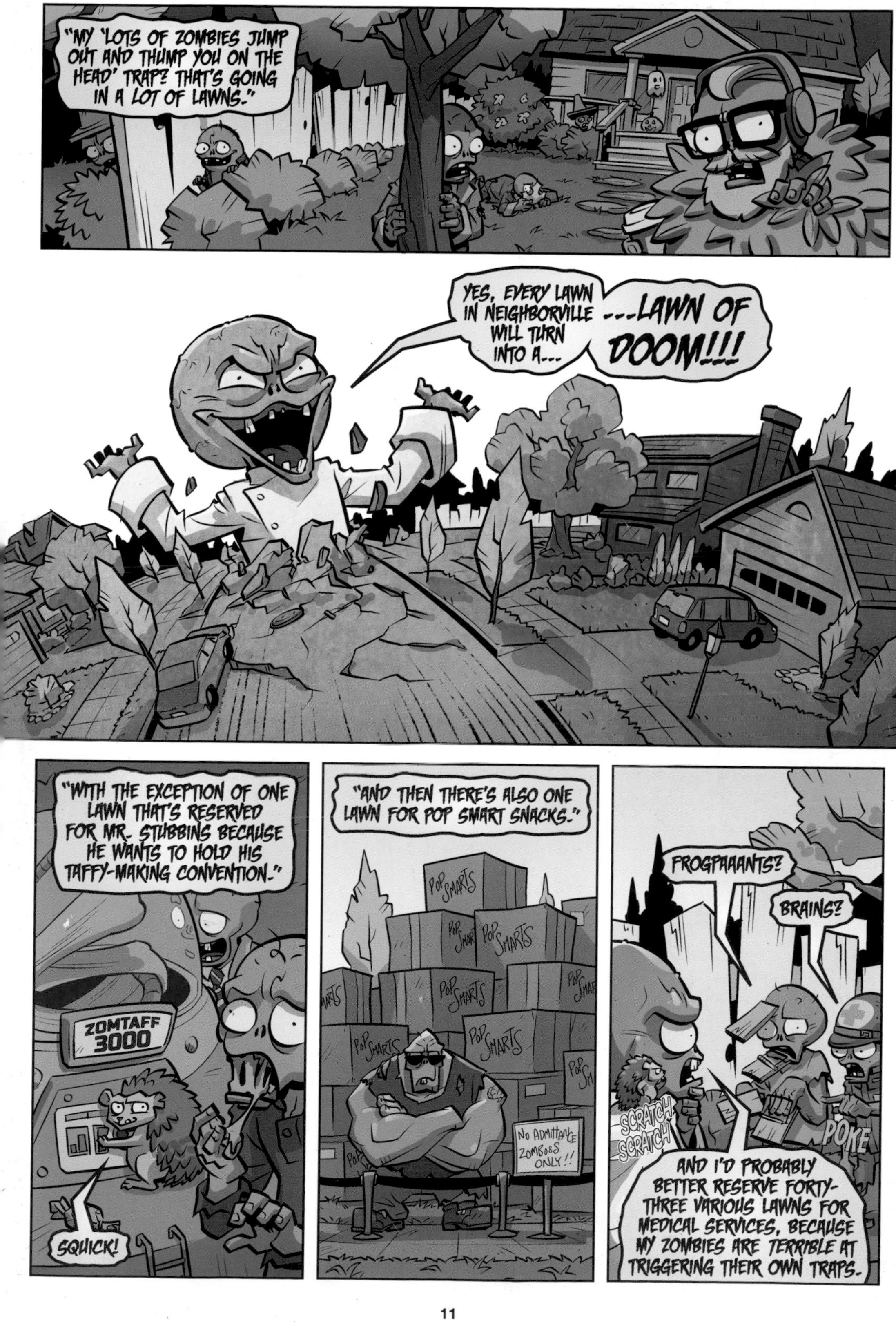
"MY 'LOTS OF ZOMBIES JUMP OUT AND THUMP YOU ON THE HEAD' TRAP? THAT'S GOING IN A LOT OF LAWNS."
YES, EVERY LAWN IN NEIGHBORVILLE WILL TURN INTO A...
...LAWN OF DOOM!!!
"WITH THE EXCEPTION OF ONE LAWN THAT'S RESERVED FOR MR. STUBBINS BECAUSE HE WANTS TO HOLD HIS TAFFY-MAKING CONVENTION."
ZOMTAFF 3000
SQUICK!
"AND THEN THERE'S ALSO ONE LAWN FOR POP SMART SNACKS."
POP SMARTS
NO ADMITTANCE ZOMBOSS ONLY!!
FROGPAAANTS?
BRAINS?
SCRATCH SCRATCH
POKE
AND I'D PROBABLY BETTER RESERVE FORTY-THREE VARIOUS LAWNS FOR MEDICAL SERVICES, BECAUSE MY ZOMBIES ARE TERRIBLE AT TRIGGERING THEIR OWN TRAPS.

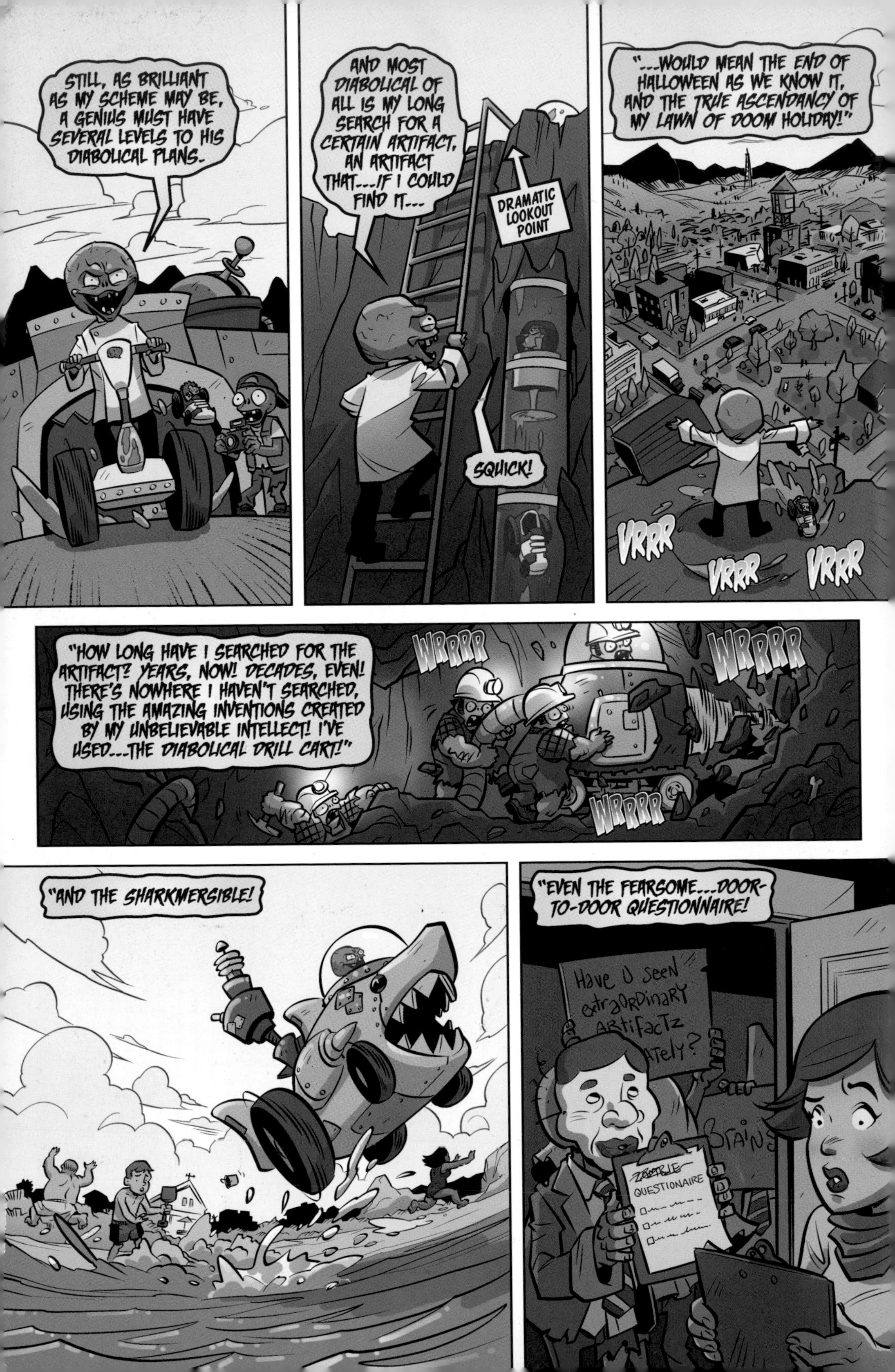
STILL, AS BRILLIANT AS MY SCHEME MAY BE, A GENIUS MUST HAVE SEVERAL LEVELS TO HIS DIABOLICAL PLANS.
AND MOST DIABOLICAL OF ALL IS MY LONG SEARCH FOR A CERTAIN ARTIFACT, AN ARTIFACT THAT...IF I COULD FIND IT...
DRAMATIC LOOKOUT POINT
SQUICK!
"...WOULD MEAN THE END OF HALLOWEEN AS WE KNOW IT, AND THE TRUE ASCENDANCY OF MY LAWN OF DOOM HOLIDAY!"
VRRR
VRRR
VRRR
"HOW LONG HAVE I SEARCHED FOR THE ARTIFACT? YEARS, NOW! DECADES, EVEN! THERE'S NOWHERE I HAVEN'T SEARCHED, USING THE AMAZING INVENTIONS CREATED BY MY UNBELIEVABLE INTELLECT! I'VE USED...THE DIABOLICAL DRILL CART!"
WRRRR
WRRRR
WRRRR
"AND THE SHARKMERSIBLE!
"EVEN THE FEARSOME...DOOR-TO-DOOR QUESTIONNAIRE!
Have U seen extraordinary Artifactz lately?
Brains
QUESTIONAIRE

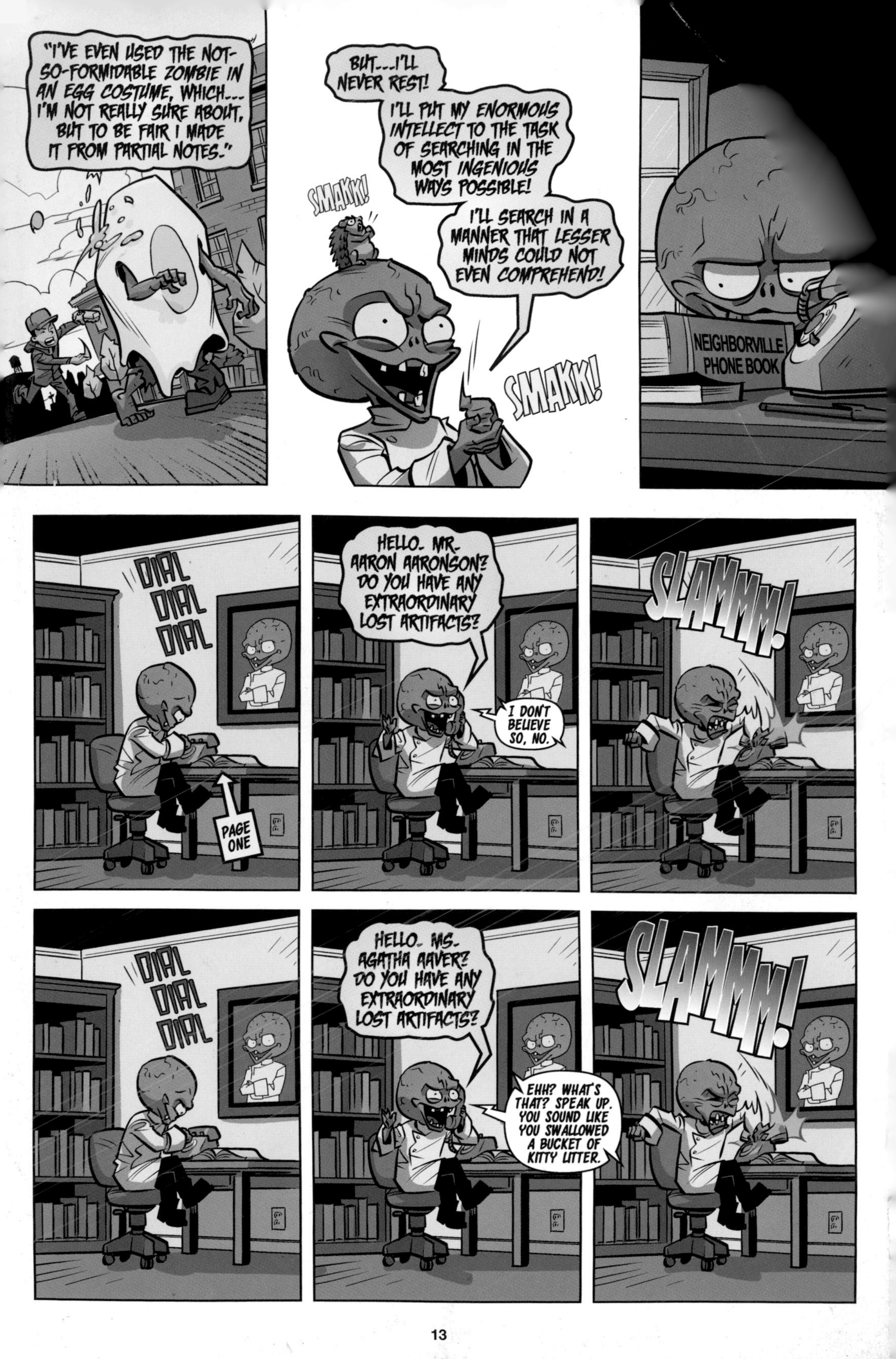

"I'VE EVEN USED THE NOT-SO-FORMIDABLE ZOMBIE IN AN EGG COSTUME, WHICH... I'M NOT REALLY SURE ABOUT, BUT TO BE FAIR I MADE IT FROM PARTIAL NOTES."
BUT...I'LL NEVER REST!
I'LL PUT MY ENORMOUS INTELLECT TO THE TASK OF SEARCHING IN THE MOST INGENIOUS WAYS POSSIBLE!
SMAKK!
I'LL SEARCH IN A MANNER THAT LESSER MINDS COULD NOT EVEN COMPREHEND!
SMAKK!
NEIGHBORVILLE PHONE BOOK
DIAL DIAL DIAL
PAGE ONE
HELLO. MR. AARON AARONSON? DO YOU HAVE ANY EXTRAORDINARY LOST ARTIFACTS?
I DON'T BELIEVE SO, NO.
SLAMMM!
DIAL DIAL DIAL
HELLO. MS. AGATHA AAVER? DO YOU HAVE ANY EXTRAORDINARY LOST ARTIFACTS?
EHH? WHAT'S THAT? SPEAK UP. YOU SOUND LIKE YOU SWALLOWED A BUCKET OF KITTY LITTER.
SLAMMM!

MEANWHILE...

...RE ARE OU?

I'M IN INTENSIVE TRAINING!

THUMP THUMP

THUMP

DISCO PIZZA

GHHHHH!

TRAINING FOR WHAT?

IT'S HALLOWEEN! SO I'M TRYING TO GET IN WORLD-CLASS CANDY-EATING SHAPE AND BEAT MY OWN WORLD RECORD OF 284 CANDY PIECES EATEN BEFORE MOM STOPS ME!

WHAT HAVE YOU BEEN DOING?

I'M TEACHING THE PLANTS HOW TO FIT IN WITH REGULAR SOCIETY.

NOT GETTING ENOUGH SUN

THEY'RE DOING PRETTY WELL, EXCEPT FOR ASSORTED PROBLEMS WITH CATS.

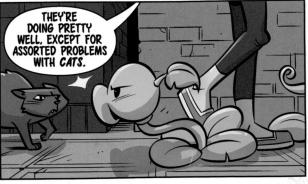

"THE CATS ARE JEALOUS BECAUSE OF HOW PEOPLE SO OFTEN PUT PLANTS ON WINDOWSILLS, MEANING THERE'S LOTS OF TERRITORIAL DISPUTES."

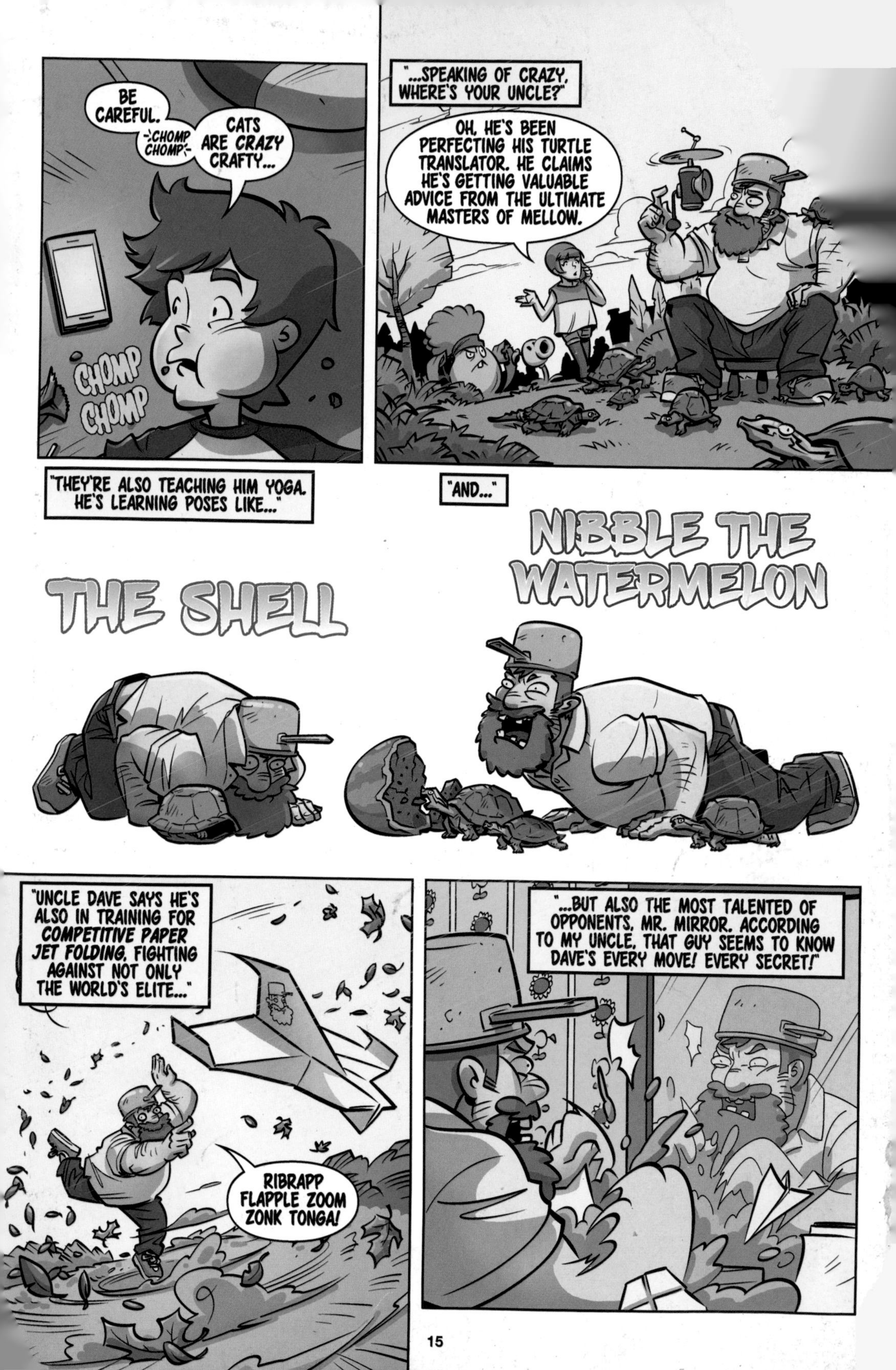
BE CAREFUL.
CHOMP CHOMP
CATS ARE CRAZY CRAFTY...
CHOMP CHOMP
"...SPEAKING OF CRAZY, WHERE'S YOUR UNCLE?"
OH, HE'S BEEN PERFECTING HIS TURTLE TRANSLATOR. HE CLAIMS HE'S GETTING VALUABLE ADVICE FROM THE ULTIMATE MASTERS OF MELLOW.
"THEY'RE ALSO TEACHING HIM YOGA. HE'S LEARNING POSES LIKE..."
THE SHELL
"AND..."
NIBBLE THE WATERMELON
"UNCLE DAVE SAYS HE'S ALSO IN TRAINING FOR COMPETITIVE PAPER JET FOLDING, FIGHTING AGAINST NOT ONLY THE WORLD'S ELITE..."
RIBRAPP FLAPPLE ZOOM ZONK TONGA!
"...BUT ALSO THE MOST TALENTED OF OPPONENTS, MR. MIRROR. ACCORDING TO MY UNCLE, THAT GUY SEEMS TO KNOW DAVE'S EVERY MOVE! EVERY SECRET!"

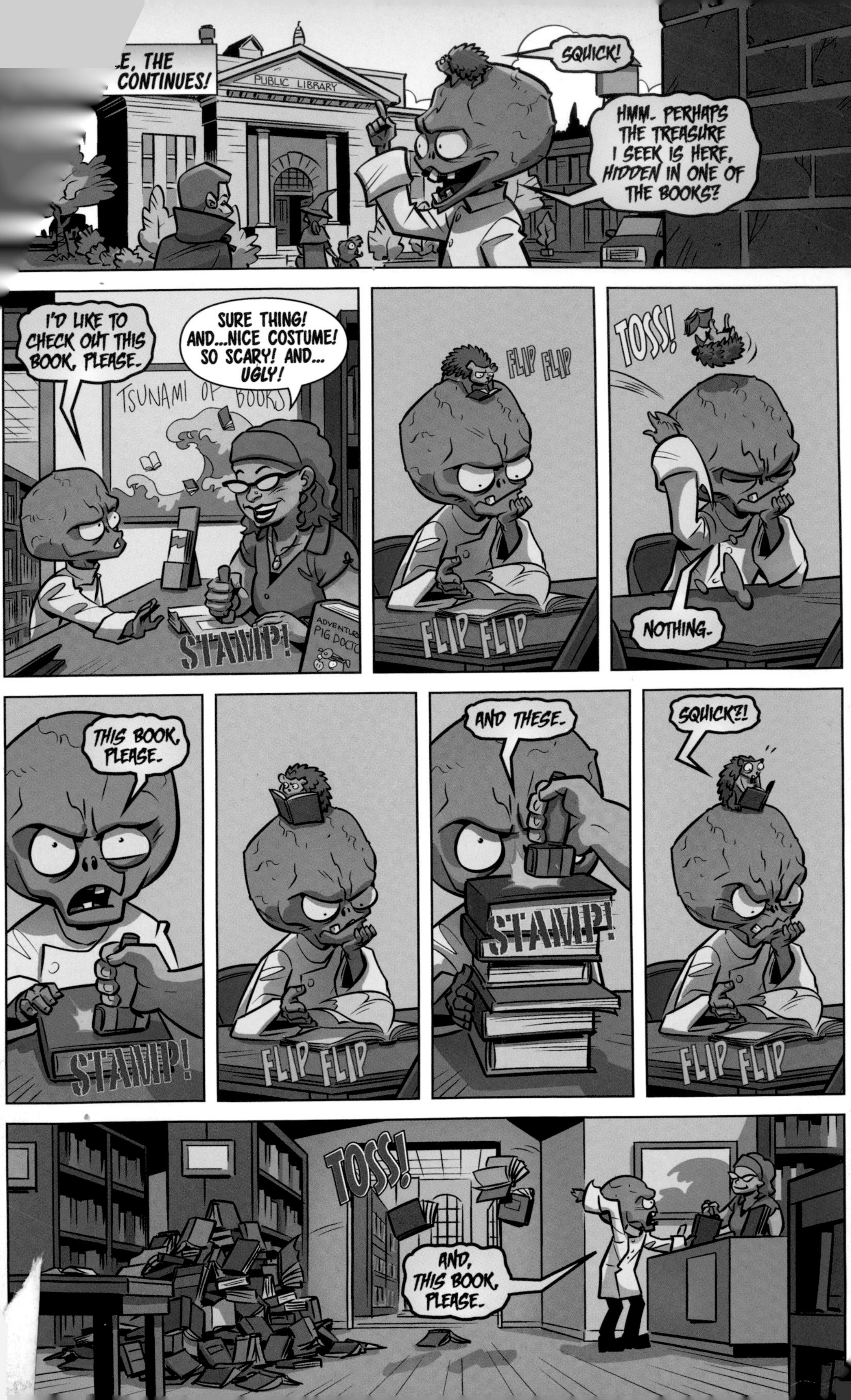

...E, THE ... CONTINUES!
PUBLIC LIBRARY
SQUICK!
HMM. PERHAPS THE TREASURE I SEEK IS HERE, HIDDEN IN ONE OF THE BOOKS?
I'D LIKE TO CHECK OUT THIS BOOK, PLEASE.
SURE THING! AND...NICE COSTUME! SO SCARY! AND... UGLY!
TSUNAMI OF BOOKS
STAMP!
FLIP FLIP
FLIP FLIP
TOSS!
NOTHING.
THIS BOOK, PLEASE.
STAMP!
FLIP FLIP
AND THESE.
STAMP!
SQUICK?!
FLIP FLIP
TOSS!
AND, THIS BOOK, PLEASE.

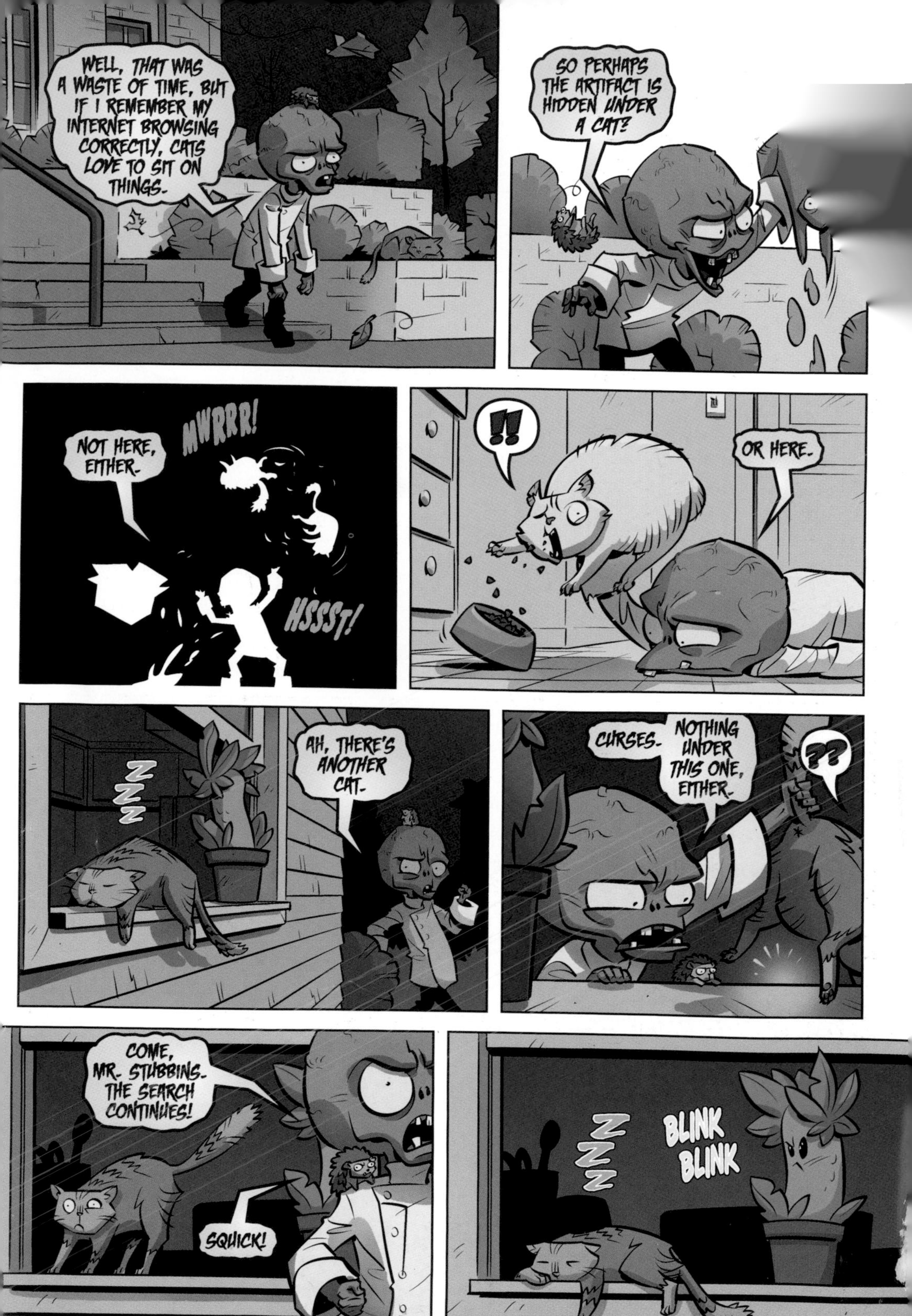
WELL, THAT WAS A WASTE OF TIME, BUT IF I REMEMBER MY INTERNET BROWSING CORRECTLY, CATS LOVE TO SIT ON THINGS.
SO PERHAPS THE ARTIFACT IS HIDDEN UNDER A CAT?
NOT HERE, EITHER.
MWRRR!
HSSST!
!!
OR HERE.
AH, THERE'S ANOTHER CAT.
Z Z Z
CURSES.
NOTHING UNDER THIS ONE, EITHER.
??
COME, MR. STUBBINS. THE SEARCH CONTINUES!
SQUICK!
Z Z Z
BLINK BLINK

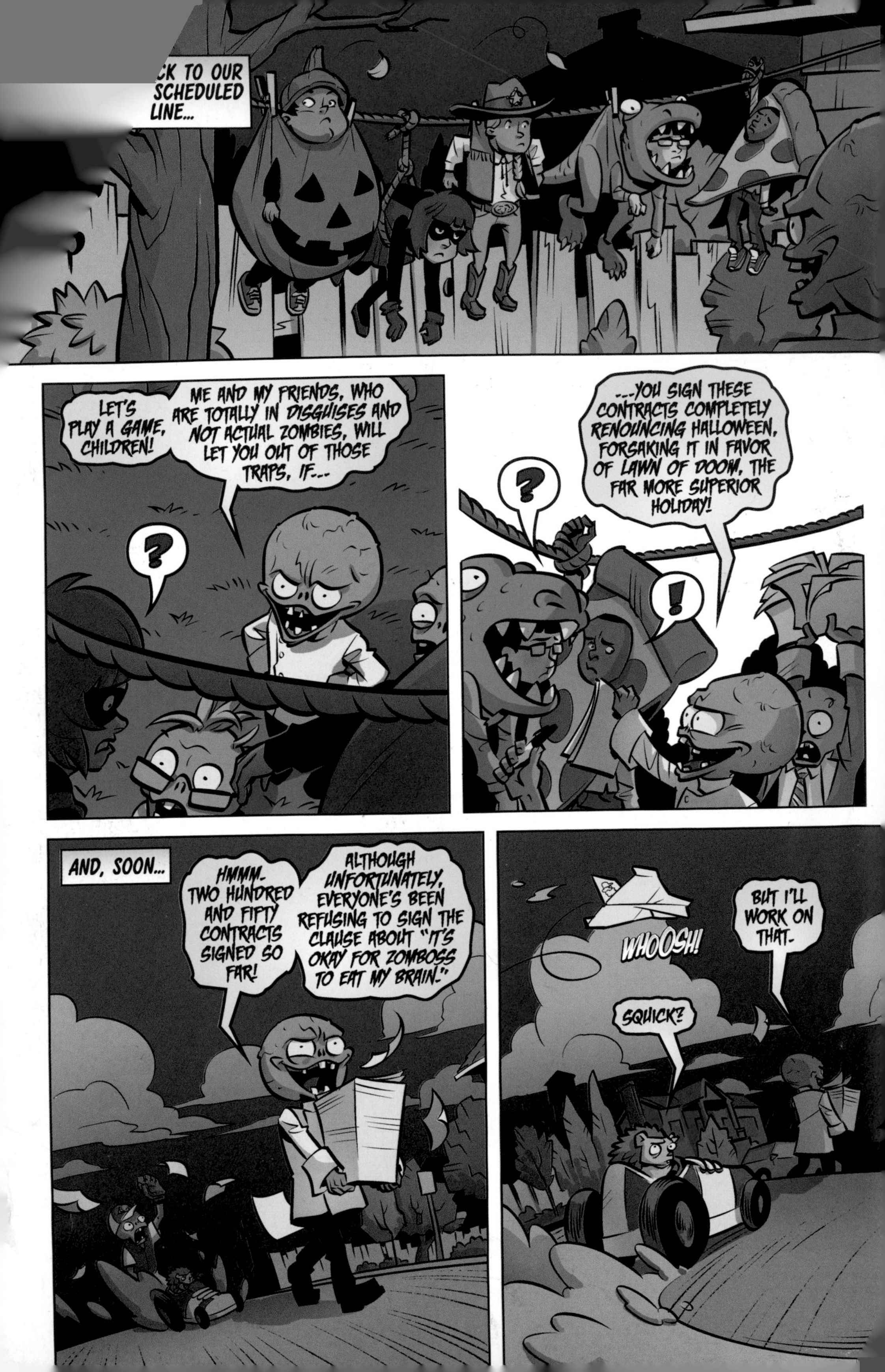
CK TO OUR
SCHEDULED
LINE...
LET'S PLAY A GAME, CHILDREN!
ME AND MY FRIENDS, WHO ARE TOTALLY IN DISGUISES AND NOT ACTUAL ZOMBIES, WILL LET YOU OUT OF THOSE TRAPS, IF...
?
...YOU SIGN THESE CONTRACTS COMPLETELY RENOUNCING HALLOWEEN, FORSAKING IT IN FAVOR OF LAWN OF DOOM, THE FAR MORE SUPERIOR HOLIDAY!
?
!
AND, SOON...
HMMM. TWO HUNDRED AND FIFTY CONTRACTS SIGNED SO FAR!
ALTHOUGH UNFORTUNATELY, EVERYONE'S BEEN REFUSING TO SIGN THE CLAUSE ABOUT "IT'S OKAY FOR ZOMBOSS TO EAT MY BRAIN."
WHOOSH!
BUT I'LL WORK ON THAT.
SQUICK?

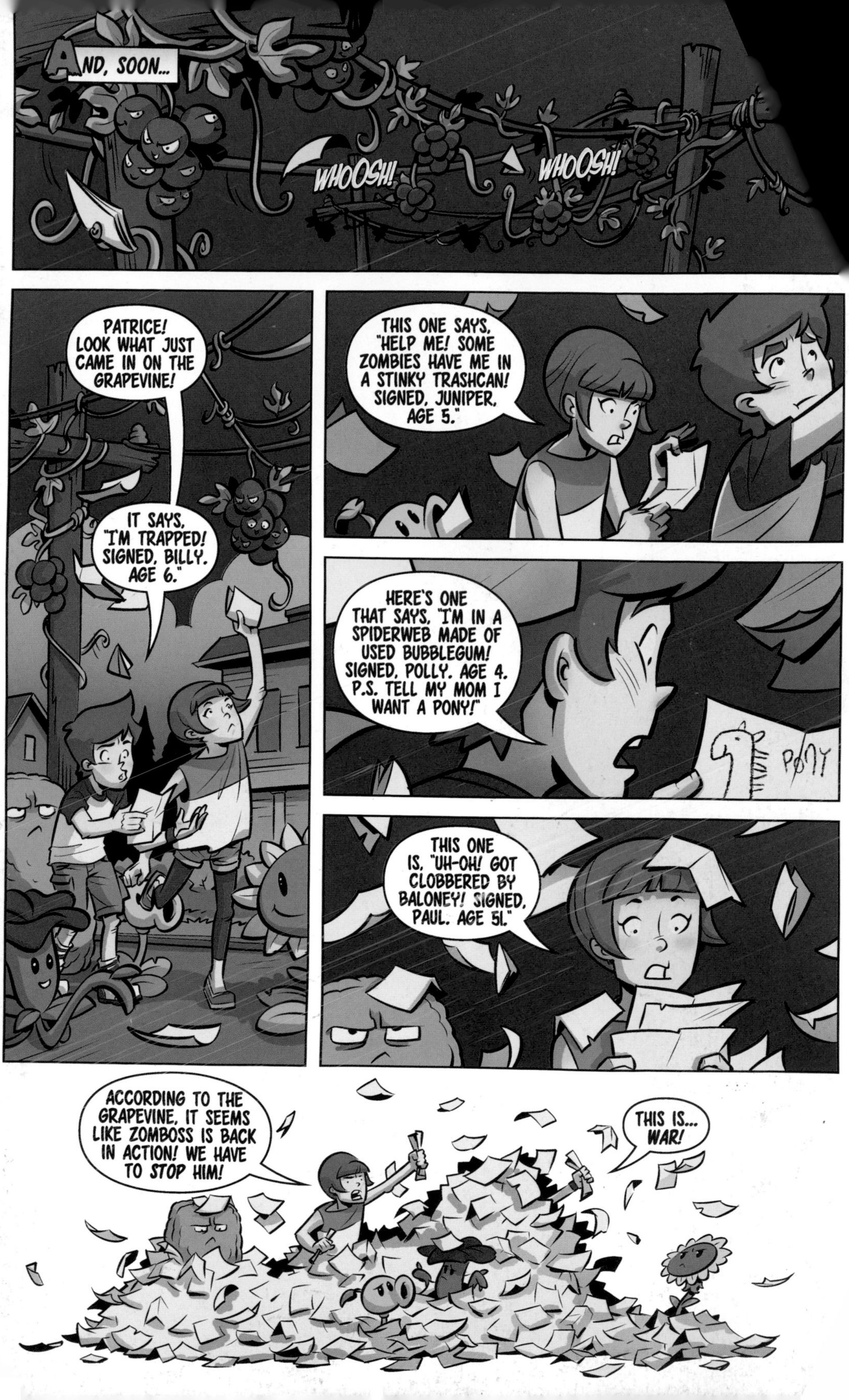
AND, SOON...
WHOOSH!
WHOOSH!
PATRICE! LOOK WHAT JUST CAME IN ON THE GRAPEVINE!
IT SAYS, "I'M TRAPPED! SIGNED, BILLY. AGE 6."
THIS ONE SAYS, "HELP ME! SOME ZOMBIES HAVE ME IN A STINKY TRASHCAN! SIGNED, JUNIPER, AGE 5."
HERE'S ONE THAT SAYS, "I'M IN A SPIDERWEB MADE OF USED BUBBLEGUM! SIGNED, POLLY. AGE 4. P.S. TELL MY MOM I WANT A PONY!"
PONY
THIS ONE IS, "UH-OH! GOT CLOBBERED BY BALONEY! SIGNED, PAUL. AGE 51."
ACCORDING TO THE GRAPEVINE, IT SEEMS LIKE ZOMBOSS IS BACK IN ACTION! WE HAVE TO STOP HIM!
THIS IS... WAR!

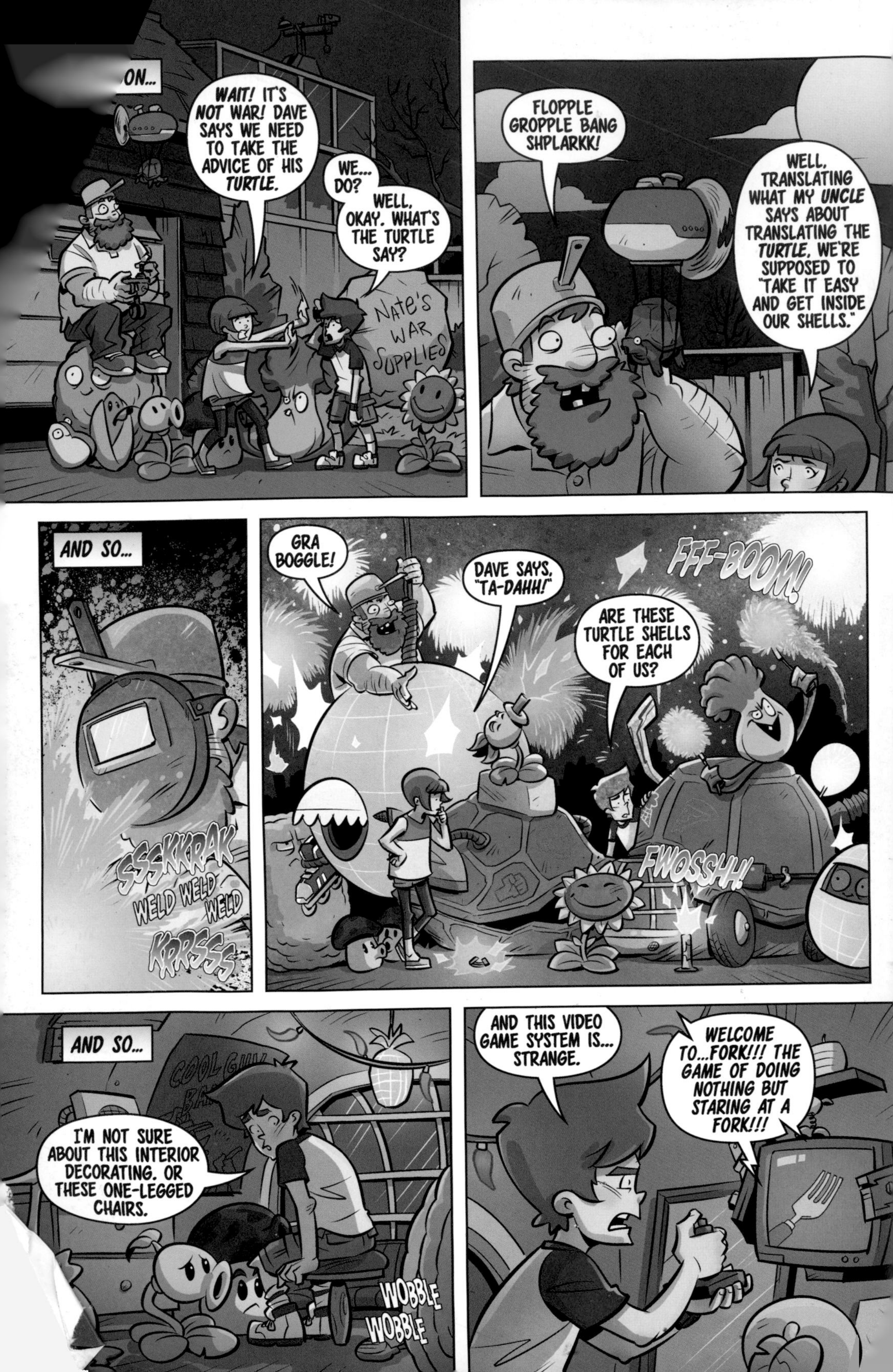
ON...
WAIT! IT'S NOT WAR! DAVE SAYS WE NEED TO TAKE THE ADVICE OF HIS TURTLE.
WE... DO?
WELL, OKAY. WHAT'S THE TURTLE SAY?
NATE'S WAR SUPPLIES
FLOPPLE GROPPLE BANG SHPLARKK!
WELL, TRANSLATING WHAT MY UNCLE SAYS ABOUT TRANSLATING THE TURTLE, WE'RE SUPPOSED TO "TAKE IT EASY AND GET INSIDE OUR SHELLS."
AND SO...
SSSKKRAK
WELD WELD WELD
KRRSSS
GRA BOGGLE!
DAVE SAYS, "TA-DAHH!"
FFF-BOOM!
ARE THESE TURTLE SHELLS FOR EACH OF US?
FWOSSHH!
AND SO...
I'M NOT SURE ABOUT THIS INTERIOR DECORATING. OR THESE ONE-LEGGED CHAIRS.
WOBBLE WOBBLE
AND THIS VIDEO GAME SYSTEM IS... STRANGE.
WELCOME TO...FORK!!! THE GAME OF DOING NOTHING BUT STARING AT A FORK!!!

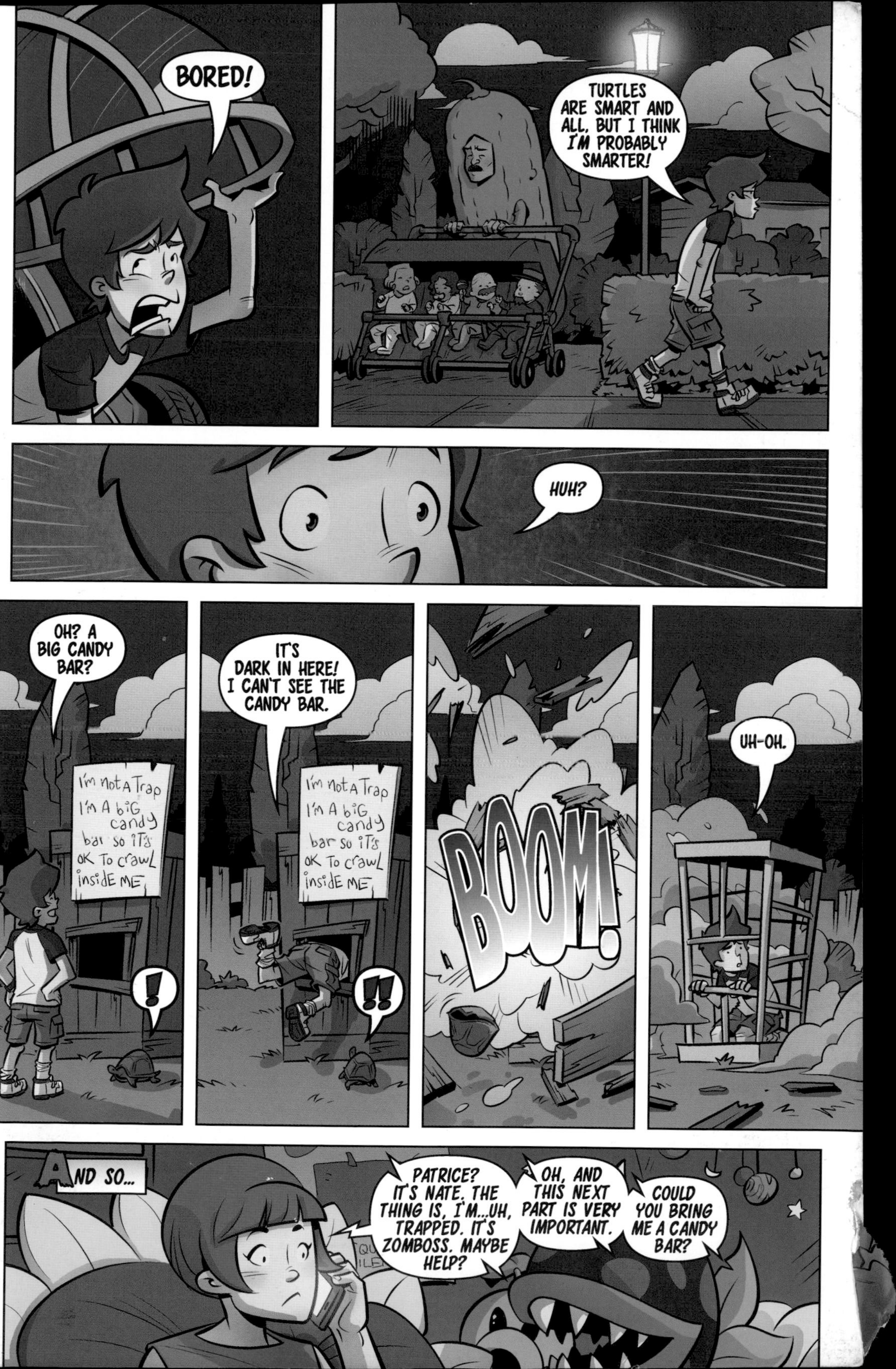
BORED!
TURTLES ARE SMART AND ALL, BUT I THINK I'M PROBABLY SMARTER!
HUH?
OH? A BIG CANDY BAR?
I'm not A Trap I'm A big candy bar so iT's oK To crawL insidE ME
!
IT'S DARK IN HERE! I CAN'T SEE THE CANDY BAR.
I'm not A Trap I'm A big candy bar so iT's oK To crawL insidE ME
!!
BOOM!
UH-OH.
AND SO...
PATRICE? IT'S NATE. THE THING IS, I'M...UH, TRAPPED. IT'S ZOMBOSS. MAYBE HELP?
OH, AND THIS NEXT PART IS VERY IMPORTANT.
COULD YOU BRING ME A CANDY BAR?

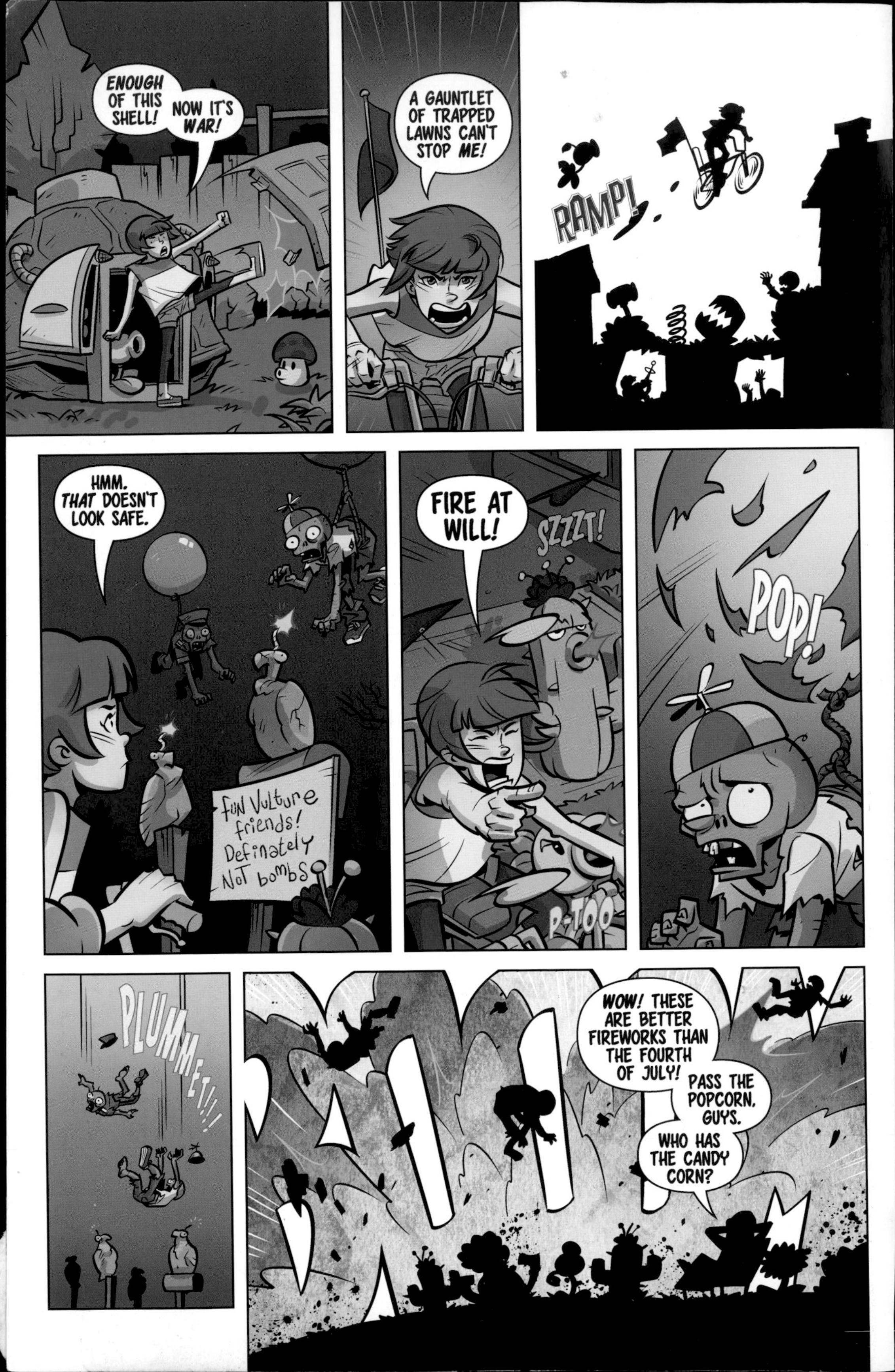
ENOUGH OF THIS SHELL!
NOW IT'S WAR!
A GAUNTLET OF TRAPPED LAWNS CAN'T STOP ME!
RAMP!
HMM. THAT DOESN'T LOOK SAFE.
fun Vulture friends! Definately Not bombs
FIRE AT WILL!
SZZZT!
P-TOO
POP!
PLUMMET!!!
WOW! THESE ARE BETTER FIREWORKS THAN THE FOURTH OF JULY!
PASS THE POPCORN, GUYS.
WHO HAS THE CANDY CORN?

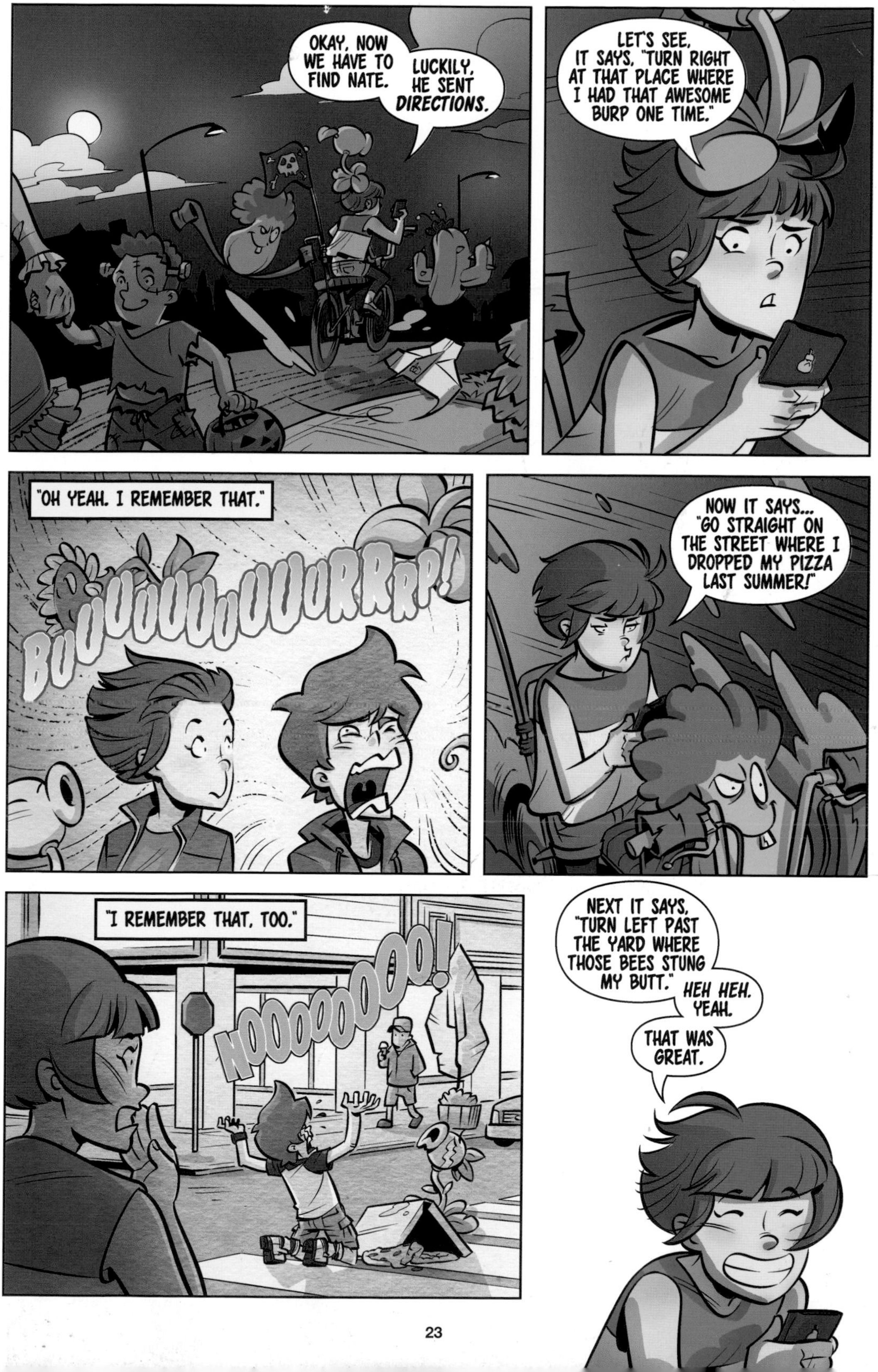
OKAY, NOW WE HAVE TO FIND NATE.
LUCKILY, HE SENT *DIRECTIONS*.
LET'S SEE, IT SAYS, "TURN RIGHT AT THAT PLACE WHERE I HAD THAT AWESOME BURP ONE TIME."
"OH YEAH. I REMEMBER THAT."
BUUUUUUUUUUURRRP!
NOW IT SAYS... "GO STRAIGHT ON THE STREET WHERE I DROPPED MY PIZZA LAST SUMMER!"
"I REMEMBER THAT, TOO."
NOOOOOOOOO!
NEXT IT SAYS, "TURN LEFT PAST THE YARD WHERE THOSE BEES STUNG MY BUTT."
HEH HEH. YEAH.
THAT WAS GREAT.

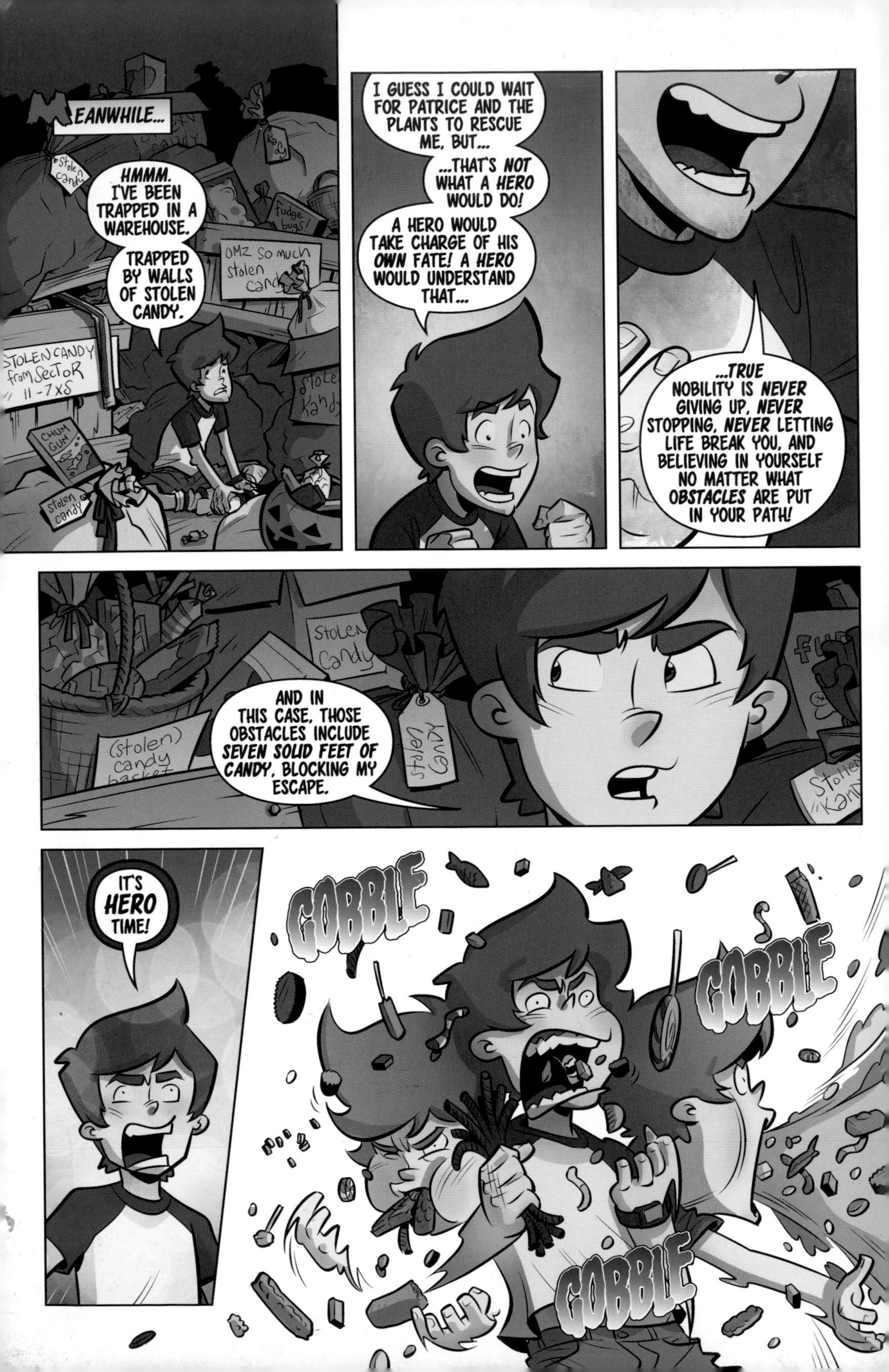
MEANWHILE...
stolen candy
kandy
HMMM. I'VE BEEN TRAPPED IN A WAREHOUSE.
TRAPPED BY WALLS OF STOLEN CANDY.
fudge bugs!
OMZ so much stolen candy
STOLEN CANDY from SECTOR 11-7XS
Stolen Kandy
CHUM GUM
stolen candy
I GUESS I COULD WAIT FOR PATRICE AND THE PLANTS TO RESCUE ME, BUT...
...THAT'S NOT WHAT A HERO WOULD DO!
A HERO WOULD TAKE CHARGE OF HIS OWN FATE! A HERO WOULD UNDERSTAND THAT...
...TRUE NOBILITY IS NEVER GIVING UP, NEVER STOPPING, NEVER LETTING LIFE BREAK YOU, AND BELIEVING IN YOURSELF NO MATTER WHAT OBSTACLES ARE PUT IN YOUR PATH!
stolen candy
(stolen) candy
AND IN THIS CASE, THOSE OBSTACLES INCLUDE SEVEN SOLID FEET OF CANDY, BLOCKING MY ESCAPE.
stolen candy
Stolen Kandy
IT'S HERO TIME!
GOBBLE
GOBBLE
GOBBLE

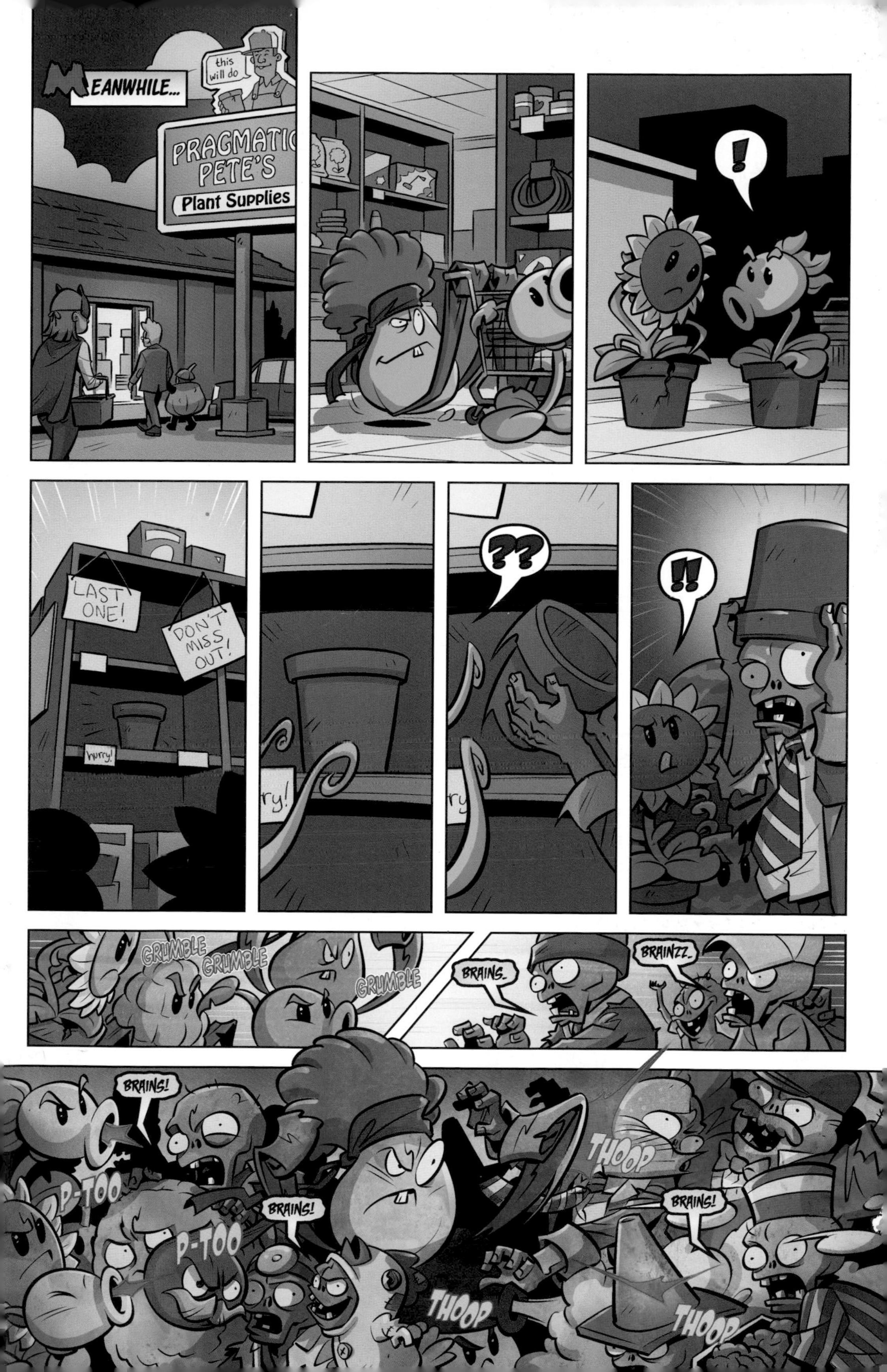
MEANWHILE...
this will do
PRAGMATIC PETE'S
Plant Supplies
!
LAST ONE!
DON'T MISS OUT!
hurry!
??
!!
GRUMBLE
GRUMBLE
GRUMBLE
BRAINS_
BRAINZZ_
BRAINS!
P-TOO
BRAINS!
P-TOO
THOOP
BRAINS!
THOOP
THOOP

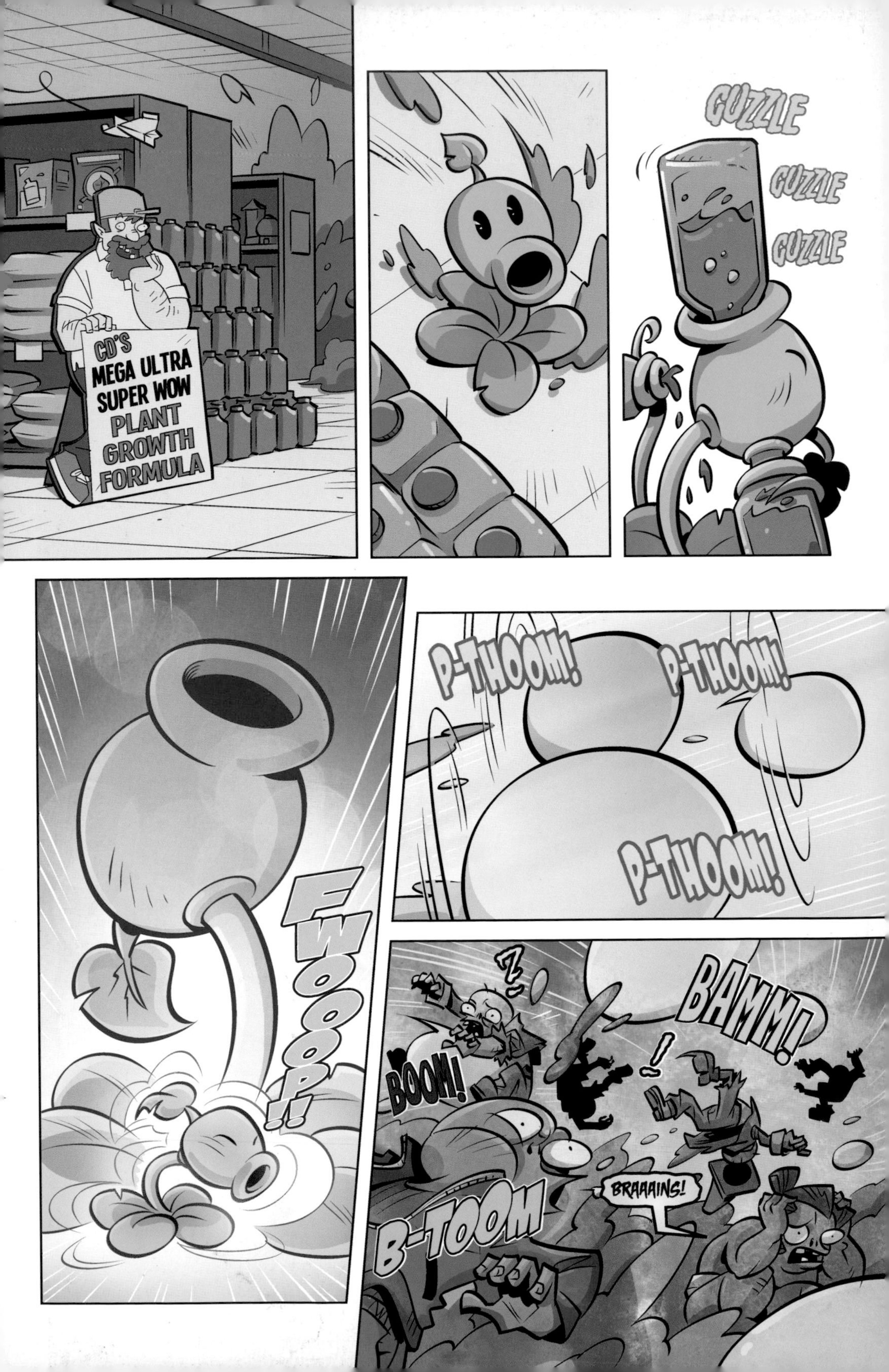
CD'S
MEGA ULTRA
SUPER WOW
PLANT
GROWTH
FORMULA
GUZZLE
GUZZLE
GUZZLE
FWOOOOP!!
P-THOOM!
P-THOOM!
P-THOOM!
BAMM!
BOOM!
B-TOOM
BRAAAINS!

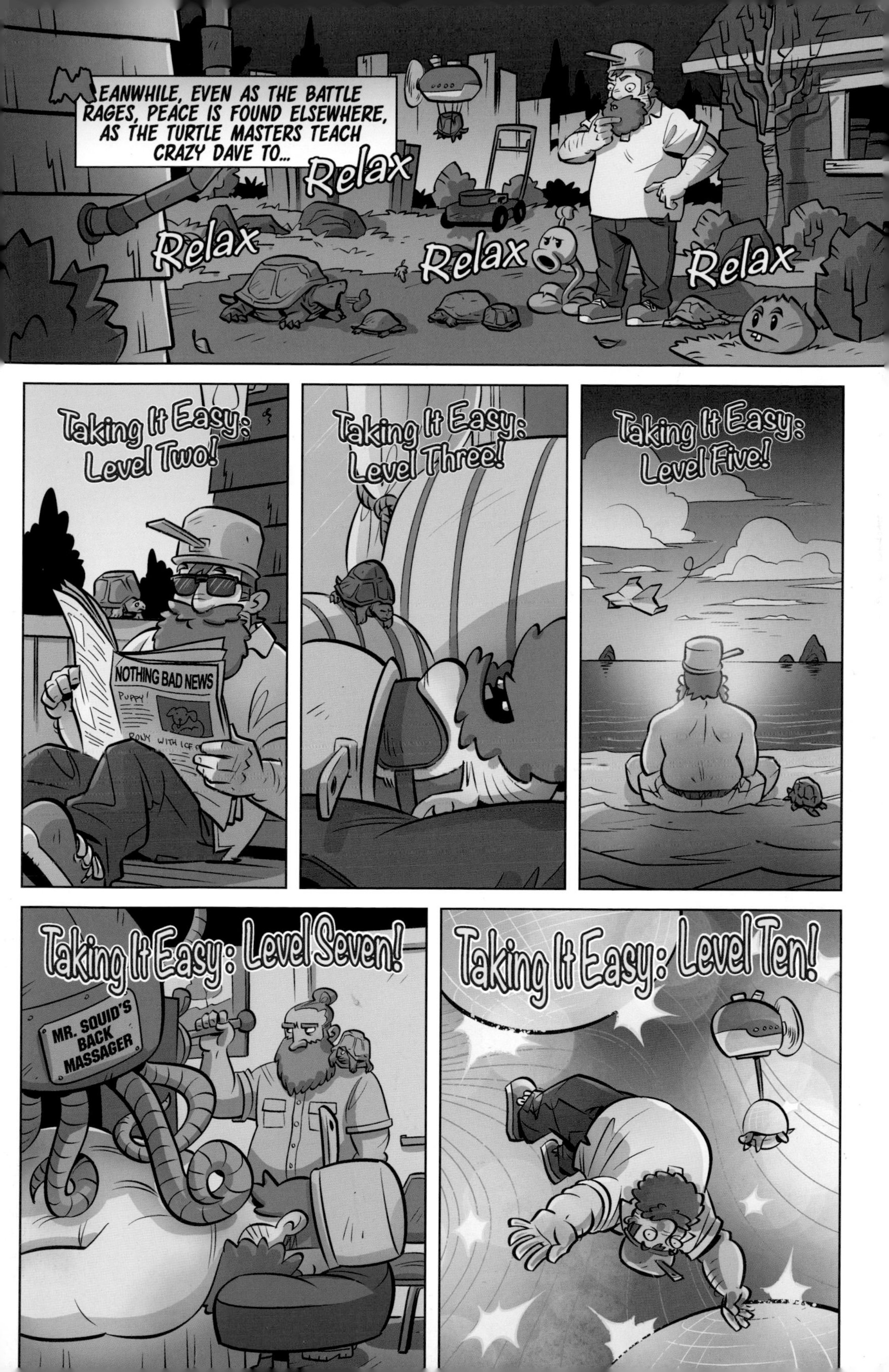
MEANWHILE, EVEN AS THE BATTLE RAGES, PEACE IS FOUND ELSEWHERE, AS THE TURTLE MASTERS TEACH CRAZY DAVE TO...
Relax
Relax
Relax
Relax
Taking It Easy: Level Two!
NOTHING BAD NEWS
PUPPY!
Taking It Easy: Level Three!
Taking It Easy: Level Five!
Taking It Easy: Level Seven!
MR. SQUID'S BACK MASSAGER
Taking It Easy: Level Ten!

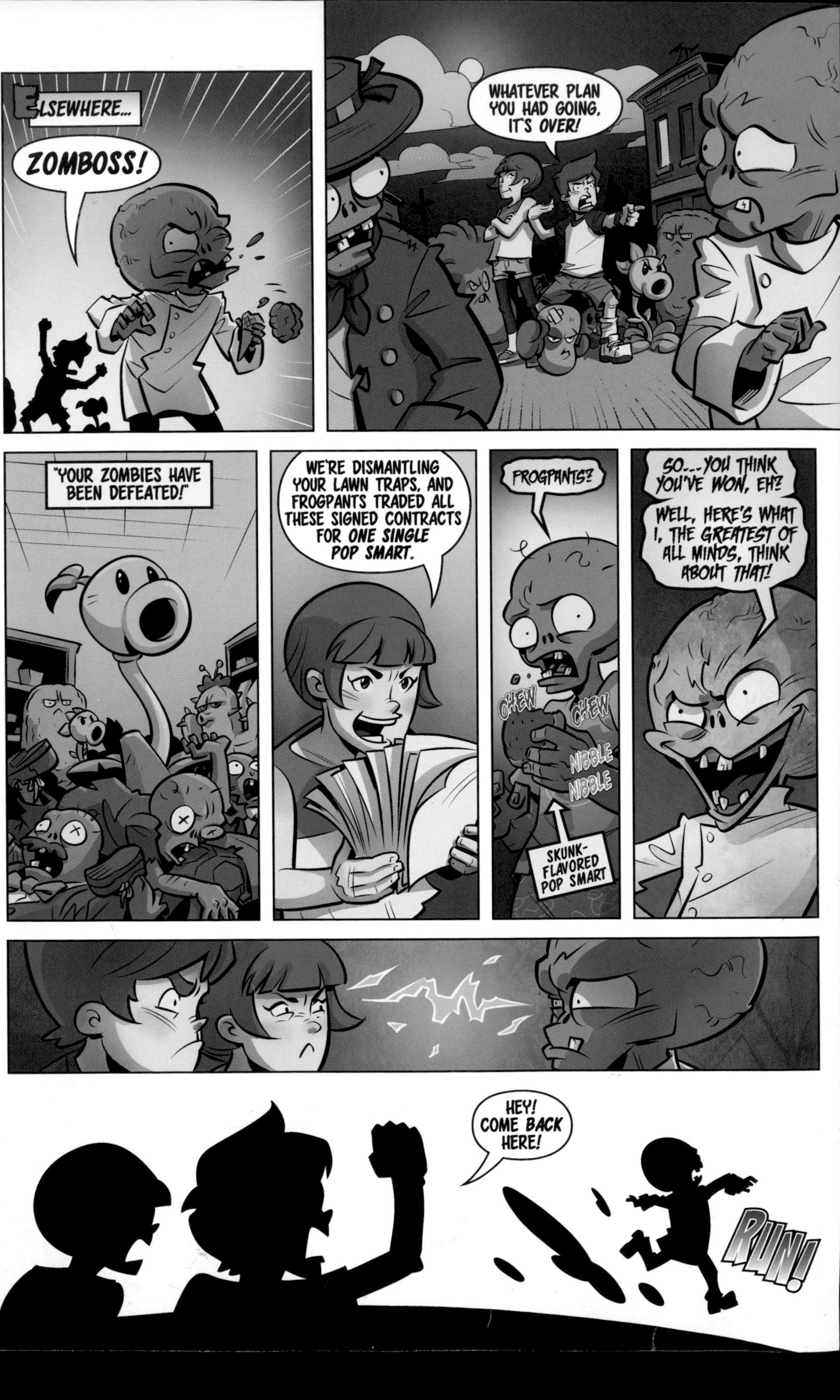
ELSEWHERE...
ZOMBOSS!
WHATEVER PLAN YOU HAD GOING, IT'S OVER!
"YOUR ZOMBIES HAVE BEEN DEFEATED!"
WE'RE DISMANTLING YOUR LAWN TRAPS, AND FROGPANTS TRADED ALL THESE SIGNED CONTRACTS FOR ONE SINGLE POP SMART.
FROGPANTS?
CHEW
CHEW
NIBBLE
NIBBLE
SKUNK-FLAVORED POP SMART
SO... YOU THINK YOU'VE WON, EH?
WELL, HERE'S WHAT I, THE GREATEST OF ALL MINDS, THINK ABOUT THAT!
HEY! COME BACK HERE!
RUN!

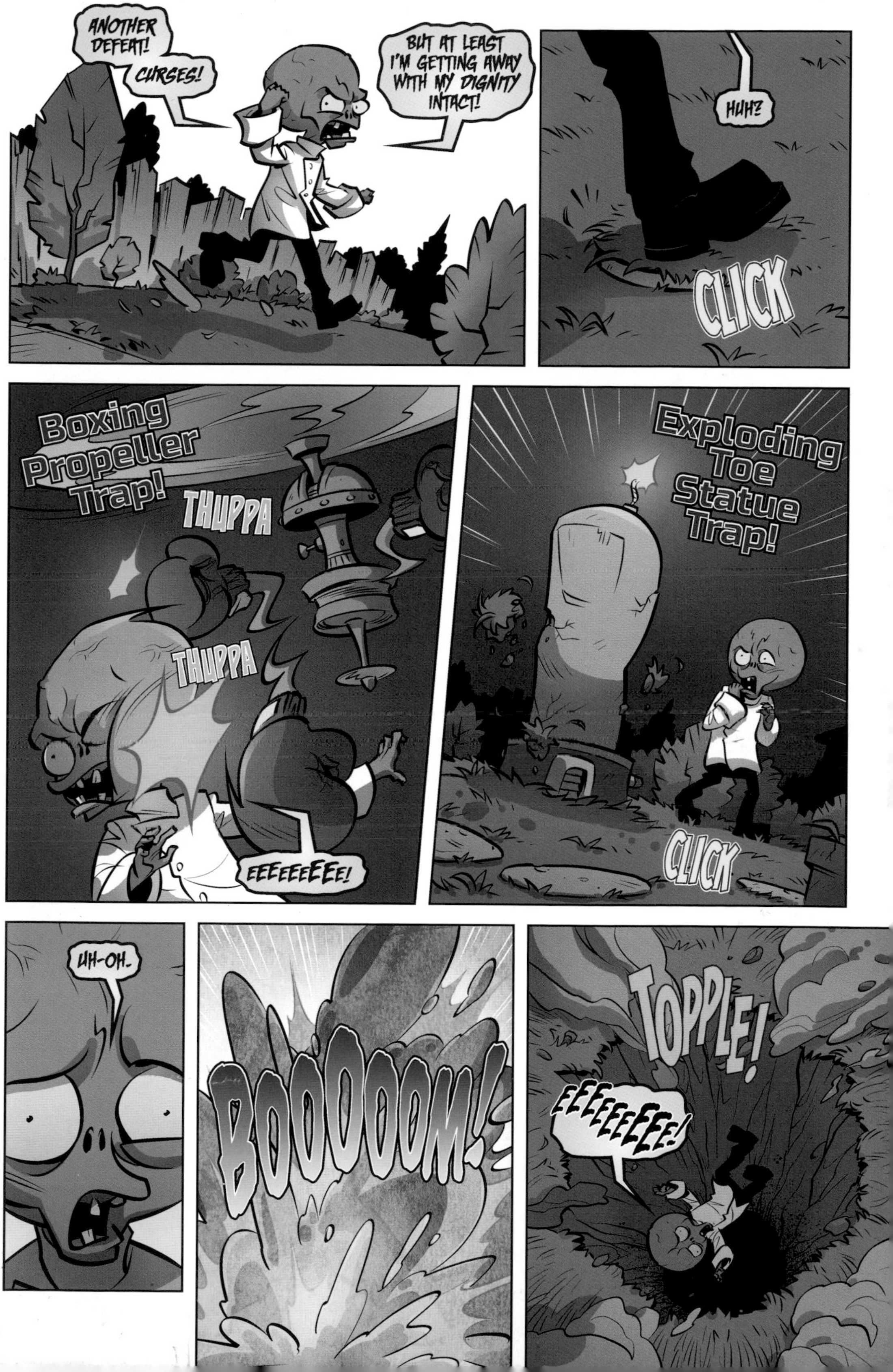
ANOTHER DEFEAT!
CURSES!
BUT AT LEAST I'M GETTING AWAY WITH MY DIGNITY INTACT!
HUH?
CLICK
Boxing Propeller Trap!
THUPPA
THUPPA
EEEEEEEEE!
Exploding Toe Statue Trap!
CLICK
UH-OH.
BOOOOOM!
TOPPLE!
EEEEEEEEE!

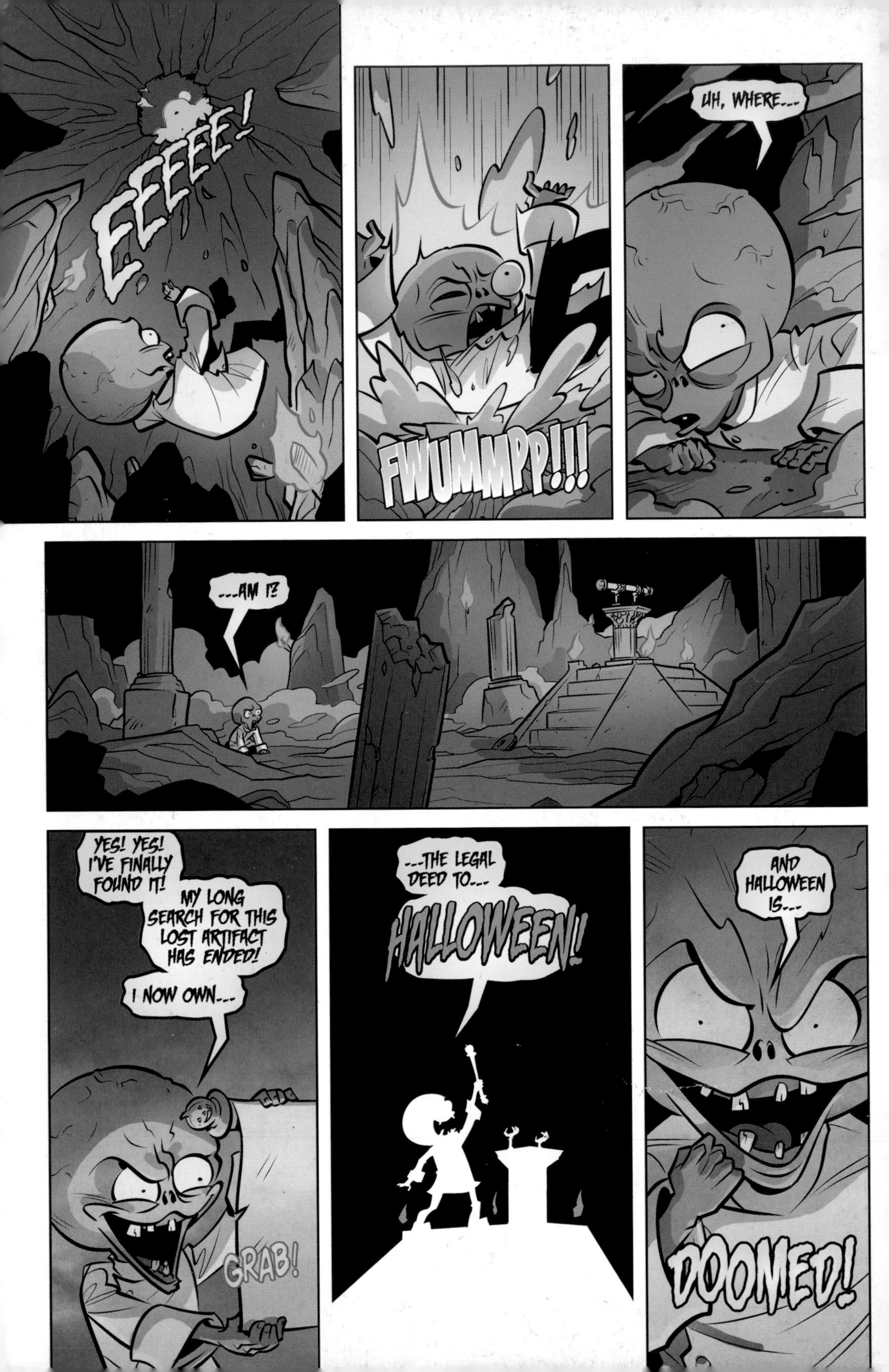
EEEEE!
FWUMMPP!!!
UH, WHERE...
...AM I!?
YES! YES! I'VE FINALLY FOUND IT!
MY LONG SEARCH FOR THIS LOST ARTIFACT HAS ENDED!
I NOW OWN...
GRAB!
...THE LEGAL DEED TO...
HALLOWEEN!!
AND HALLOWEEN IS...
DOOMED!

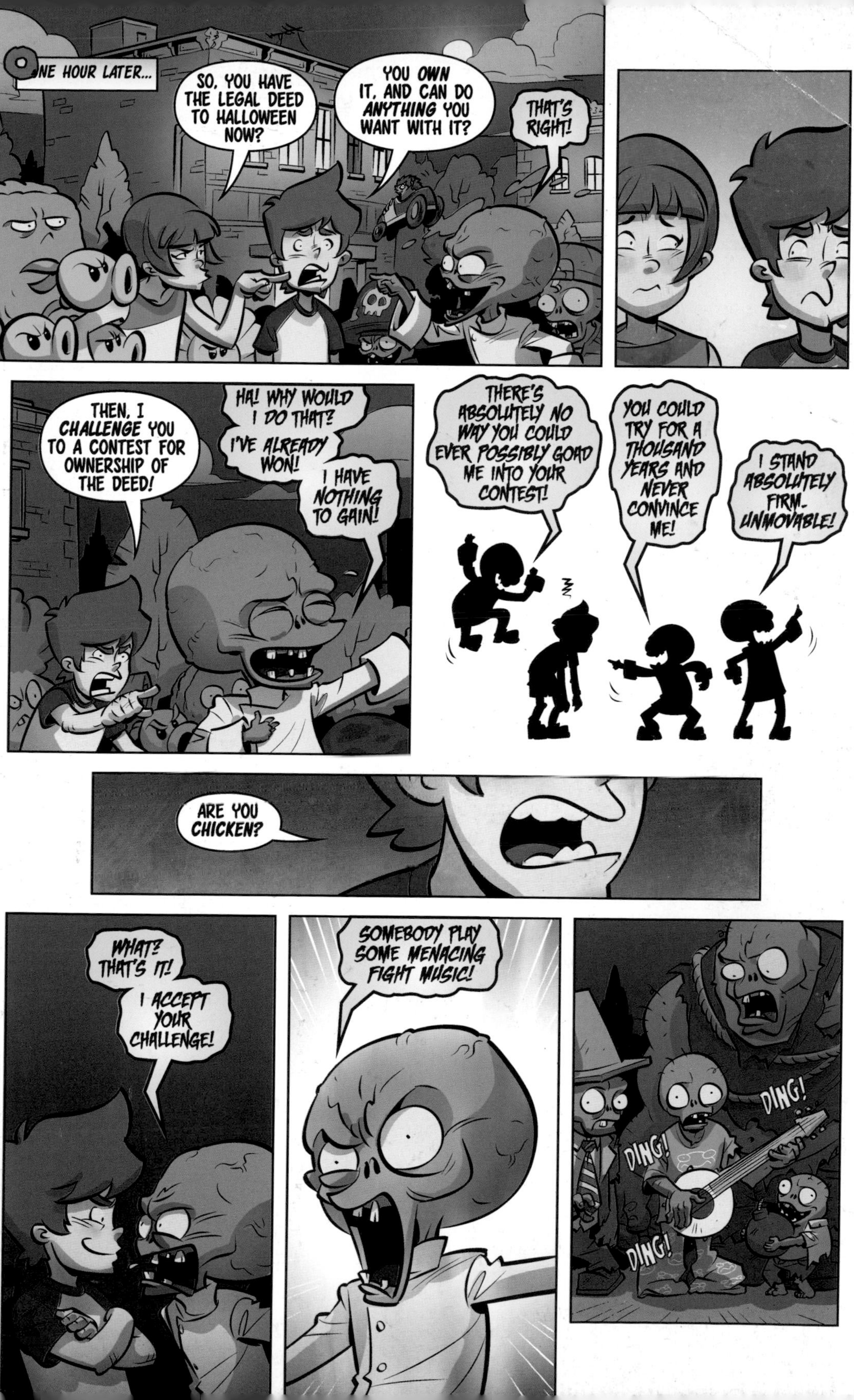
ONE HOUR LATER...
SO, YOU HAVE THE LEGAL DEED TO HALLOWEEN NOW?
YOU OWN IT, AND CAN DO ANYTHING YOU WANT WITH IT?
THAT'S RIGHT!
THEN, I CHALLENGE YOU TO A CONTEST FOR OWNERSHIP OF THE DEED!
HA! WHY WOULD I DO THAT?
I'VE ALREADY WON!
I HAVE NOTHING TO GAIN!
THERE'S ABSOLUTELY NO WAY YOU COULD EVER POSSIBLY GOAD ME INTO YOUR CONTEST!
YOU COULD TRY FOR A THOUSAND YEARS AND NEVER CONVINCE ME!
I STAND ABSOLUTELY FIRM. UNMOVABLE!
ARE YOU CHICKEN?
WHAT? THAT'S IT!
I ACCEPT YOUR CHALLENGE!
SOMEBODY PLAY SOME MENACING FIGHT MUSIC!
DING!
DING!
DING!

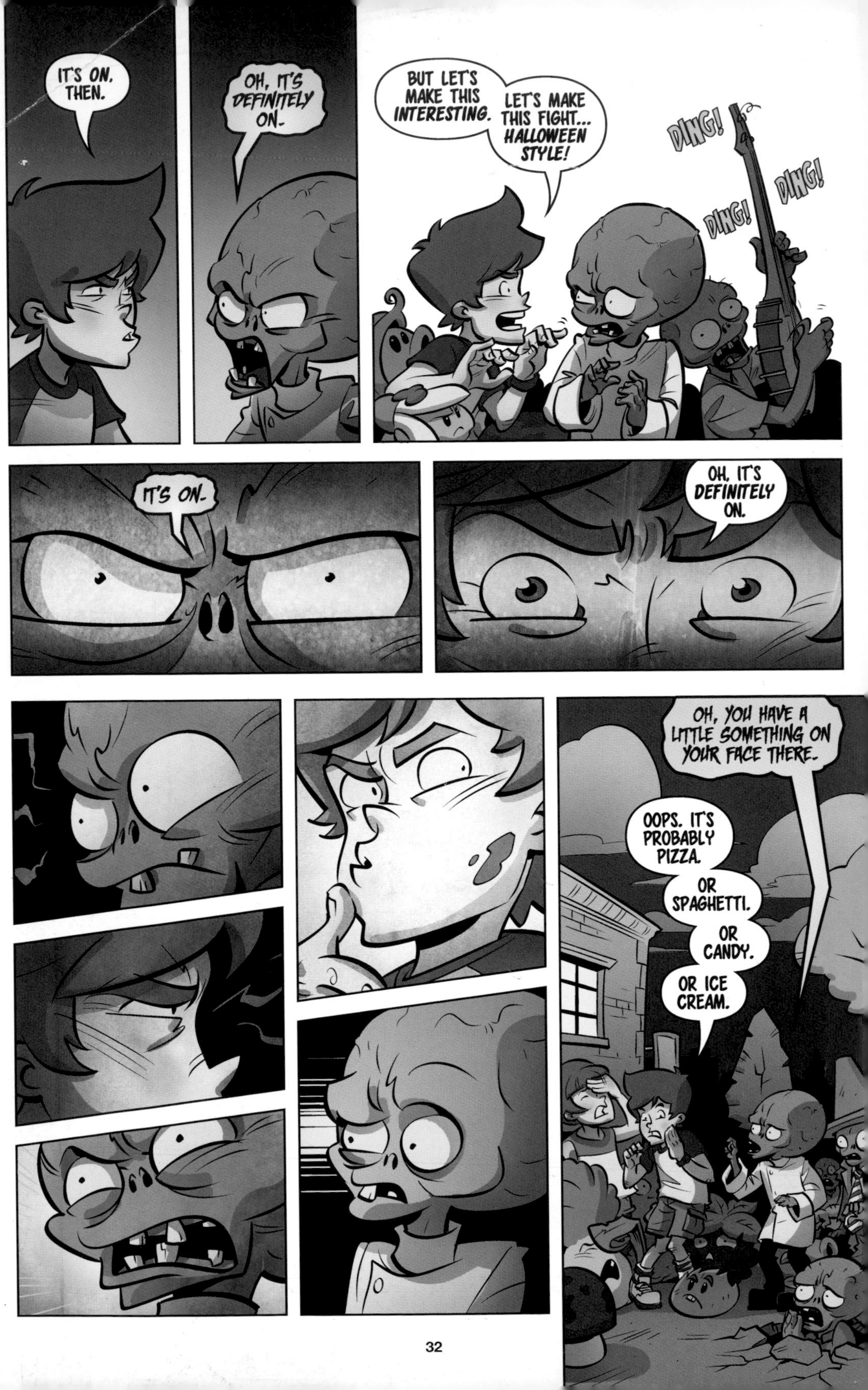

IT'S ON. THEN.
OH, IT'S DEFINITELY ON.
BUT LET'S MAKE THIS INTERESTING.
LET'S MAKE THIS FIGHT... HALLOWEEN STYLE!
DING!
DING!
DING!
IT'S ON.
OH, IT'S DEFINITELY ON.
OH, YOU HAVE A LITTLE SOMETHING ON YOUR FACE THERE.
OOPS. IT'S PROBABLY PIZZA.
OR SPAGHETTI.
OR CANDY.
OR ICE CREAM.

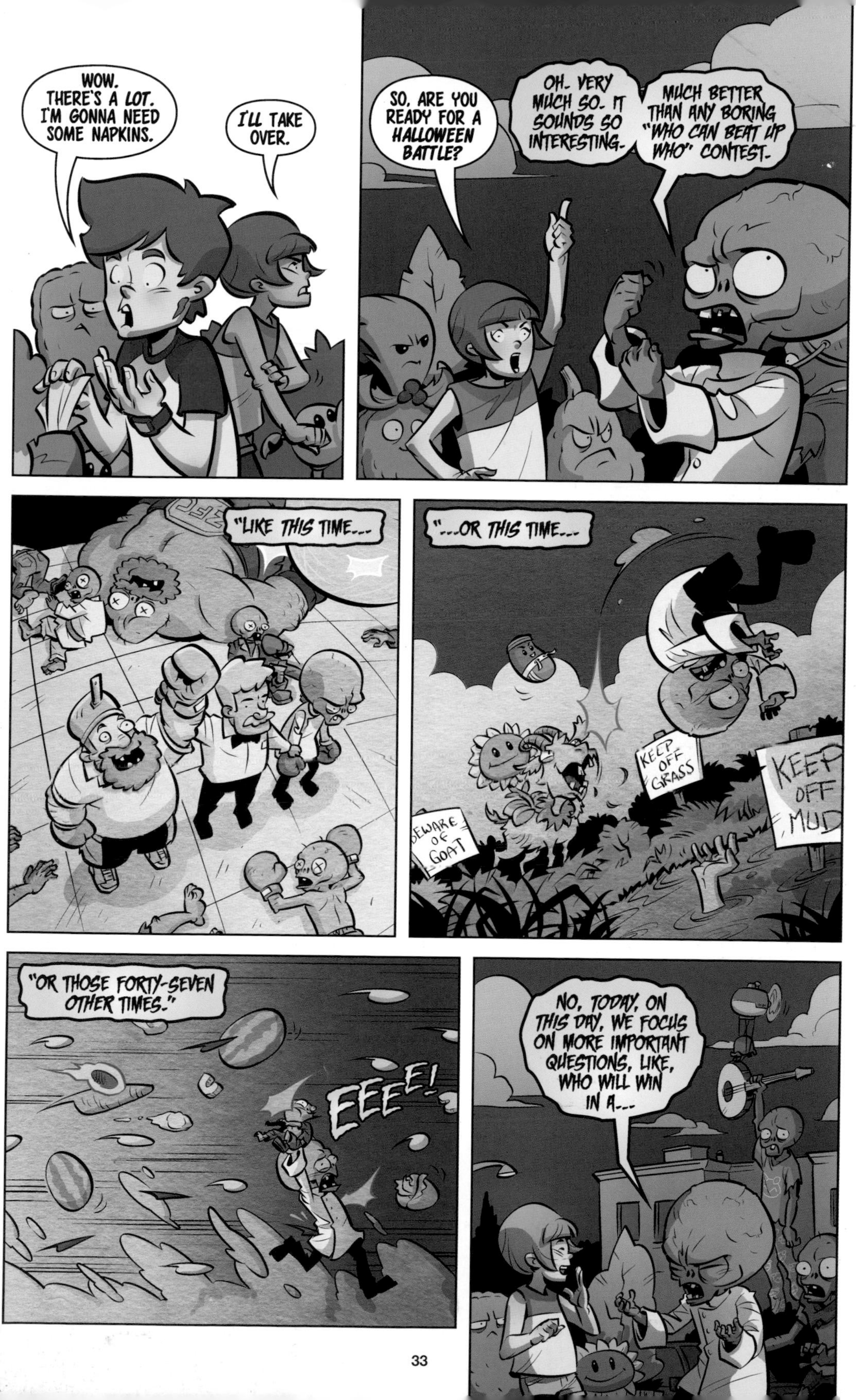
WOW. THERE'S A LOT. I'M GONNA NEED SOME NAPKINS.
I'LL TAKE OVER.
SO, ARE YOU READY FOR A HALLOWEEN BATTLE?
OH. VERY MUCH SO. IT SOUNDS SO INTERESTING.
MUCH BETTER THAN ANY BORING "WHO CAN BEAT UP WHO" CONTEST.
"LIKE THIS TIME...
"...OR THIS TIME...
KEEP OFF GRASS
KEEP OFF MUD
BEWARE OF GOAT
"OR THOSE FORTY-SEVEN OTHER TIMES."
EEEEE!
NO, TODAY, ON THIS DAY, WE FOCUS ON MORE IMPORTANT QUESTIONS, LIKE, WHO WILL WIN IN A...

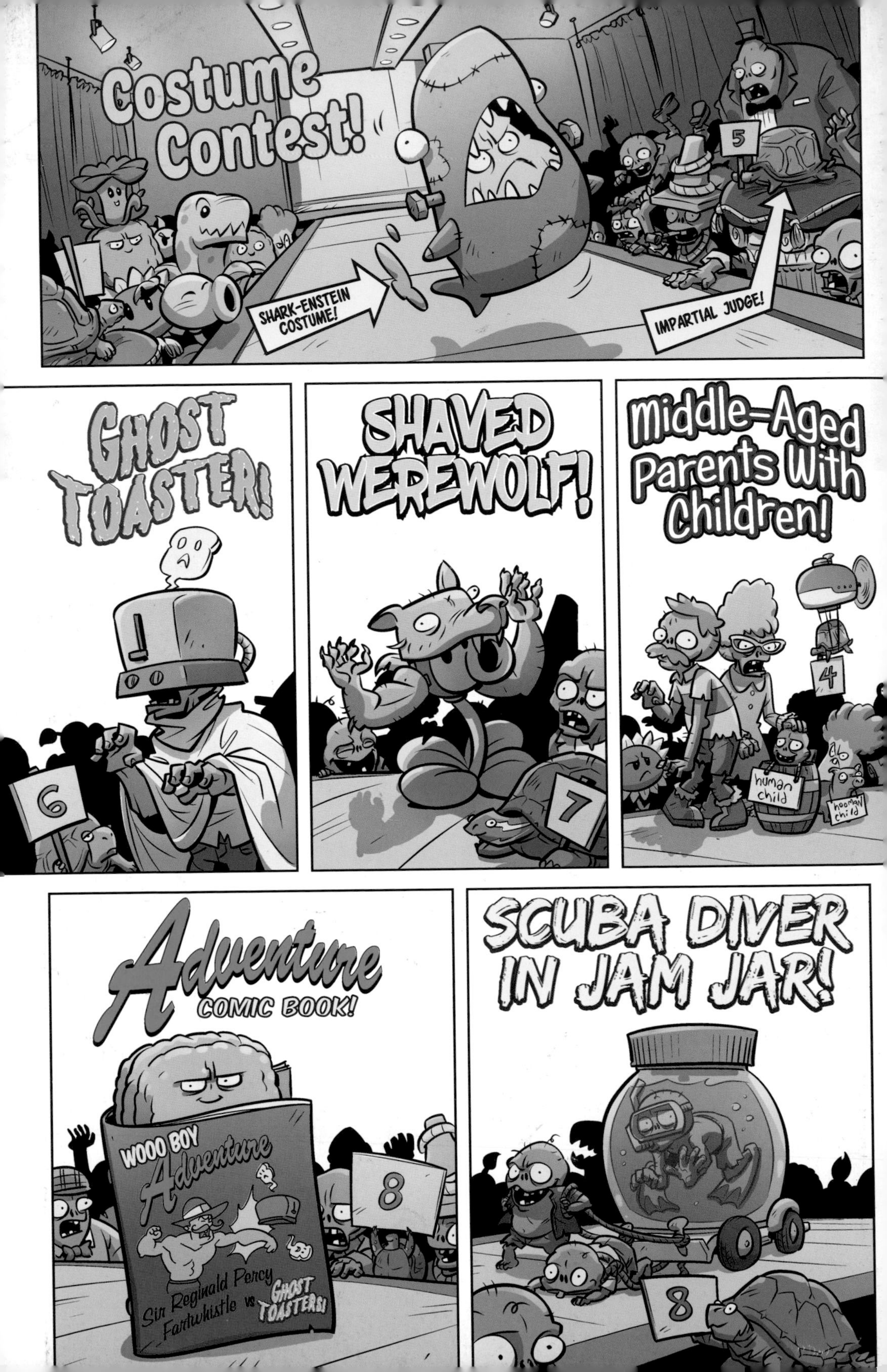
Costume Contest!
SHARK-ENSTEIN COSTUME!
5
IMPARTIAL JUDGE!
GHOST TOASTER!
6
SHAVED WEREWOLF!
7
Middle-Aged Parents With Children!
4
human child
hooman child
Adventure COMIC BOOK!
WOOO BOY Adventure
Sir Reginald Percy Fartwhistle vs GHOST TOASTERS!
8
SCUBA DIVER IN JAM JAR!
8

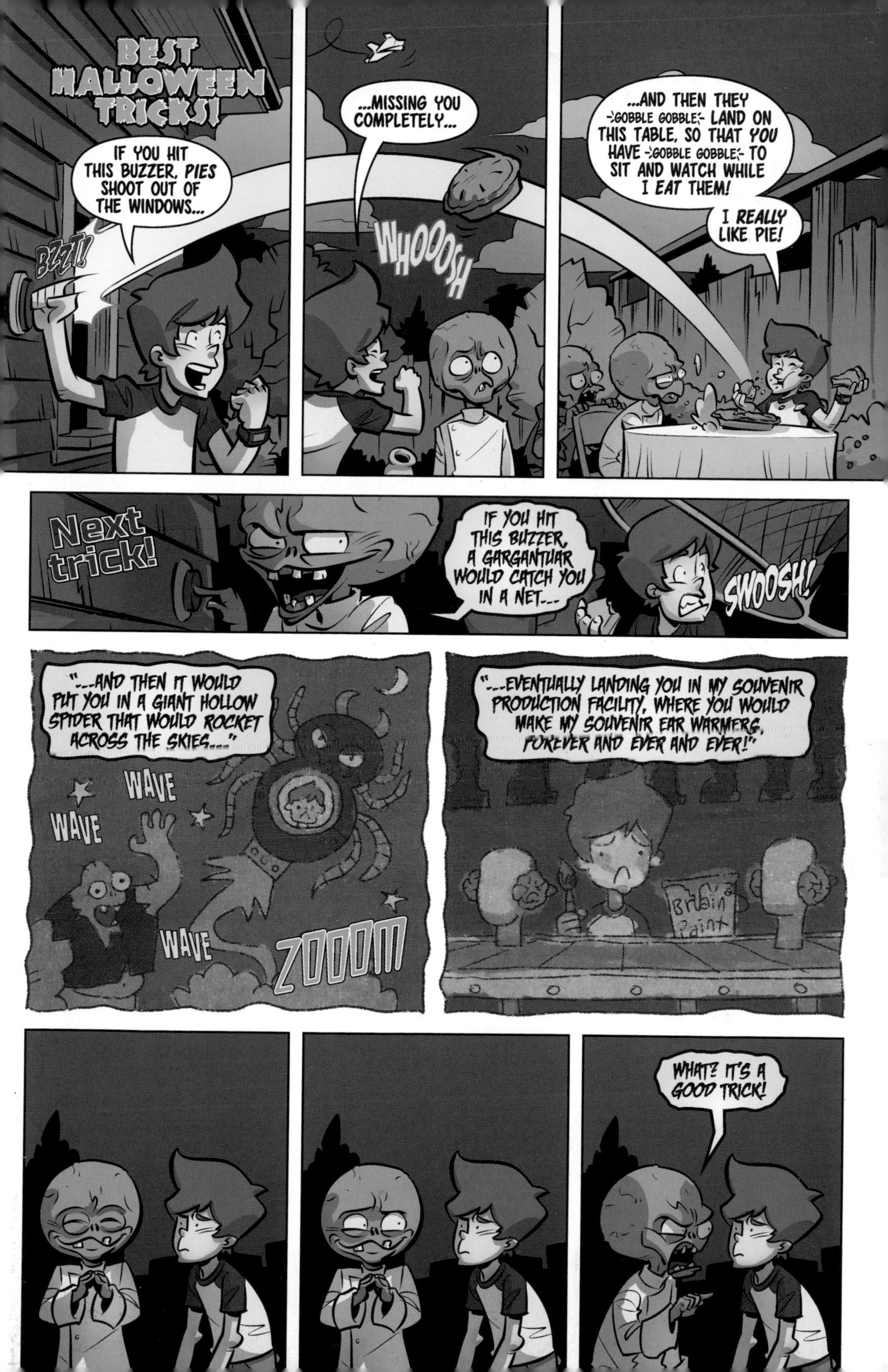

BEST HALLOWEEN TRICKS!
IF YOU HIT THIS BUZZER, PIES SHOOT OUT OF THE WINDOWS...
BZZT!
...MISSING YOU COMPLETELY...
WHOOOSH
...AND THEN THEY -GOBBLE GOBBLE- LAND ON THIS TABLE, SO THAT YOU HAVE -GOBBLE GOBBLE- TO SIT AND WATCH WHILE I EAT THEM!
I REALLY LIKE PIE!
Next trick!
IF YOU HIT THIS BUZZER, A GARGANTUAR WOULD CATCH YOU IN A NET...
SWOOSH!
"...AND THEN IT WOULD PUT YOU IN A GIANT HOLLOW SPIDER THAT WOULD ROCKET ACROSS THE SKIES..."
WAVE
WAVE
WAVE
ZOOOM
"...EVENTUALLY LANDING YOU IN MY SOUVENIR PRODUCTION FACILITY, WHERE YOU WOULD MAKE MY SOUVENIR EAR WARMERS, FOREVER AND EVER AND EVER!"
Brain Paint
WHAT? IT'S A GOOD TRICK!

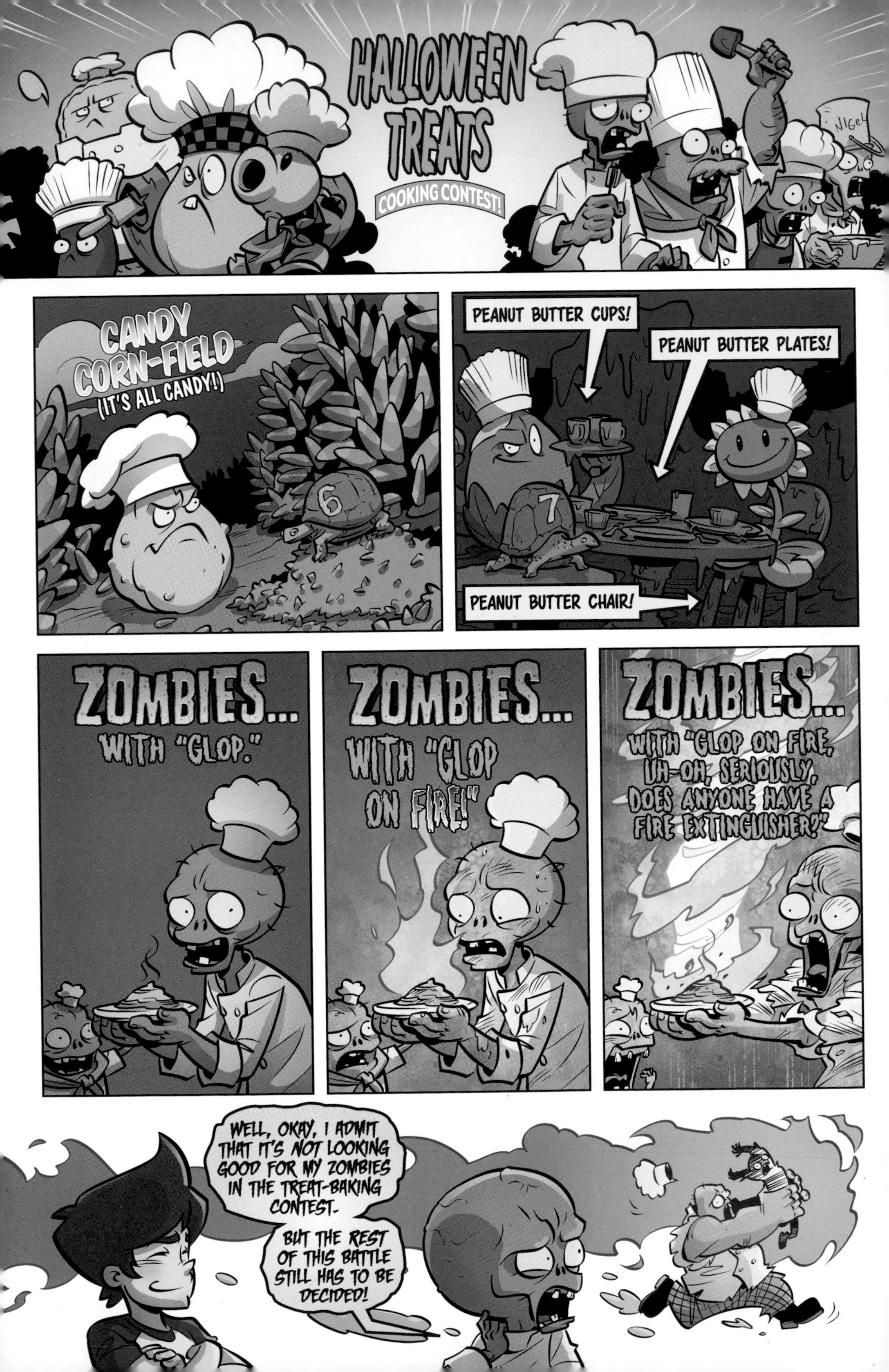

HALLOWEEN TREATS
COOKING CONTEST!
NIGEL
CANDY CORN-FIELD
(IT'S ALL CANDY!)
6
PEANUT BUTTER CUPS!
PEANUT BUTTER PLATES!
7
PEANUT BUTTER CHAIR!
ZOMBIES... WITH "GLOP."
ZOMBIES... WITH "GLOP ON FIRE!"
ZOMBIES... WITH "GLOP ON FIRE, UH-OH, SERIOUSLY, DOES ANYONE HAVE A FIRE EXTINGUISHER!"
WELL, OKAY, I ADMIT THAT IT'S NOT LOOKING GOOD FOR MY ZOMBIES IN THE TREAT-BAKING CONTEST.
BUT THE REST OF THIS BATTLE STILL HAS TO BE DECIDED!

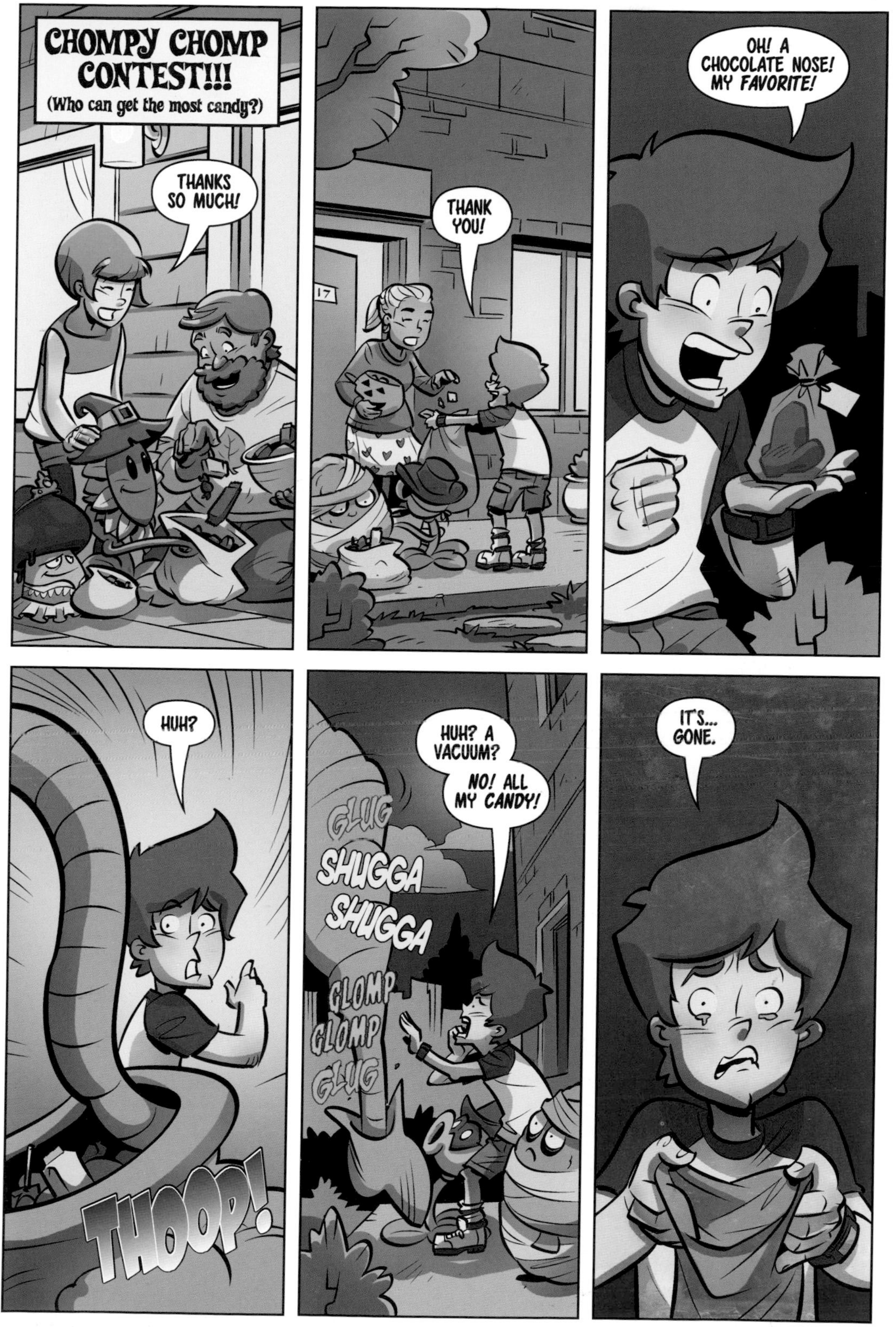
CHOMPY CHOMP CONTEST!!!
(Who can get the most candy?)
THANKS SO MUCH!
THANK YOU!
OH! A CHOCOLATE NOSE! MY FAVORITE!
HUH?
THOOP!
HUH? A VACUUM?
NO! ALL MY CANDY!
GLUG
SHUGGA
SHUGGA
GLOMP
GLOMP
GLUG
IT'S... GONE.

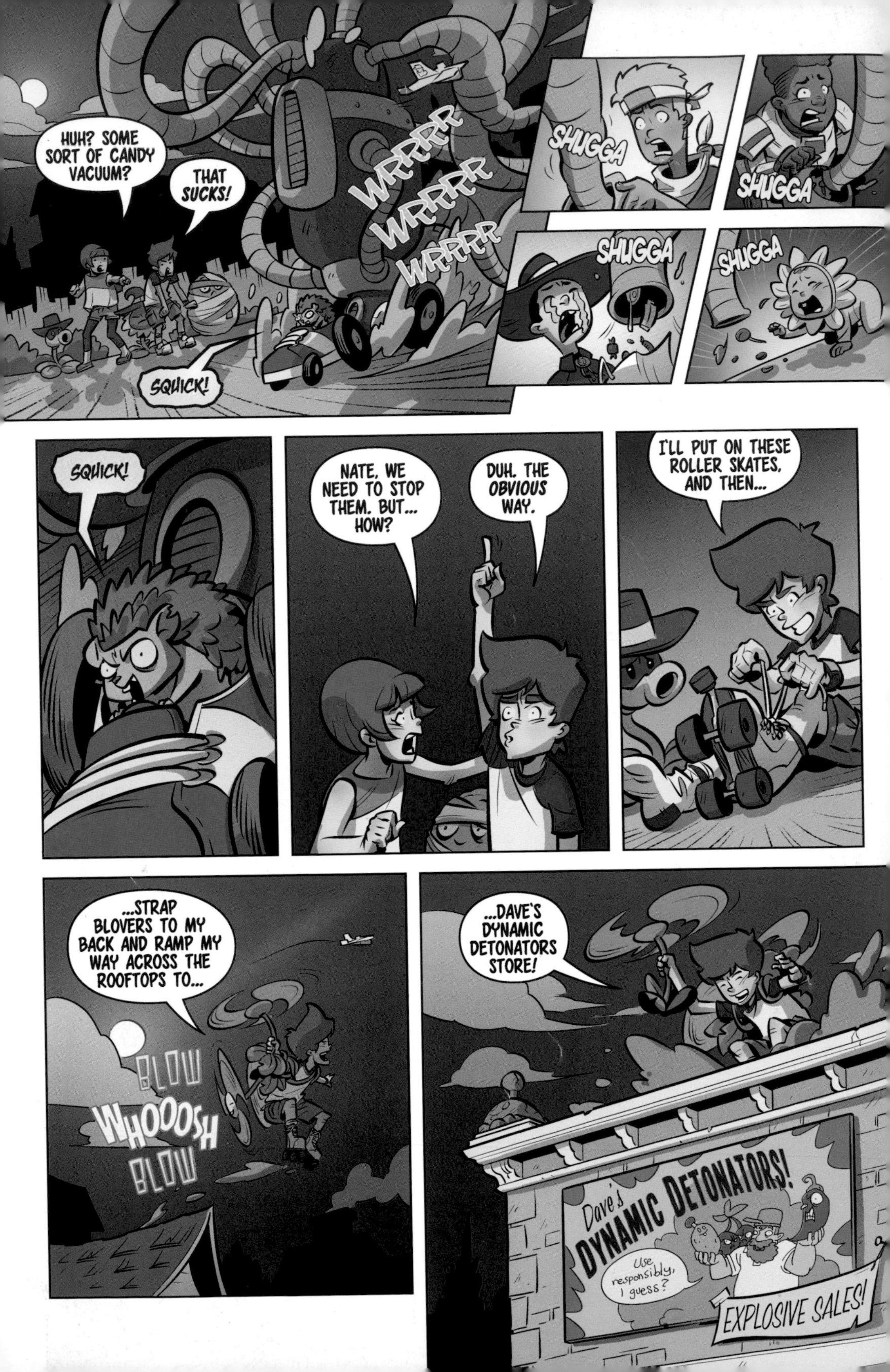
HUH? SOME SORT OF CANDY VACUUM?
THAT SUCKS!
WRRRRR
WRRRRR
WRRRRR
SQUICK!
SHUGGA
SHUGGA
SHUGGA
SHUGGA
SQUICK!
NATE, WE NEED TO STOP THEM. BUT... HOW?
DUH. THE OBVIOUS WAY.
I'LL PUT ON THESE ROLLER SKATES, AND THEN...
...STRAP BLOVERS TO MY BACK AND RAMP MY WAY ACROSS THE ROOFTOPS TO...
BLOW
WHOOOSH
BLOW
...DAVE'S DYNAMIC DETONATORS STORE!
Dave's DYNAMIC DETONATORS!
Use responsibly, I guess?
EXPLOSIVE SALES!

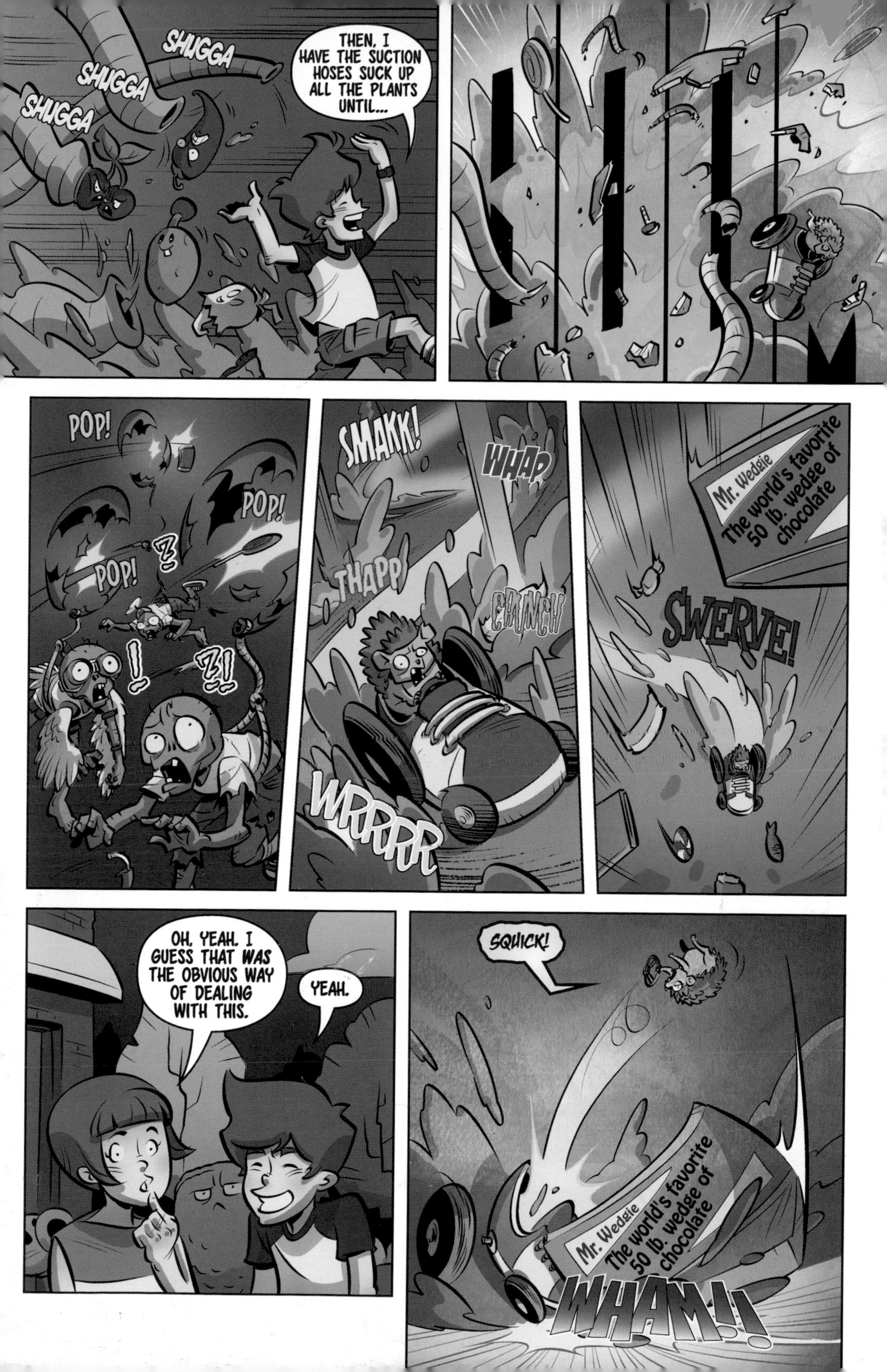
SHUGGA
SHUGGA
SHUGGA
THEN, I HAVE THE SUCTION HOSES SUCK UP ALL THE PLANTS UNTIL...
POP!
POP!
POP!
Z
!
Z!
SMAKK!
WHAP
THAPP
CRUNCH
WRRRRR
Mr. Wedgie
The world's favorite 50 lb. wedge of chocolate
SWERVE!
OH, YEAH. I GUESS THAT WAS THE OBVIOUS WAY OF DEALING WITH THIS.
YEAH.
SQUICK!
Mr. Wedgie
The world's favorite 50 lb. wedge of chocolate
WHAM!!

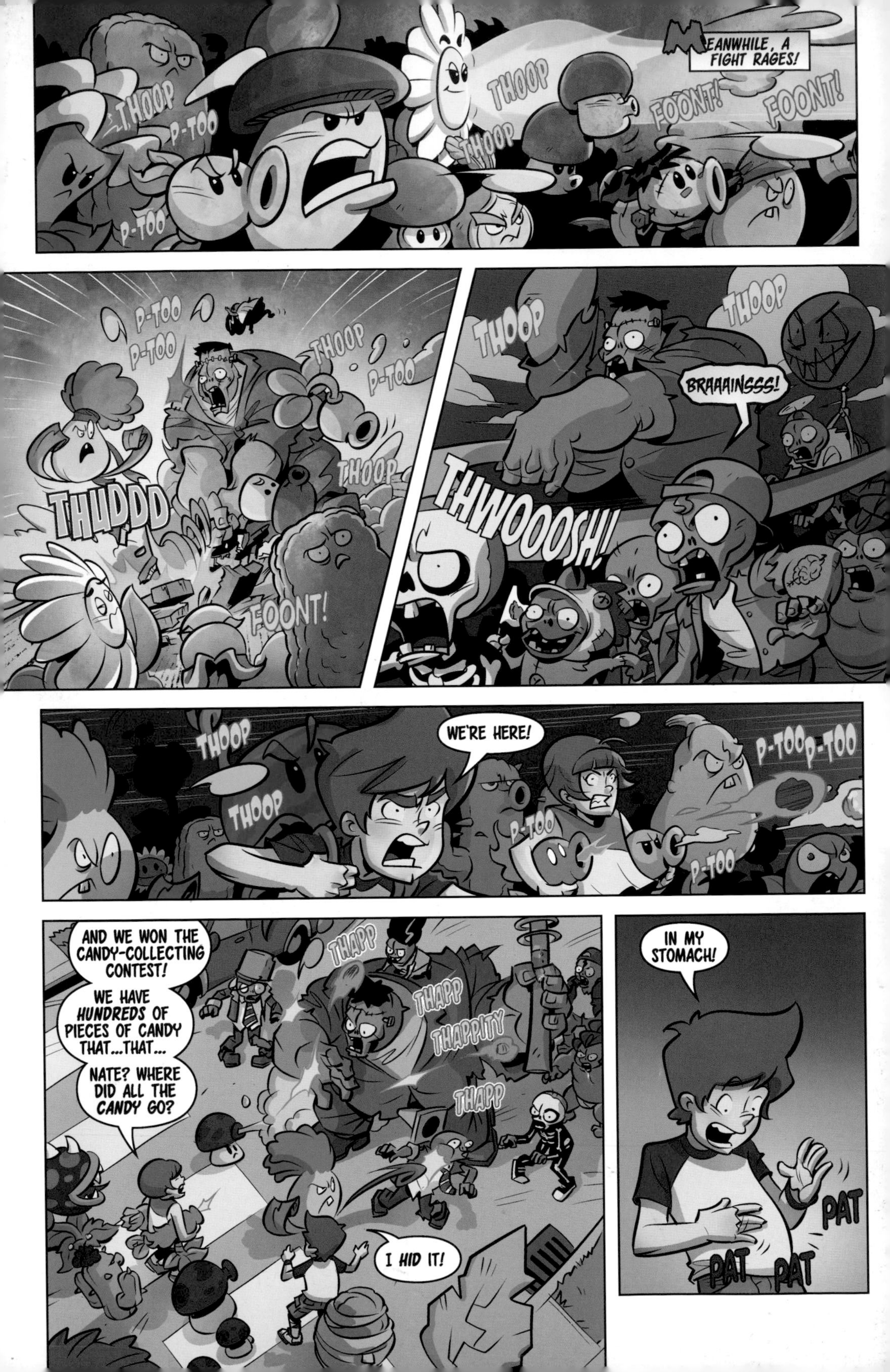
MEANWHILE, A FIGHT RAGES!
THOOP
P-TOO
P-TOO
THOOP
THOOP
FOONT!
FOONT!
P-TOO
P-TOO
THOOP
P-TOO
THOOP
THUDDD
FOONT!
THOOP
THOOP
BRAAAINSSS!
THWOOOSH!
THOOP
THOOP
WE'RE HERE!
P-TOO
P-TOO
P-TOO
P-TOO
AND WE WON THE CANDY-COLLECTING CONTEST!
WE HAVE *HUNDREDS* OF PIECES OF CANDY THAT...THAT...
NATE? WHERE DID ALL THE *CANDY* GO?
THAPP
THAPP
THAPPITY
THAPP
I HID IT!
IN MY STOMACH!
PAT
PAT
PAT

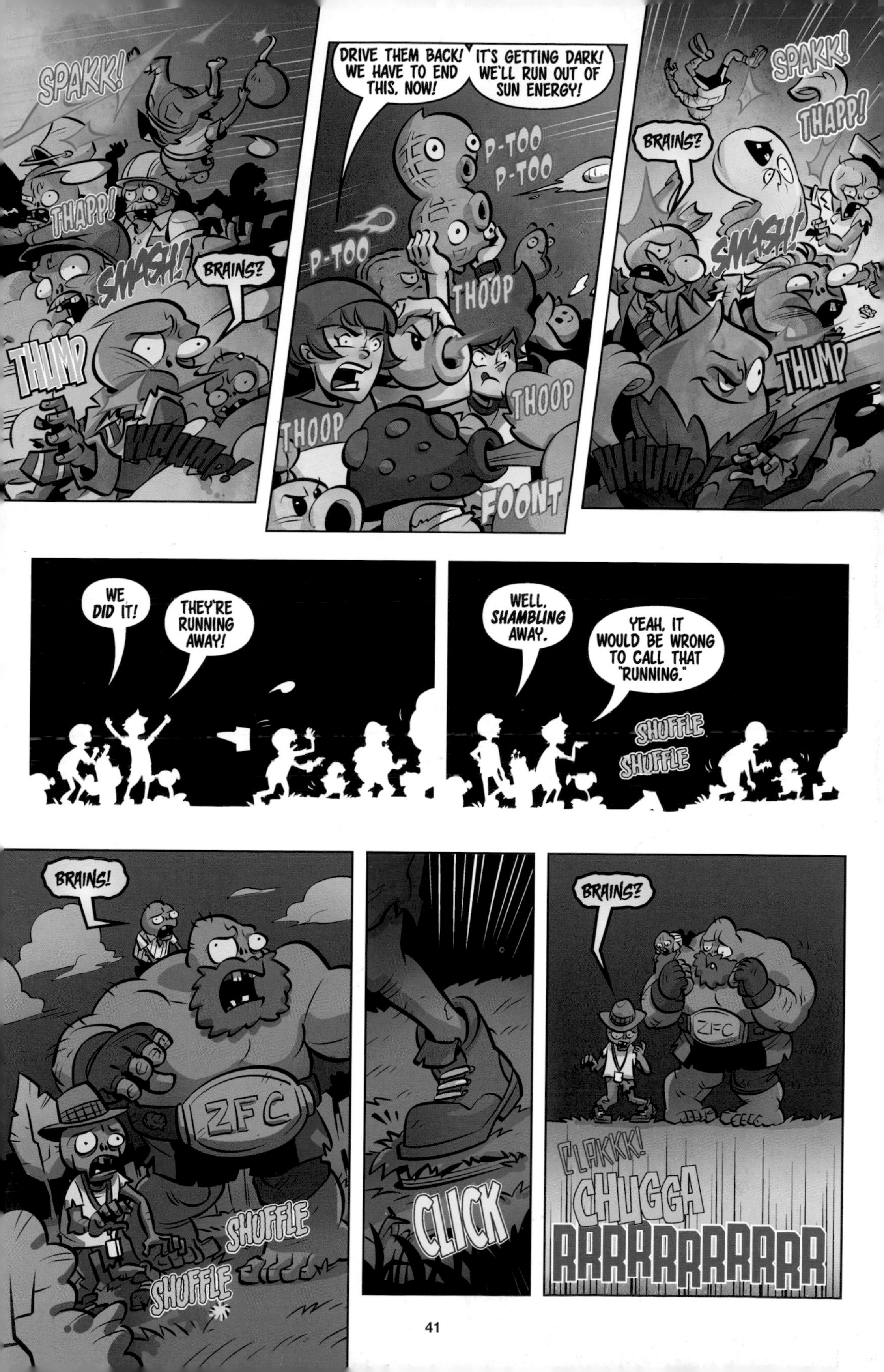

SPAKK!
THAPP!
SMASH!
BRAINS?
THUMP
WHUMP!
DRIVE THEM BACK! WE HAVE TO END THIS, NOW!
IT'S GETTING DARK! WE'LL RUN OUT OF SUN ENERGY!
P-TOO
P-TOO
P-TOO
THOOP
THOOP
THOOP
FOONT
SPAKK!
THAPP!
BRAINS?
SMASH!
THUMP
WHUMP!
WE DID IT!
THEY'RE RUNNING AWAY!
WELL, SHAMBLING AWAY.
YEAH, IT WOULD BE WRONG TO CALL THAT "RUNNING."
SHUFFLE
SHUFFLE
BRAINS!
SHUFFLE
SHUFFLE
CLICK
BRAINS?
CLAKKK!
CHUGGA
RRRRRRRRRRR

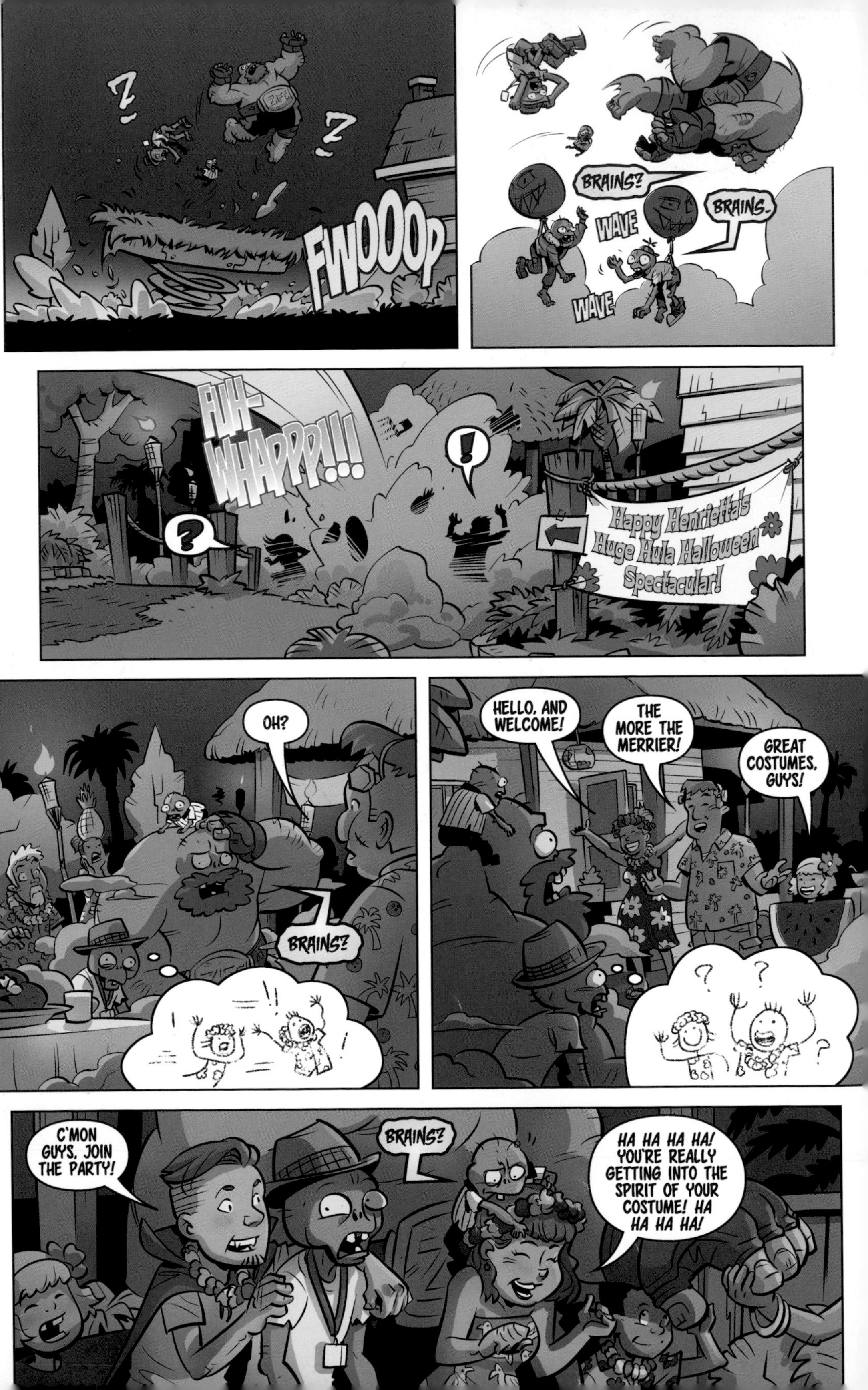
Z
Z
FWOOOP
BRAINS?
WAVE
BRAINS.
WAVE
FUH-WHAPPP!!!
?
!
Happy Henrietta's Huge Hula Halloween Spectacular!
OH?
BRAINS?
HELLO, AND WELCOME!
THE MORE THE MERRIER!
GREAT COSTUMES, GUYS!
C'MON GUYS, JOIN THE PARTY!
BRAINS?
HA HA HA HA! YOU'RE REALLY GETTING INTO THE SPIRIT OF YOUR COSTUME! HA HA HA HA!

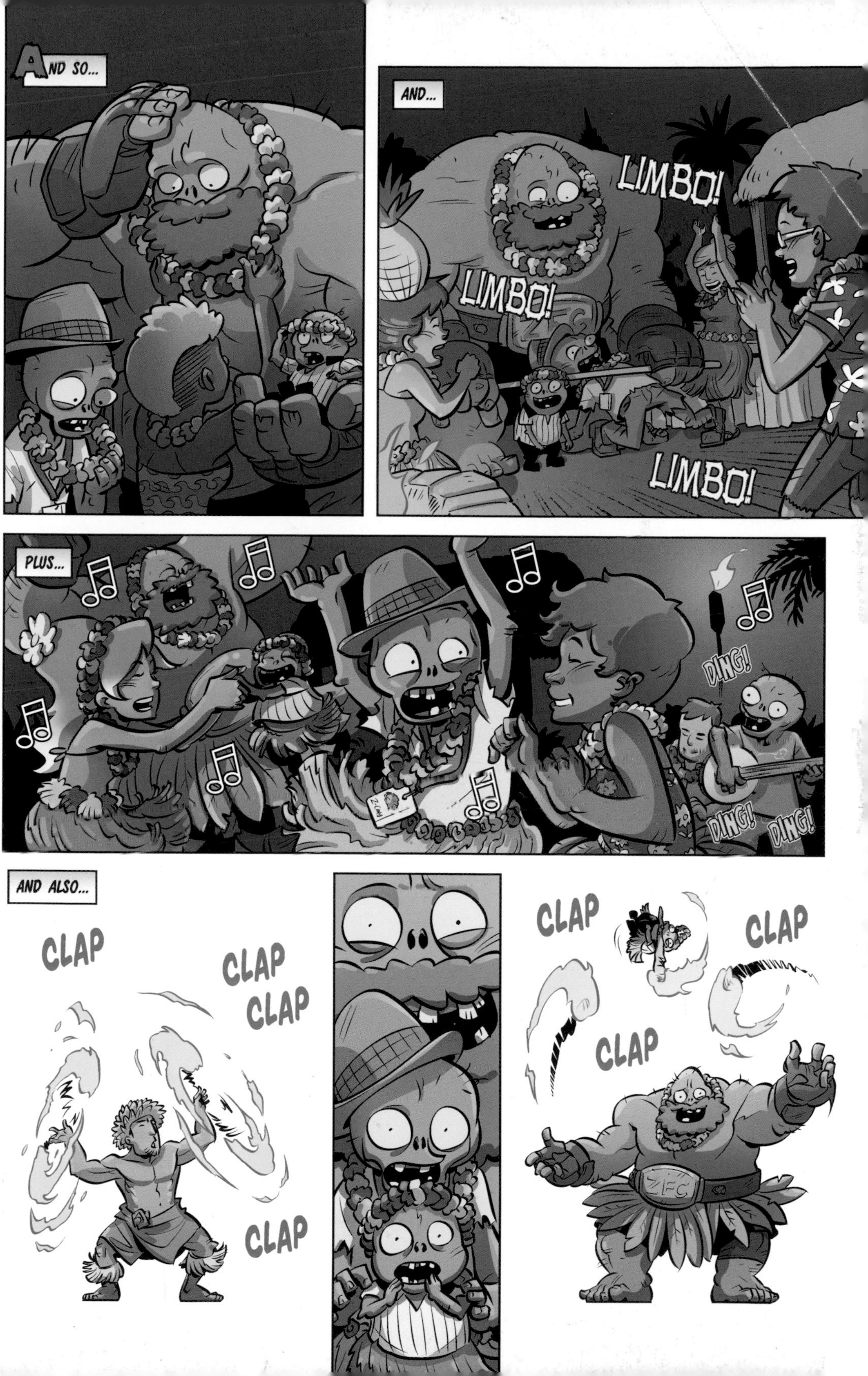
AND SO...
AND...
LIMBO!
LIMBO!
LIMBO!
PLUS...
DING!
DING!
DING!
AND ALSO...
CLAP
CLAP
CLAP
CLAP
CLAP
CLAP
CLAP
ZFC

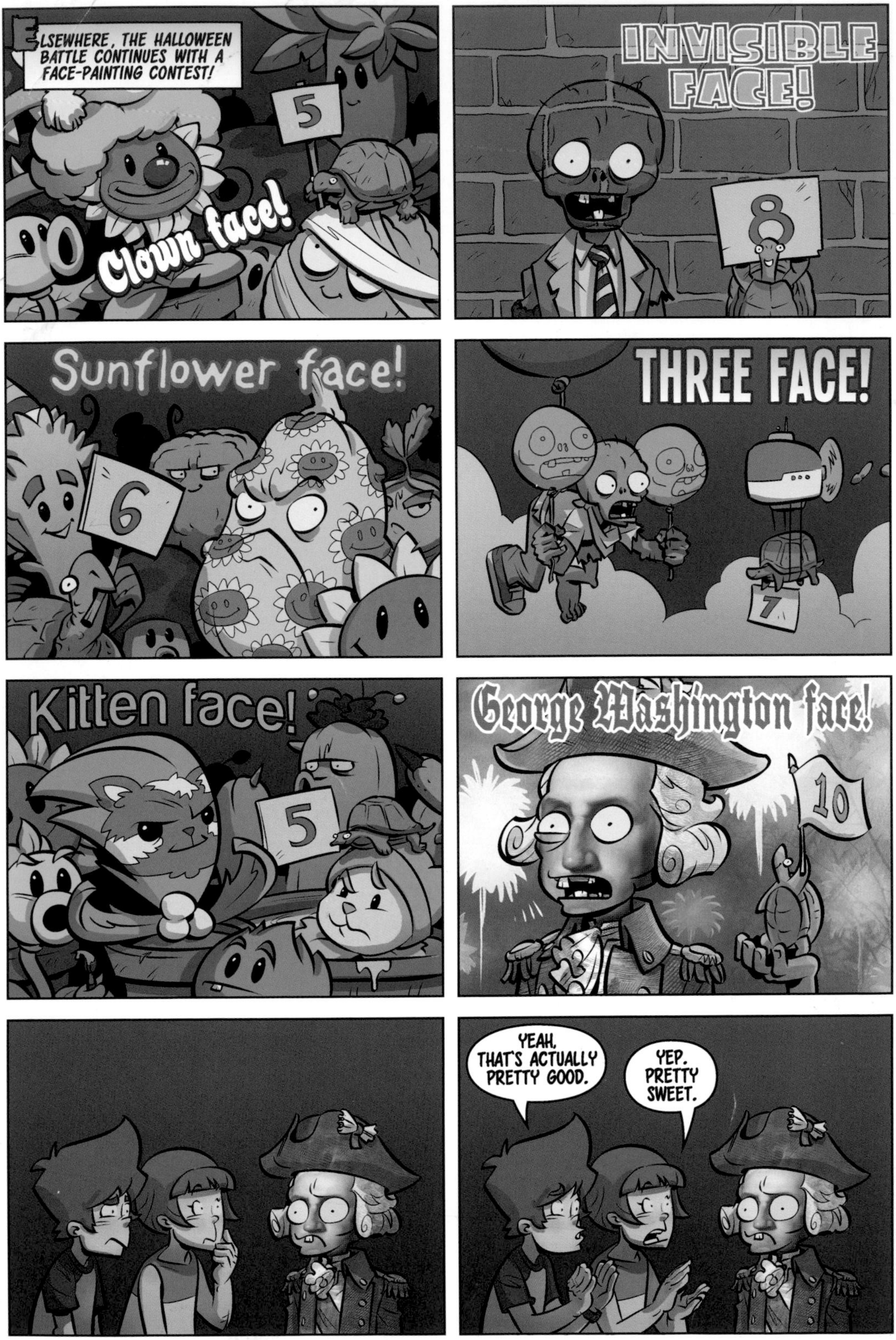
ELSEWHERE, THE HALLOWEEN BATTLE CONTINUES WITH A FACE-PAINTING CONTEST!
5
Clown face!
INVISIBLE FACE!
8
Sunflower face!
6
THREE FACE!
7
Kitten face!
5
George Washington face!
10
YEAH, THAT'S ACTUALLY PRETTY GOOD.
YEP. PRETTY SWEET.

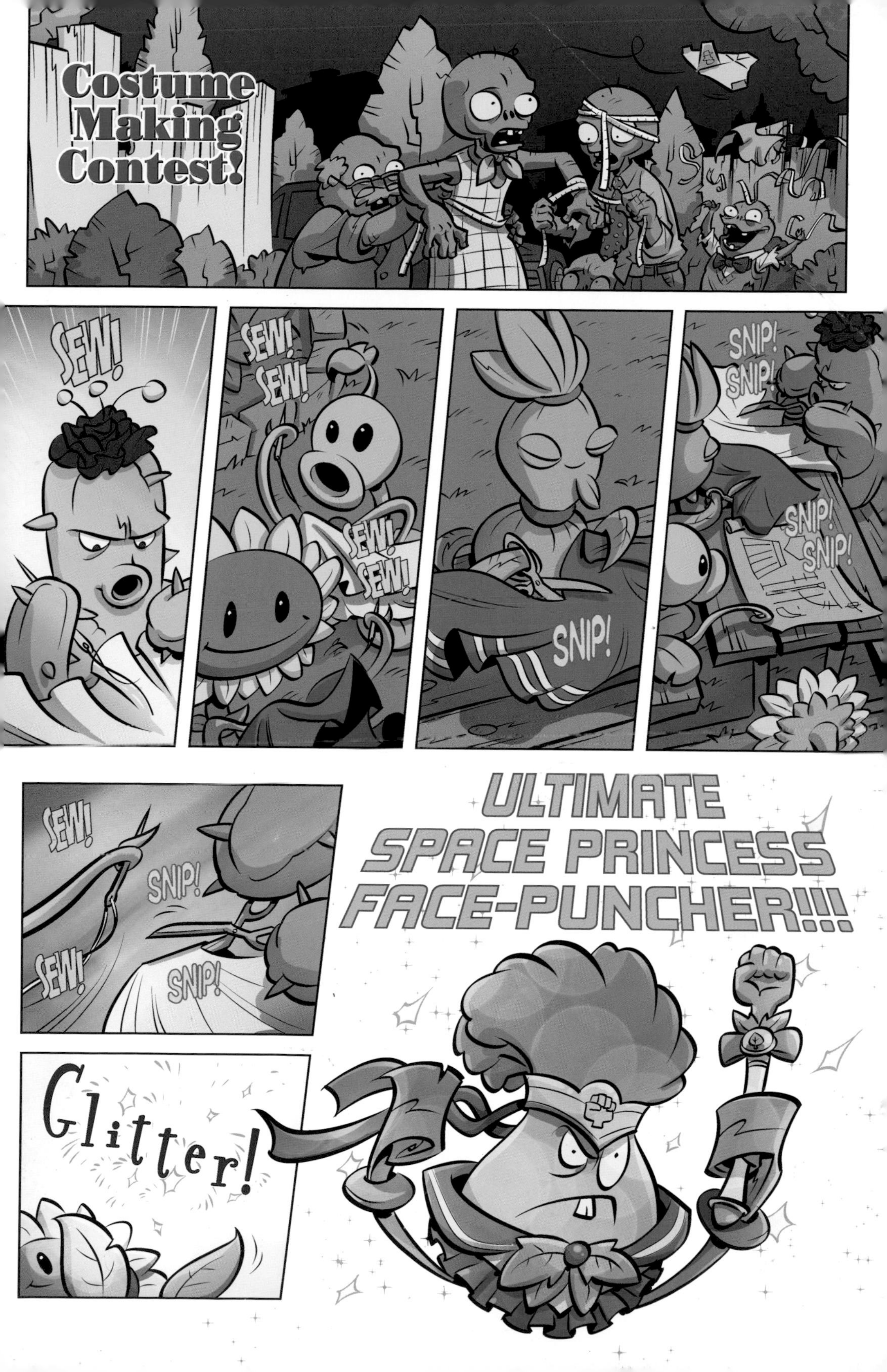
Costume Making Contest!
SEW!
SEW! SEW!
SEW! SEW!
SNIP!
SNIP! SNIP!
SNIP! SNIP!
SEW!
SNIP!
SEW!
SNIP!
ULTIMATE SPACE PRINCESS FACE-PUNCHER!!!
Glitter!

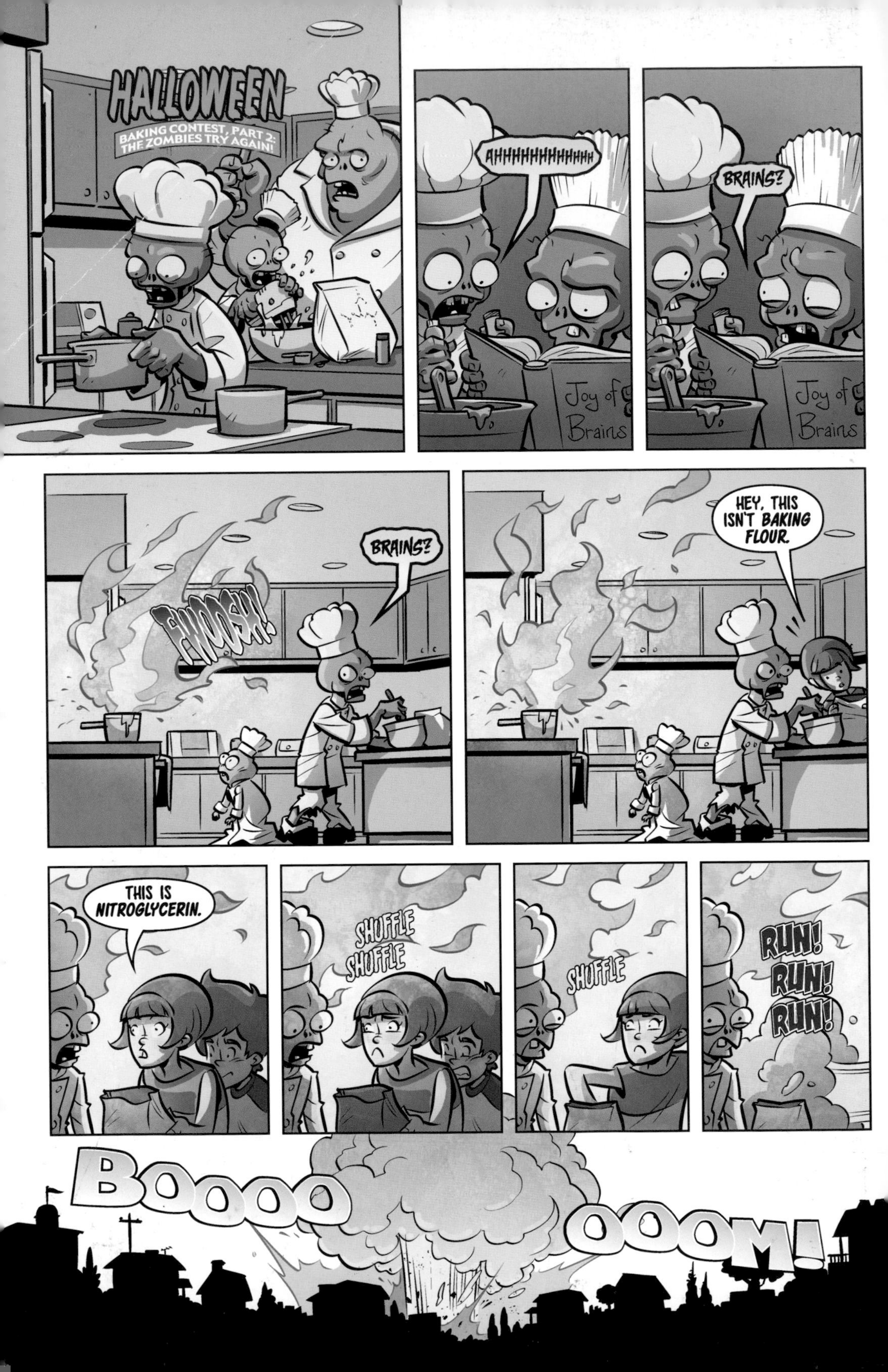
HALLOWEEN
BAKING CONTEST, PART 2: THE ZOMBIES TRY AGAIN!
AHHHHHHHHHHHH
Joy of Brains
BRAINS?
Joy of Brains
BRAINS?
FWOOSH!
HEY, THIS ISN'T BAKING FLOUR.
THIS IS NITROGLYCERIN.
SHUFFLE SHUFFLE
SHUFFLE
RUN! RUN! RUN!
BOOOOOOOOOM!

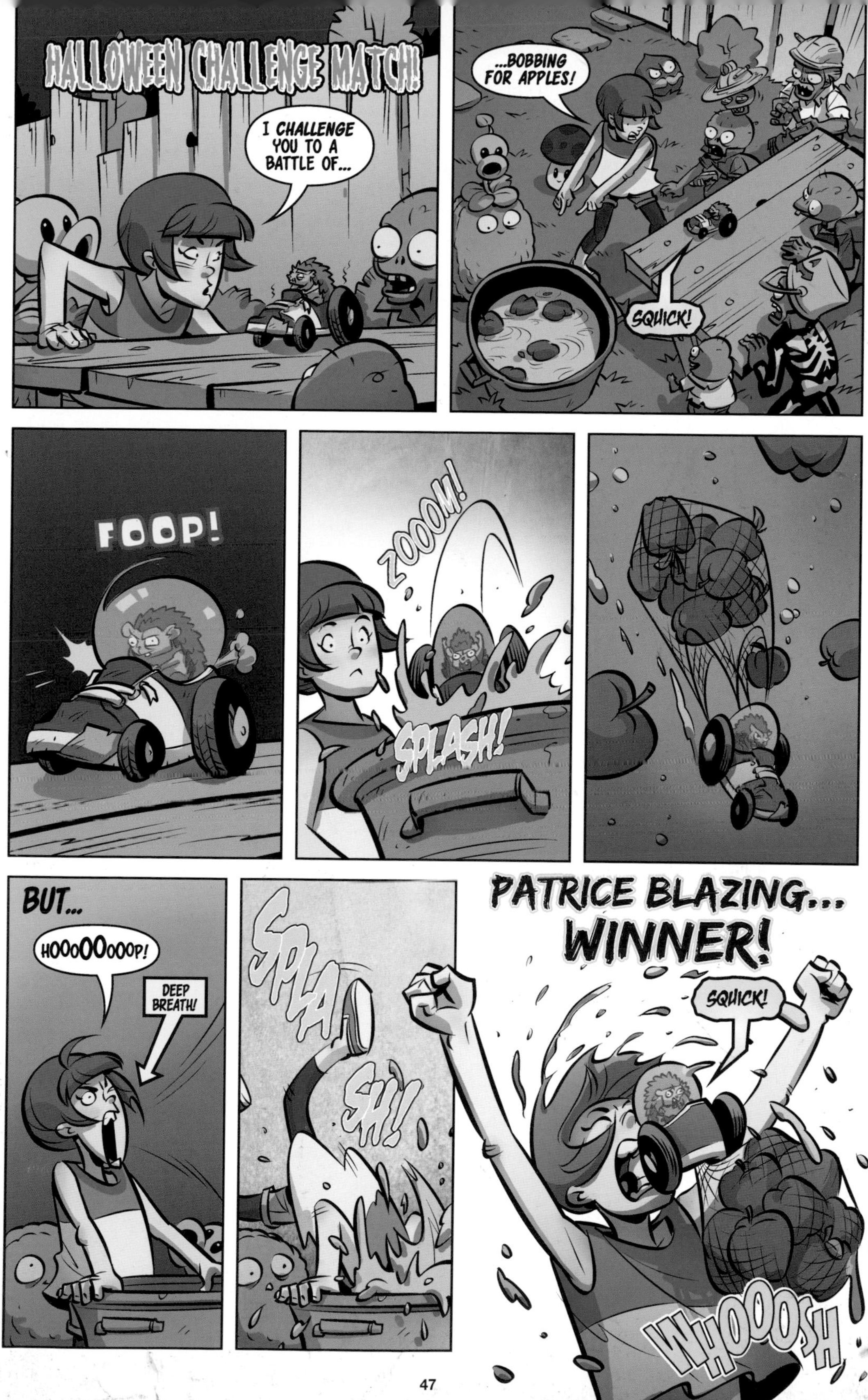
HALLOWEEN CHALLENGE MATCH!
I CHALLENGE YOU TO A BATTLE OF...
...BOBBING FOR APPLES!
SQUICK!
FOOP!
ZOOOM!
SPLASH!
BUT...
HOOOOOOOOP!
DEEP BREATH!
SPLASH!
PATRICE BLAZING... WINNER!
SQUICK!
WHOOOSH

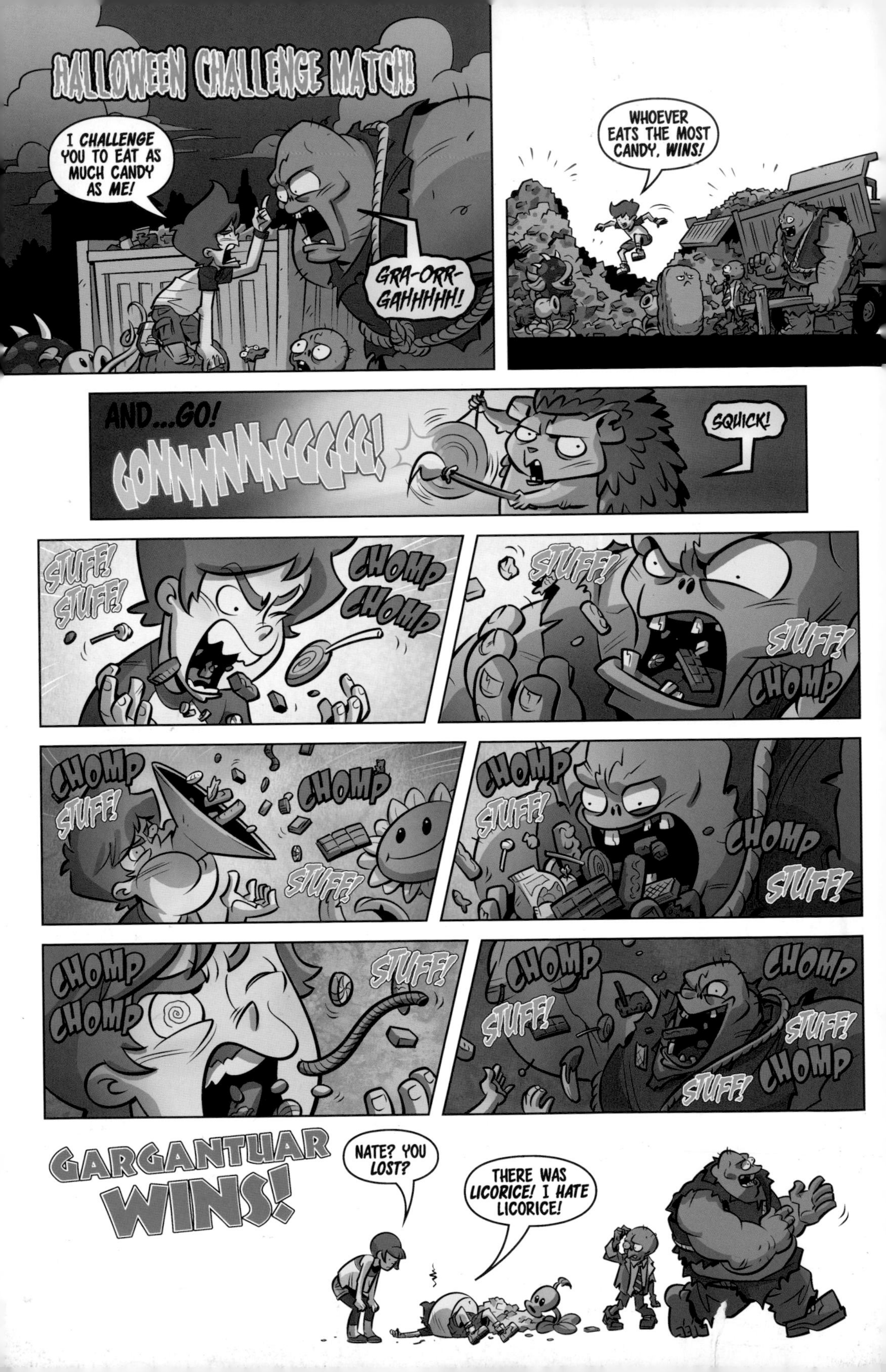
HALLOWEEN CHALLENGE MATCH!
I CHALLENGE YOU TO EAT AS MUCH CANDY AS ME!
GRA-ORR-GAHHHHH!
WHOEVER EATS THE MOST CANDY, WINS!
AND...GO!
GONNNNNNGGGGG!
SQUICK!
STUFF! STUFF!
CHOMP CHOMP
STUFF!
STUFF!
CHOMP
CHOMP
STUFF!
CHOMP
STUFF!
CHOMP
STUFF!
CHOMP
STUFF!
CHOMP CHOMP
STUFF!
CHOMP
STUFF!
CHOMP
STUFF!
CHOMP
STUFF!
GARGANTUAR WINS!
NATE? YOU LOST?
THERE WAS LICORICE! I HATE LICORICE!

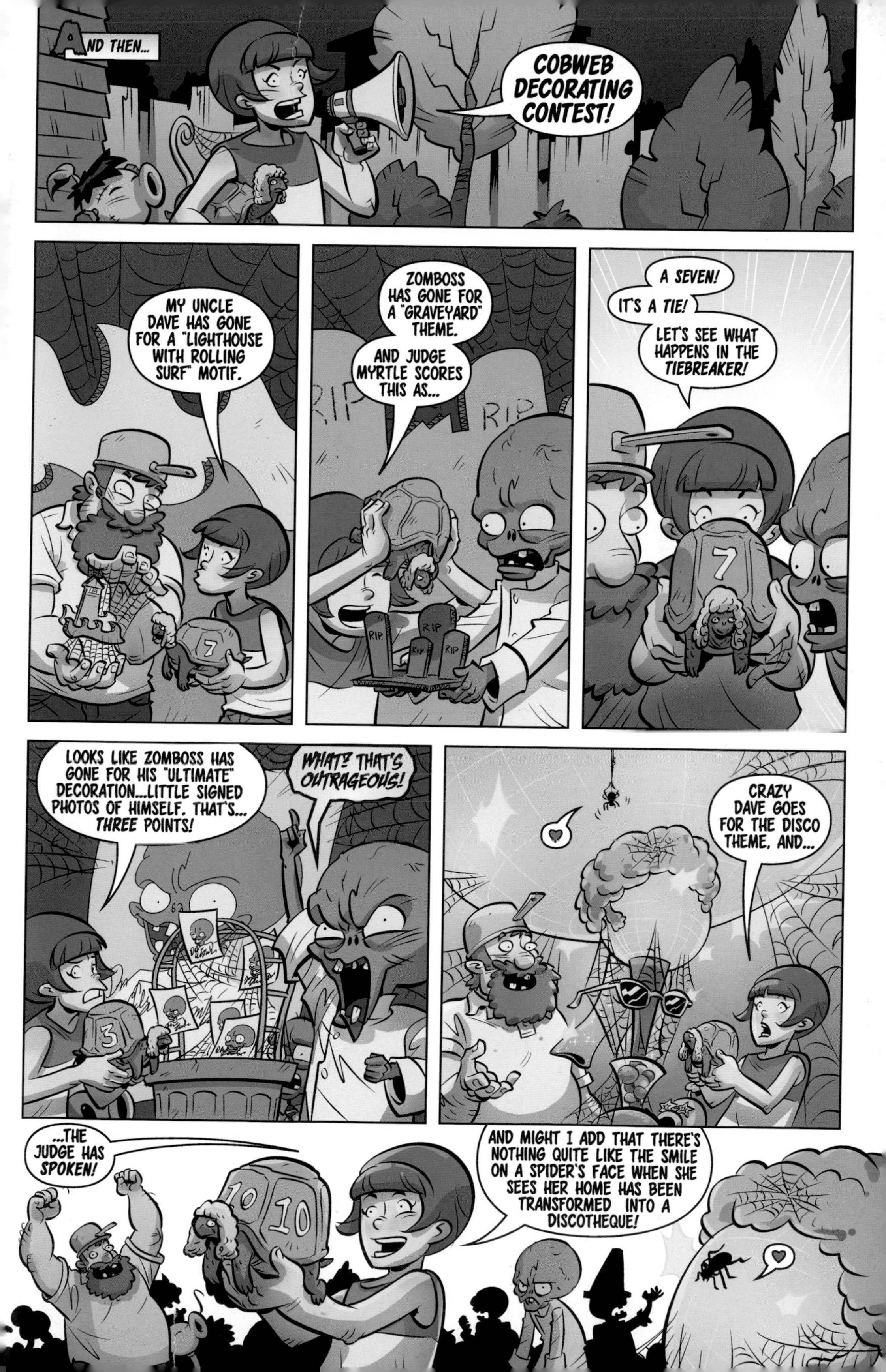
AND THEN...
COBWEB DECORATING CONTEST!
MY UNCLE DAVE HAS GONE FOR A "LIGHTHOUSE WITH ROLLING SURF" MOTIF.
ZOMBOSS HAS GONE FOR A "GRAVEYARD" THEME.
AND JUDGE MYRTLE SCORES THIS AS...
A SEVEN!
IT'S A TIE!
LET'S SEE WHAT HAPPENS IN THE TIEBREAKER!
LOOKS LIKE ZOMBOSS HAS GONE FOR HIS "ULTIMATE" DECORATION...LITTLE SIGNED PHOTOS OF HIMSELF. THAT'S... THREE POINTS!
WHAT? THAT'S OUTRAGEOUS!
CRAZY DAVE GOES FOR THE DISCO THEME, AND...
...THE JUDGE HAS SPOKEN!
AND MIGHT I ADD THAT THERE'S NOTHING QUITE LIKE THE SMILE ON A SPIDER'S FACE WHEN SHE SEES HER HOME HAS BEEN TRANSFORMED INTO A DISCOTHEQUE!

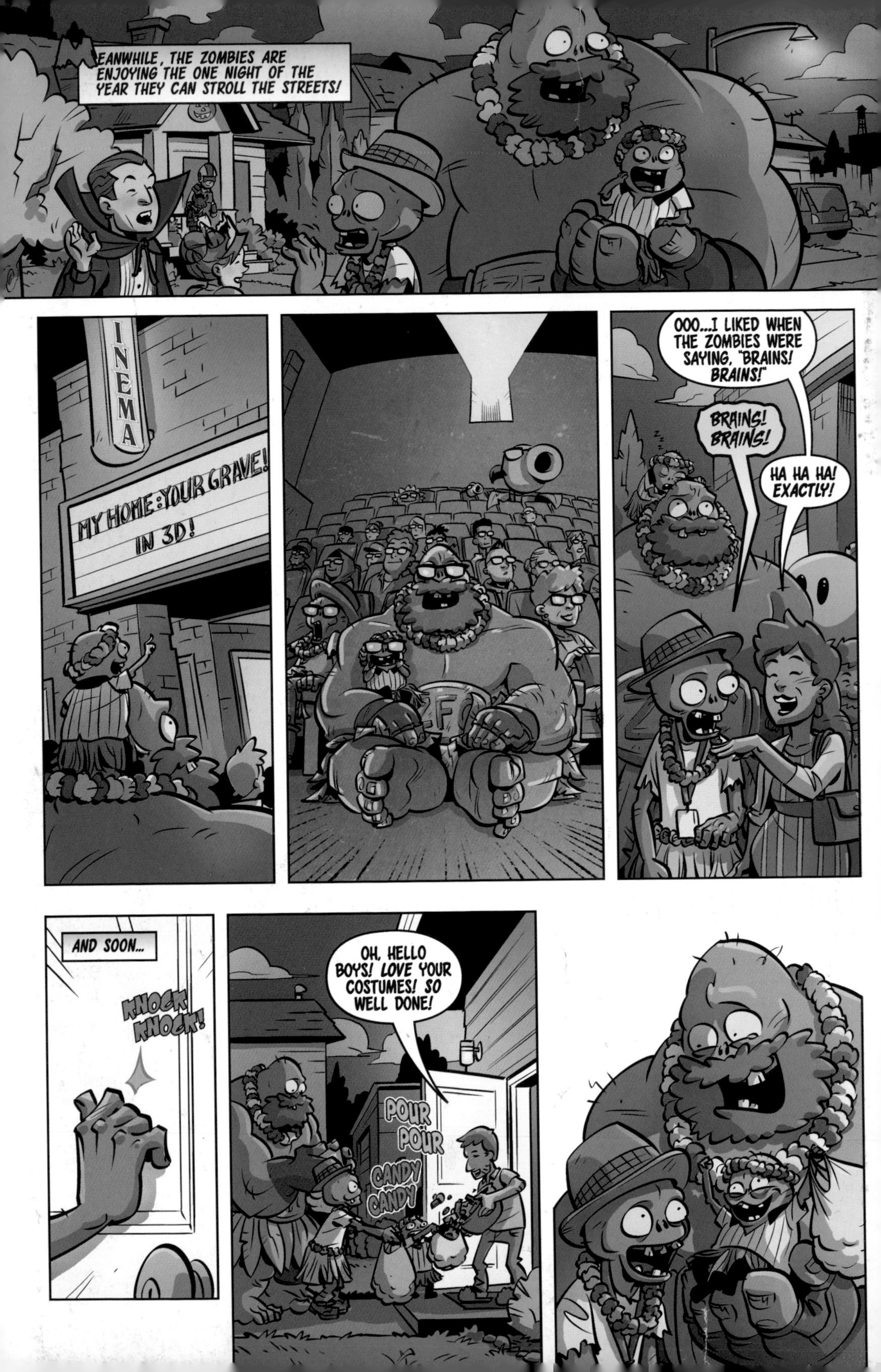
MEANWHILE, THE ZOMBIES ARE ENJOYING THE ONE NIGHT OF THE YEAR THEY CAN STROLL THE STREETS!
CINEMA
MY HOME: YOUR GRAVE! IN 3D!
OOO...I LIKED WHEN THE ZOMBIES WERE SAYING, "BRAINS! BRAINS!"
BRAINS! BRAINS!
HA HA HA! EXACTLY!
AND SOON...
KNOCK KNOCK!
OH, HELLO BOYS! LOVE YOUR COSTUMES! SO WELL DONE!
POUR POUR
CANDY CANDY

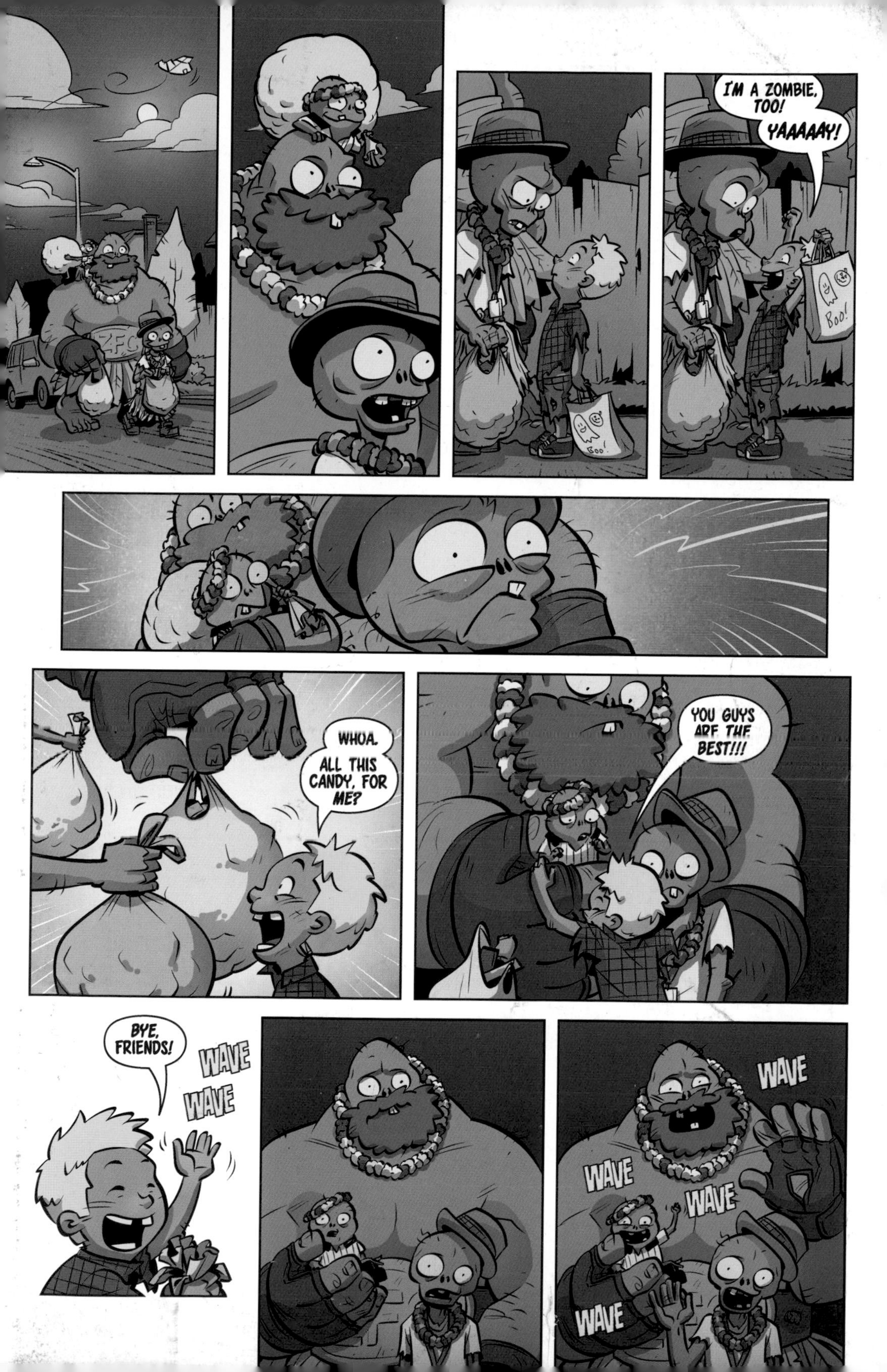
I'M A ZOMBIE, TOO!
YAAAAAY!
Boo!
WHOA. ALL THIS CANDY, FOR ME?
YOU GUYS ARE THE BEST!!!
BYE, FRIENDS!
WAVE
WAVE
WAVE
WAVE
WAVE
WAVE

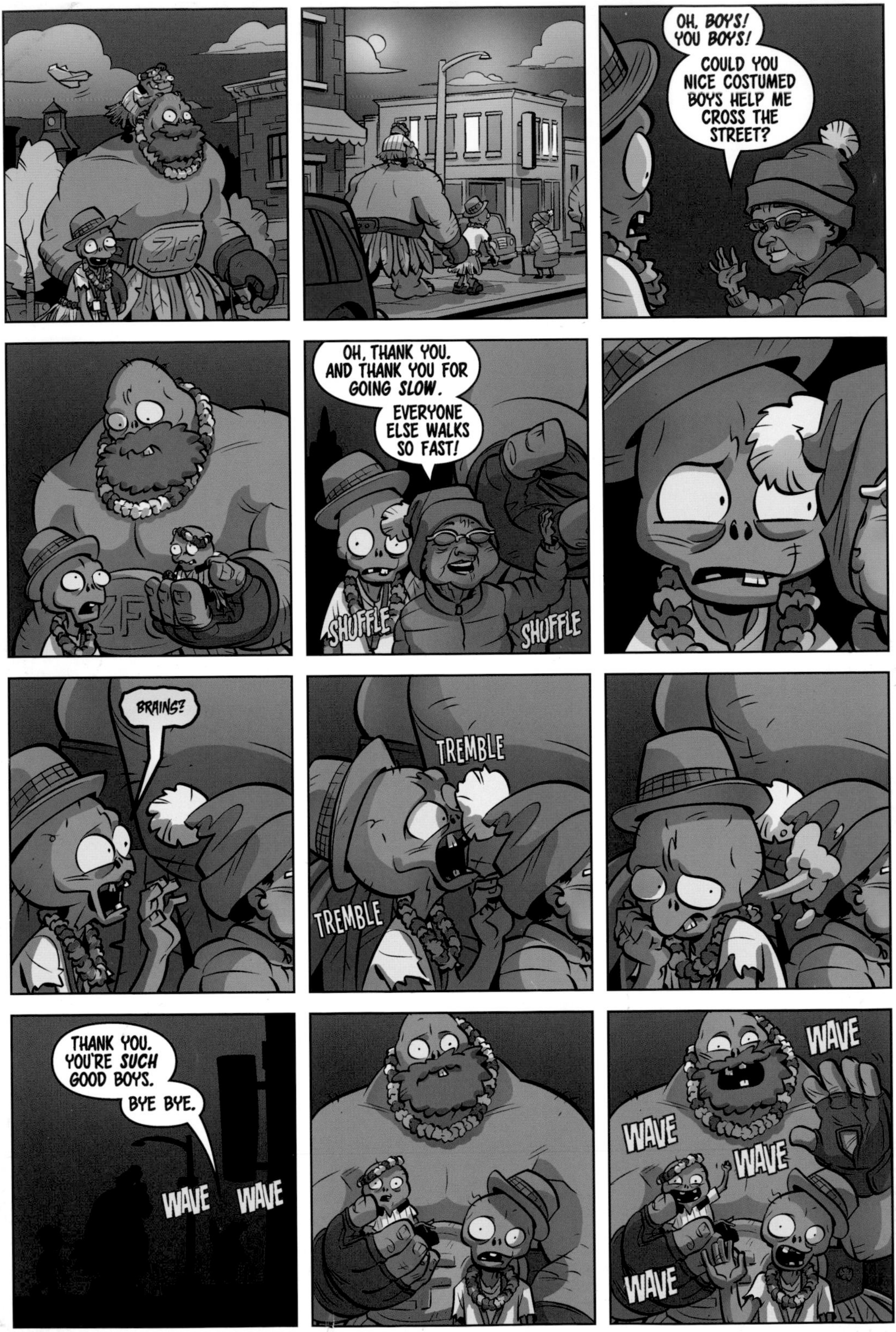
OH, BOYS! YOU BOYS!
COULD YOU NICE COSTUMED BOYS HELP ME CROSS THE STREET?
OH, THANK YOU. AND THANK YOU FOR GOING SLOW.
EVERYONE ELSE WALKS SO FAST!
SHUFFLE
SHUFFLE
BRAINS?
TREMBLE
TREMBLE
THANK YOU. YOU'RE SUCH GOOD BOYS.
BYE BYE.
WAVE
WAVE
WAVE
WAVE
WAVE
WAVE

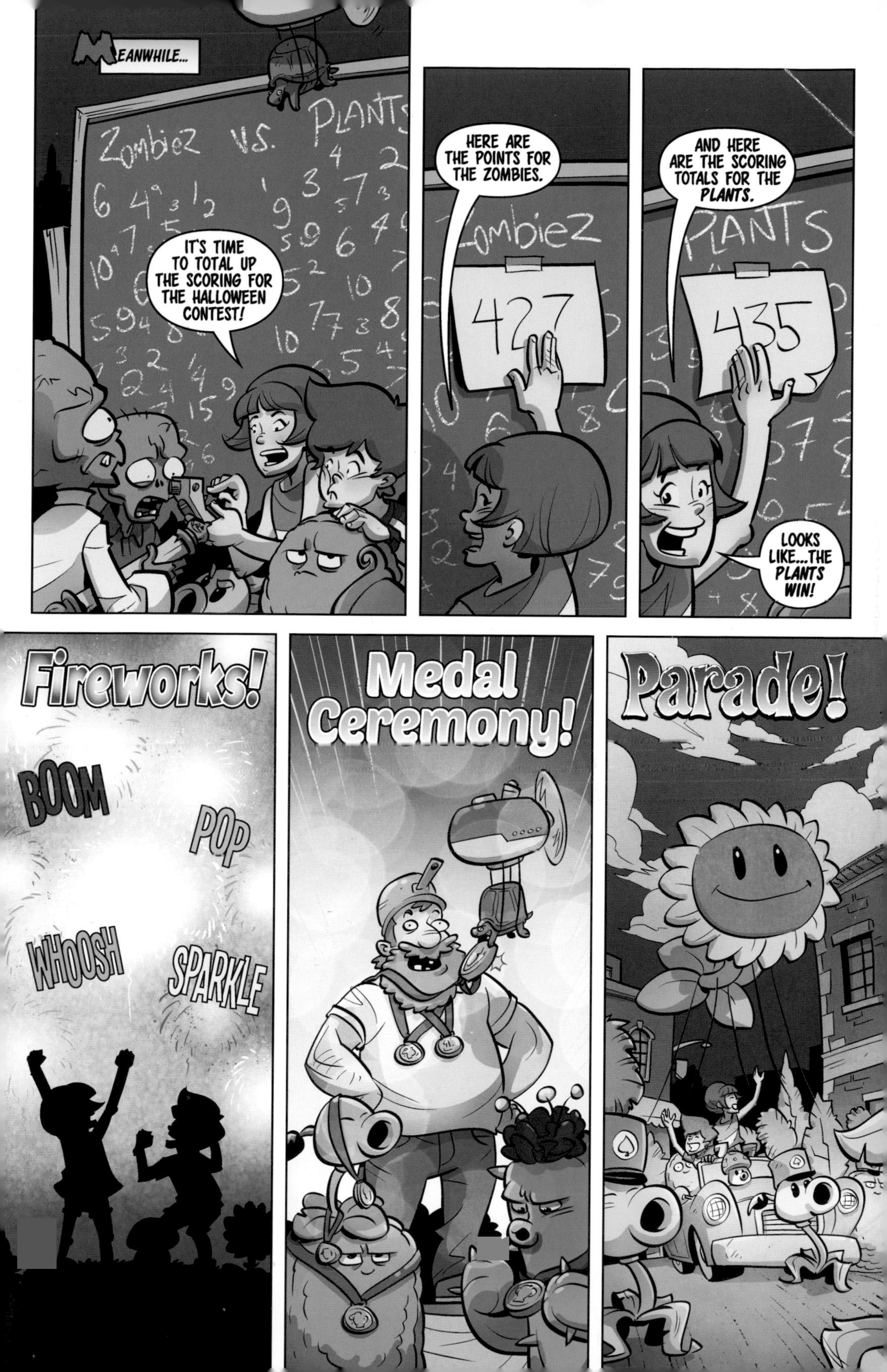
MEANWHILE...
Zombiez V.S. PLANTS
IT'S TIME TO TOTAL UP THE SCORING FOR THE HALLOWEEN CONTEST!
HERE ARE THE POINTS FOR THE ZOMBIES.
Zombiez
427
AND HERE ARE THE SCORING TOTALS FOR THE PLANTS.
PLANTS
435
LOOKS LIKE...THE PLANTS WIN!
Fireworks!
BOOM
POP
WHOOSH
SPARKLE
Medal Ceremony!
Parade!

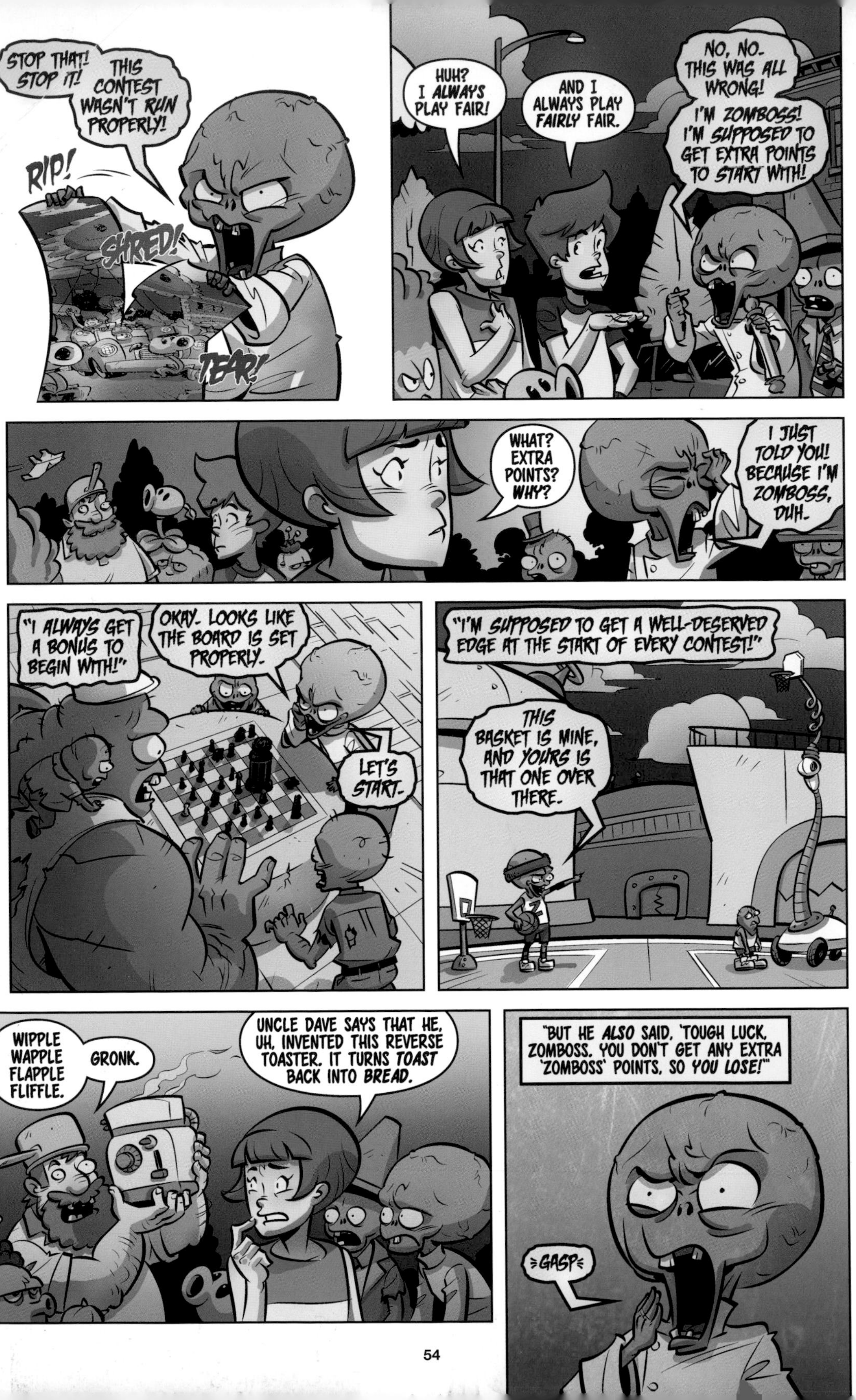

STOP THAT! STOP IT!
THIS CONTEST WASN'T RUN PROPERLY!
RIP!
SHRED!
TEAR!
HUH? I ALWAYS PLAY FAIR!
AND I ALWAYS PLAY FAIRLY FAIR.
NO, NO. THIS WAS ALL WRONG!
I'M ZOMBOSS! I'M SUPPOSED TO GET EXTRA POINTS TO START WITH!
WHAT? EXTRA POINTS? WHY?
I JUST TOLD YOU! BECAUSE I'M ZOMBOSS, DUH.
"I ALWAYS GET A BONUS TO BEGIN WITH!"
OKAY. LOOKS LIKE THE BOARD IS SET PROPERLY.
LET'S START.
"I'M SUPPOSED TO GET A WELL-DESERVED EDGE AT THE START OF EVERY CONTEST!"
THIS BASKET IS MINE, AND YOURS IS THAT ONE OVER THERE.
WIPPLE WAPPLE FLAPPLE FLIFFLE.
GRONK.
UNCLE DAVE SAYS THAT HE, UH, INVENTED THIS REVERSE TOASTER. IT TURNS TOAST BACK INTO BREAD.
"BUT HE ALSO SAID, 'TOUGH LUCK, ZOMBOSS. YOU DON'T GET ANY EXTRA 'ZOMBOSS' POINTS, SO YOU LOSE!'"
GASP

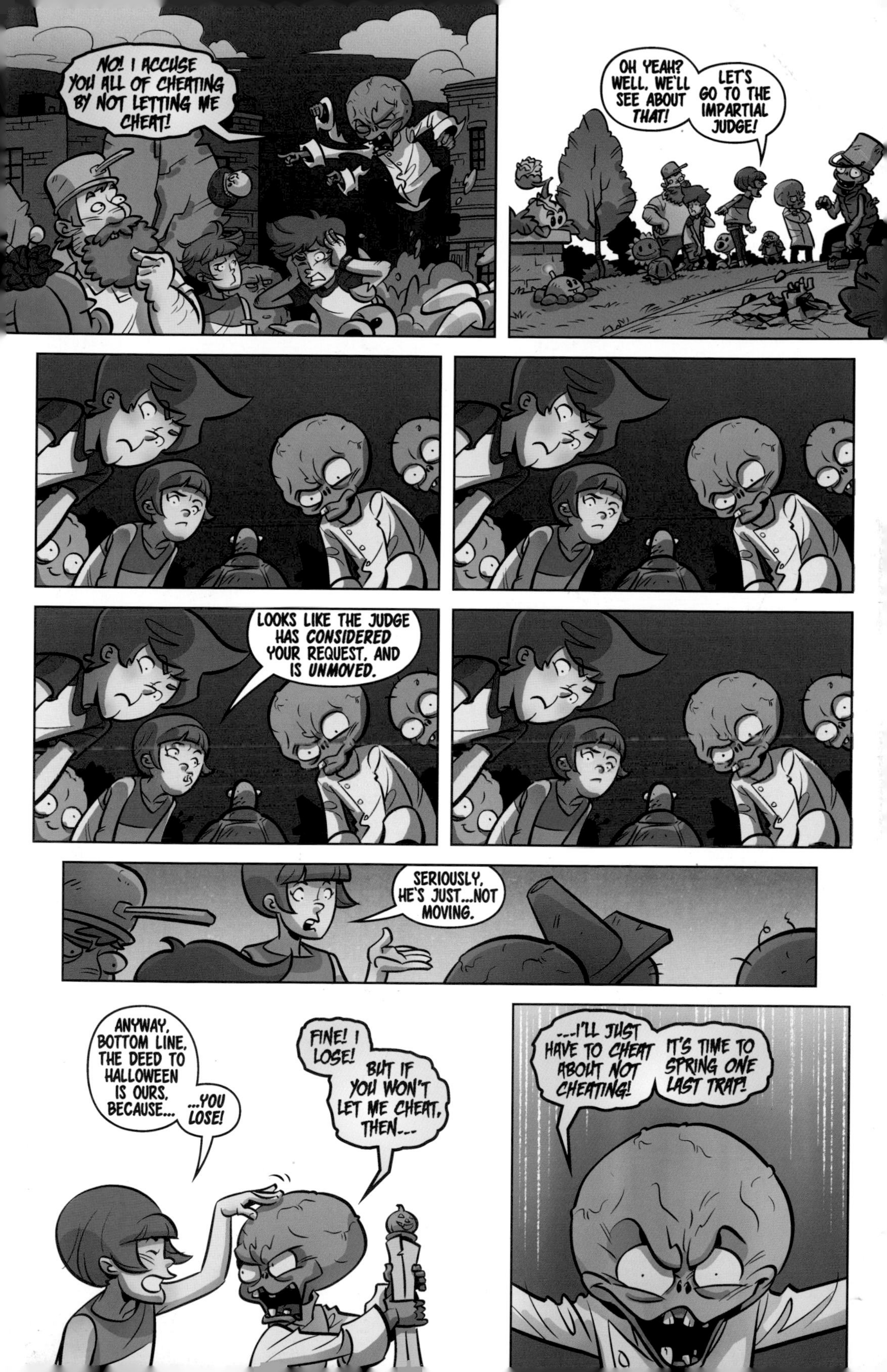
NO! I ACCUSE YOU ALL OF CHEATING BY NOT LETTING ME CHEAT!
OH YEAH? WELL, WE'LL SEE ABOUT THAT!
LET'S GO TO THE IMPARTIAL JUDGE!
LOOKS LIKE THE JUDGE HAS CONSIDERED YOUR REQUEST, AND IS UNMOVED.
SERIOUSLY, HE'S JUST...NOT MOVING.
ANYWAY, BOTTOM LINE, THE DEED TO HALLOWEEN IS OURS, BECAUSE...
...YOU LOSE!
FINE! I LOSE!
BUT IF YOU WON'T LET ME CHEAT, THEN...
...I'LL JUST HAVE TO CHEAT ABOUT NOT CHEATING!
IT'S TIME TO SPRING ONE LAST TRAP!

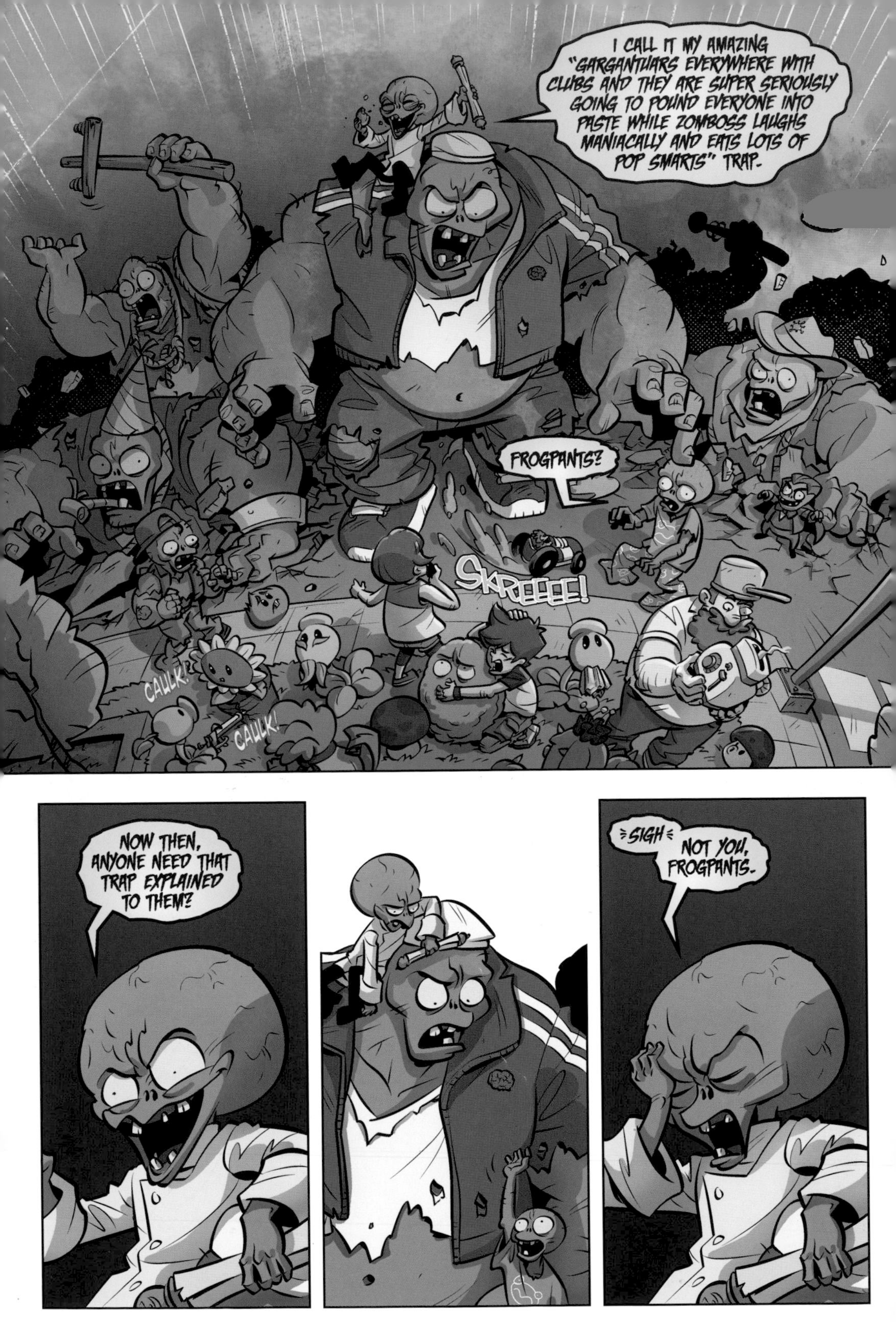
I CALL IT MY AMAZING "GARGANTUARS EVERYWHERE WITH CLUBS AND THEY ARE SUPER SERIOUSLY GOING TO POUND EVERYONE INTO PASTE WHILE ZOMBOSS LAUGHS MANIACALLY AND EATS LOTS OF POP SMARTS" TRAP.
FROGPANTS?
SKREEEEE!
CAULK!
CAULK!
NOW THEN, ANYONE NEED THAT TRAP EXPLAINED TO THEM?
SIGH
NOT YOU, FROGPANTS.

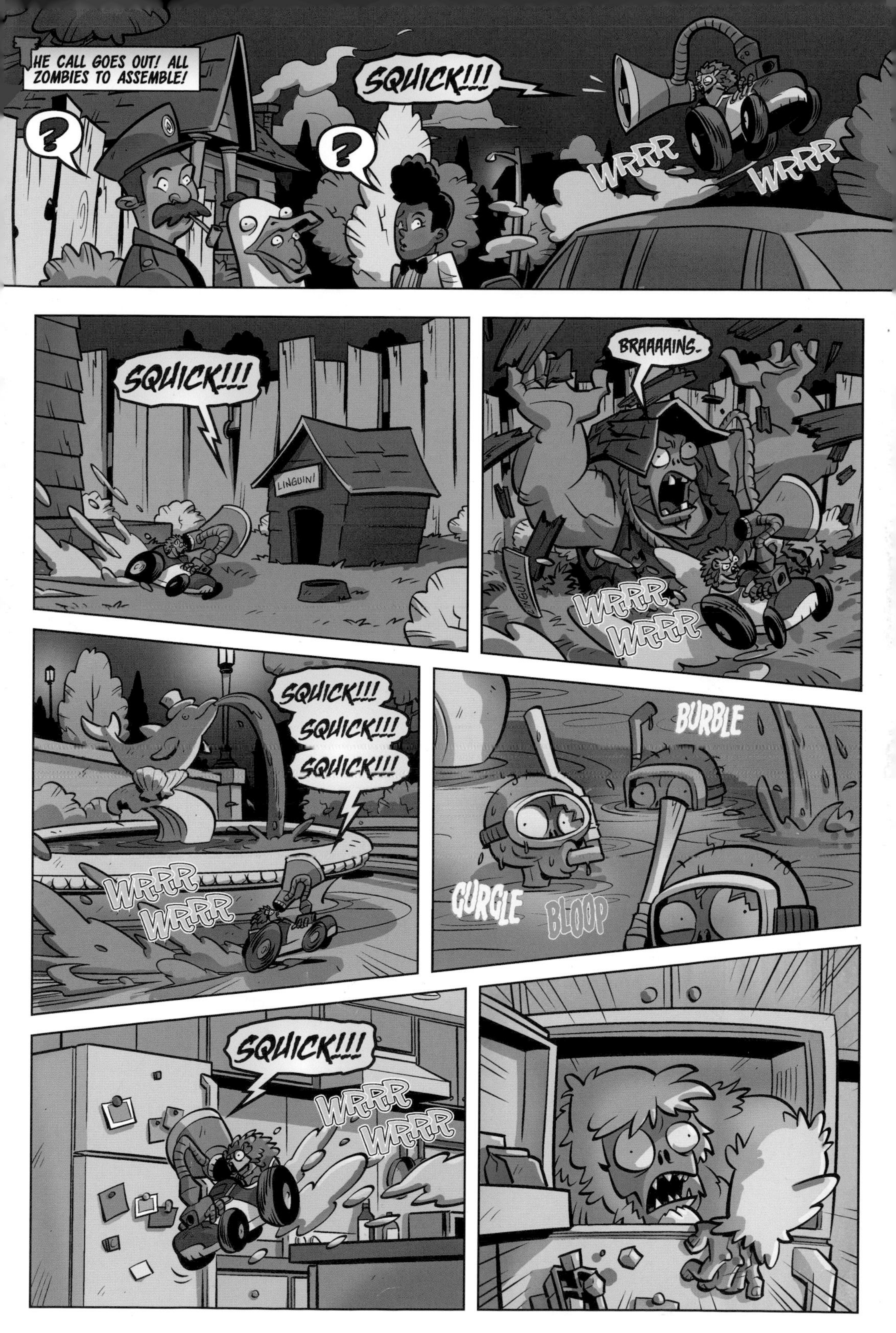
THE CALL GOES OUT! ALL ZOMBIES TO ASSEMBLE!
?
SQUICK!!!
?
WRRR
WRRR
SQUICK!!!
LINGUINI
BRAAAAINS.
LINGUINI
WRRR
WRRR
SQUICK!!!
SQUICK!!!
SQUICK!!!
WRRR
WRRR
BURBLE
GURGLE
BLOOP
SQUICK!!!
WRRR
WRRR

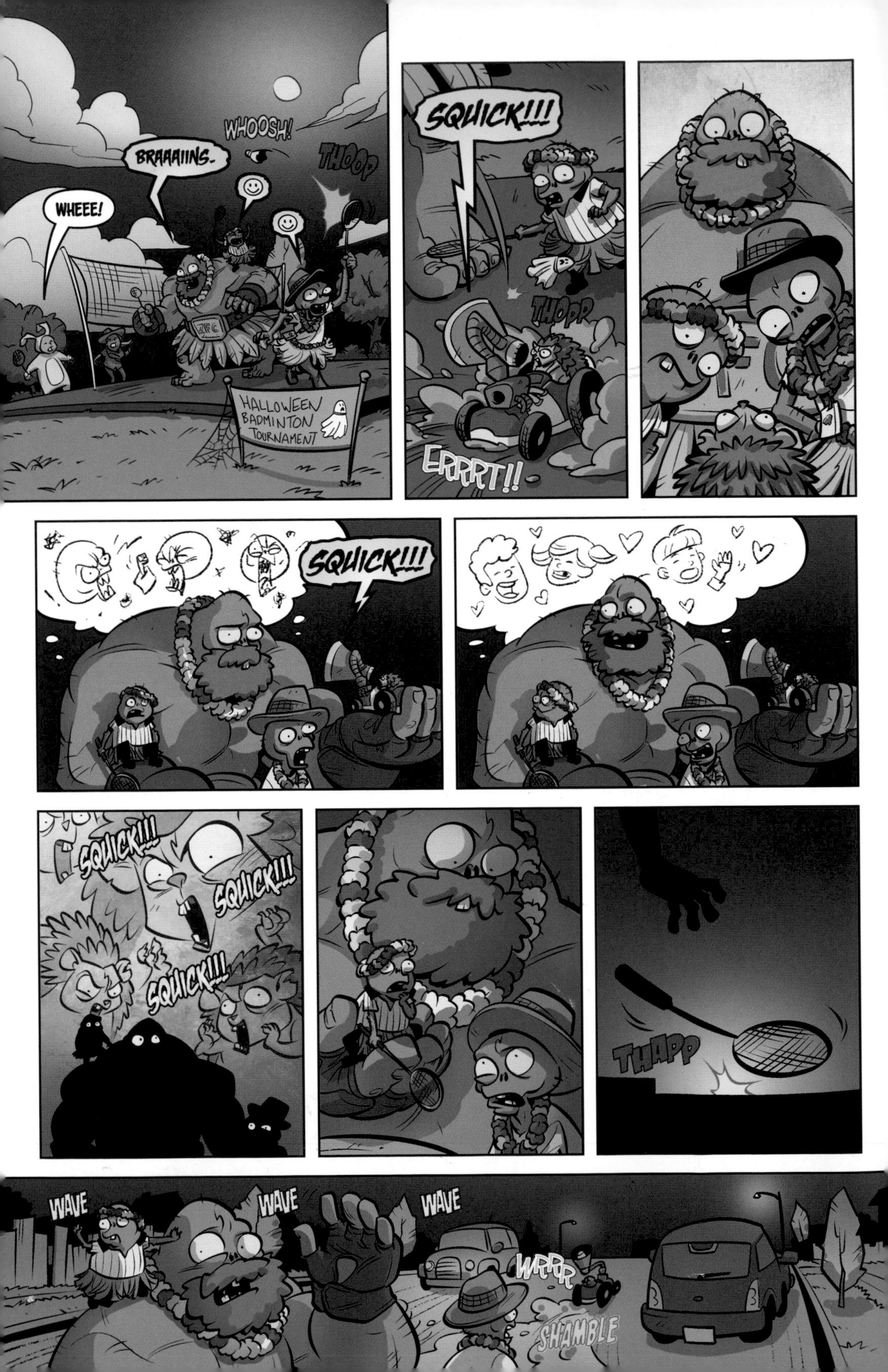
WHEEE!
BRAAAIINS.
WHOOSH!
THOOP
HALLOWEEN BADMINTON TOURNAMENT
ZFC
SQUICK!!!
THOPP
ERRRT!!
SQUICK!!!
SQUICK!!!
SQUICK!!!
SQUICK!!!
THAPP
WAVE
WAVE
WAVE
WRRRR
SHAMBLE

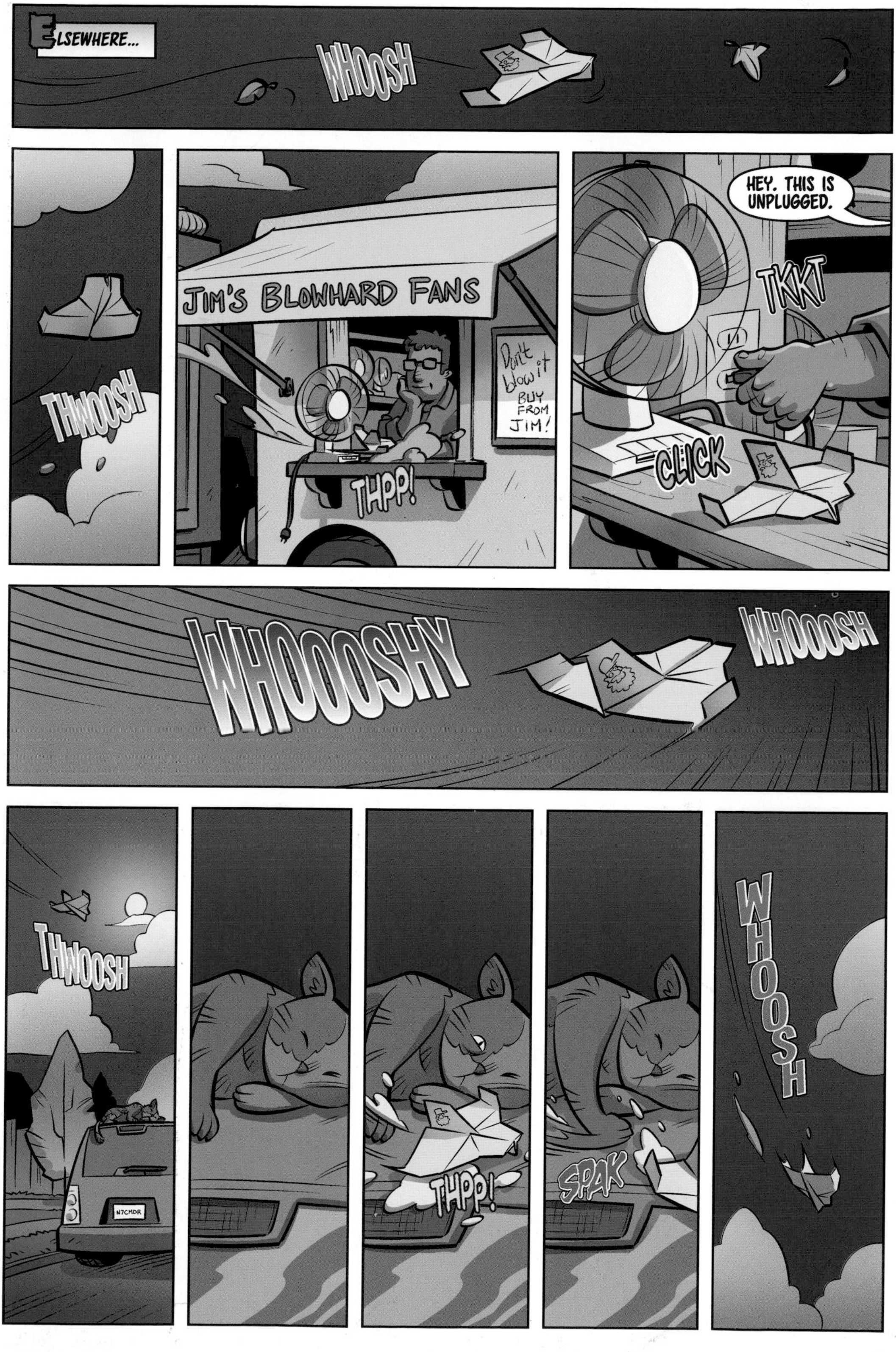
ELSEWHERE...
WHOOSH
THWOOSH
JIM'S BLOWHARD FANS
Don't blow it BUY FROM JIM!
THPP!
HEY. THIS IS UNPLUGGED.
TKKT
CLICK
WHOOOSHY
WHOOOSH
THWOOSH
N7CMDR
THPP!
SPAK
WHOOOSH

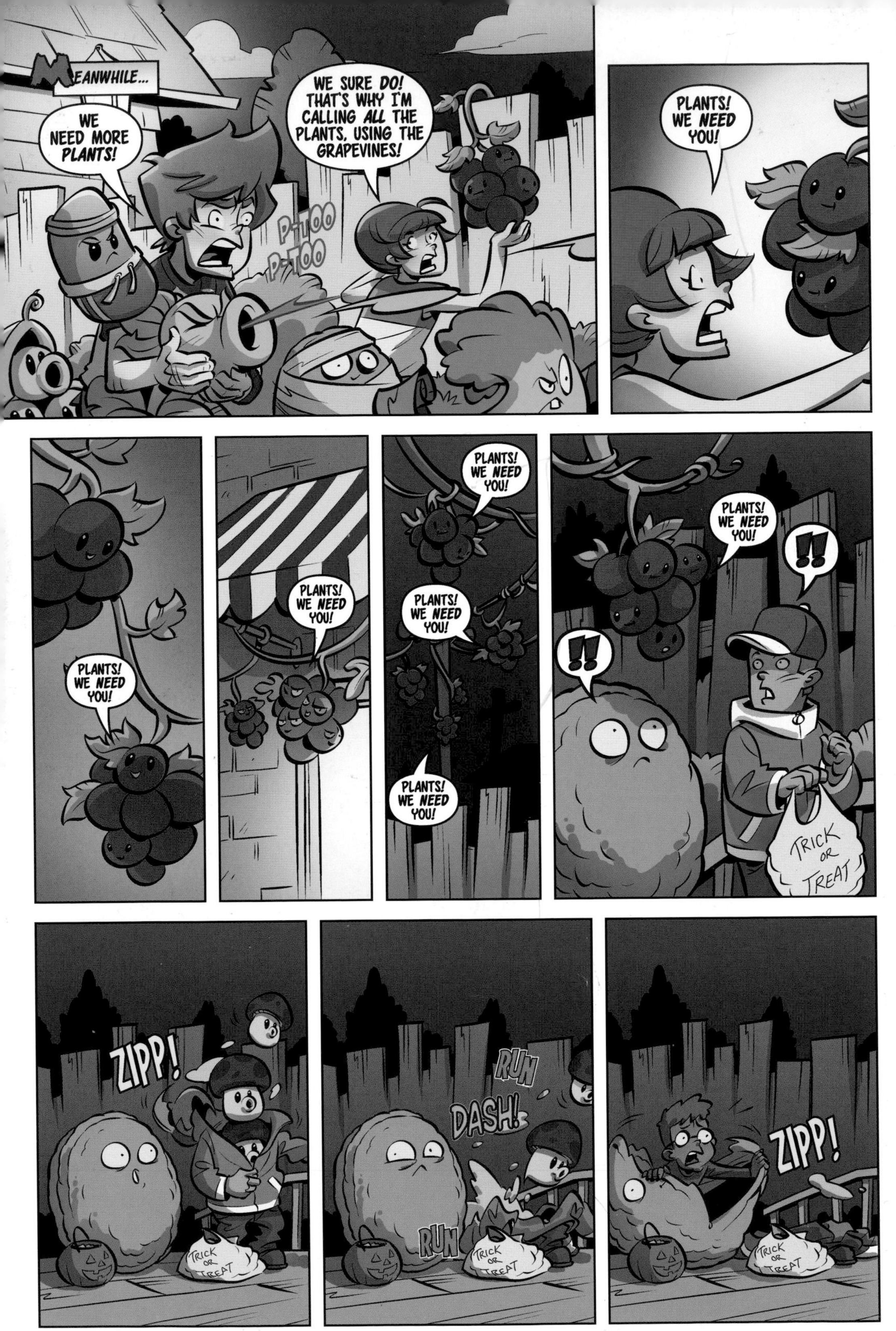
MEANWHILE...
WE NEED MORE PLANTS!
WE SURE DO! THAT'S WHY I'M CALLING ALL THE PLANTS, USING THE GRAPEVINES!
P-TOO P-TOO
PLANTS! WE NEED YOU!
PLANTS! WE NEED YOU!
PLANTS! WE NEED YOU!
PLANTS! WE NEED YOU!
PLANTS! WE NEED YOU!
PLANTS! WE NEED YOU!
PLANTS! WE NEED YOU!
!!
!!
TRICK OR TREAT
ZIPP!
TRICK OR TREAT
RUN
DASH!
RUN
TRICK OR TREAT
ZIPP!
TRICK OR TREAT

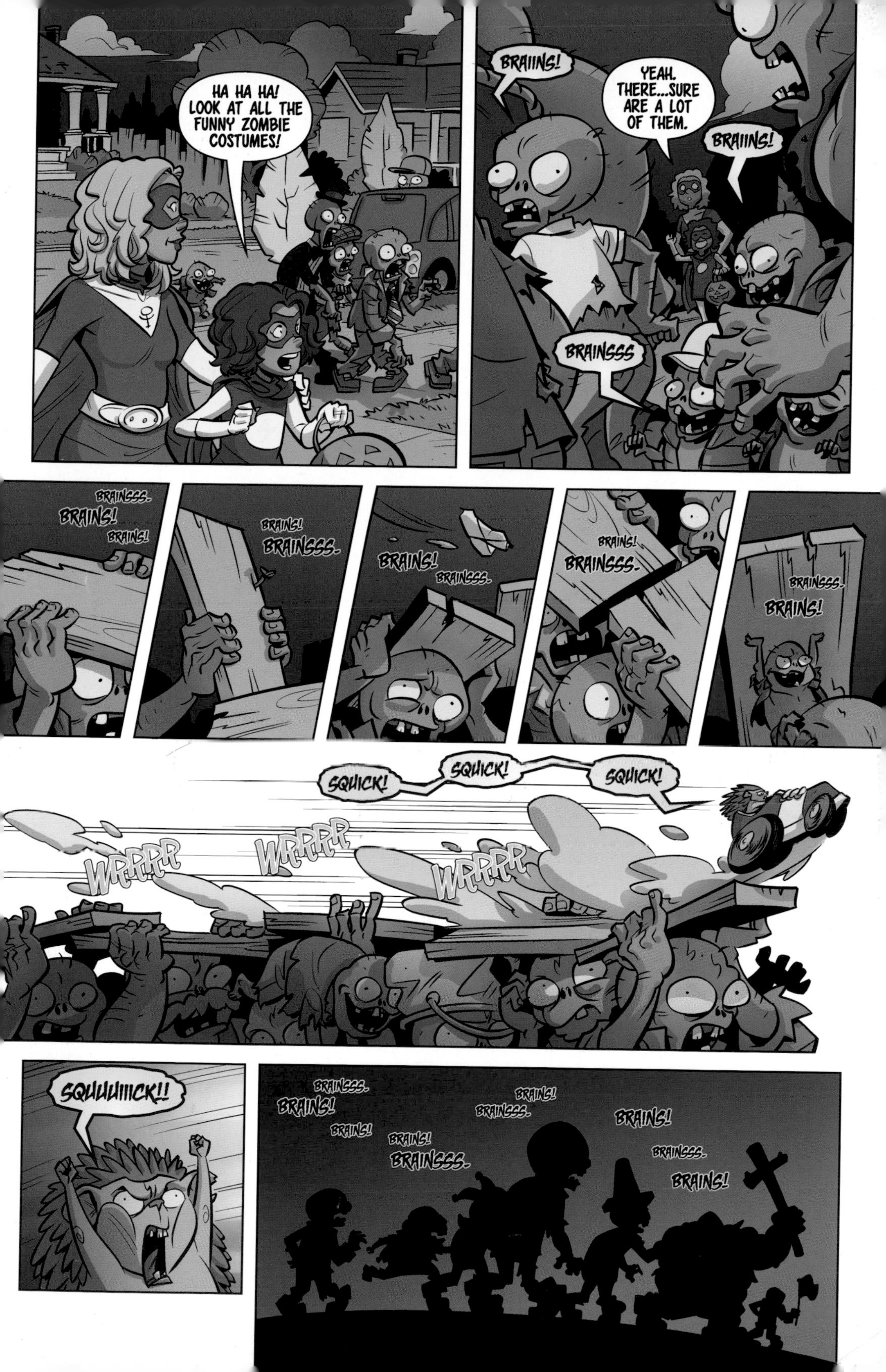
HA HA HA! LOOK AT ALL THE FUNNY ZOMBIE COSTUMES!
BRAIINS!
YEAH. THERE...SURE ARE A LOT OF THEM.
BRAIINS!
BRAINSSS
BRAINSSS.
BRAINS!
BRAINS!
BRAINS!
BRAINSSS.
BRAINS!
BRAINSSS.
BRAINS!
BRAINSSS.
BRAINSSS.
BRAINS!
SQUICK!
SQUICK!
SQUICK!
WRRRR
WRRRR
WRRRR
SQUUUIIICK!!
BRAINSSS.
BRAINS!
BRAINS!
BRAINS!
BRAINSSS.
BRAINS!
BRAINSSS.
BRAINS!
BRAINSSS.
BRAINS!

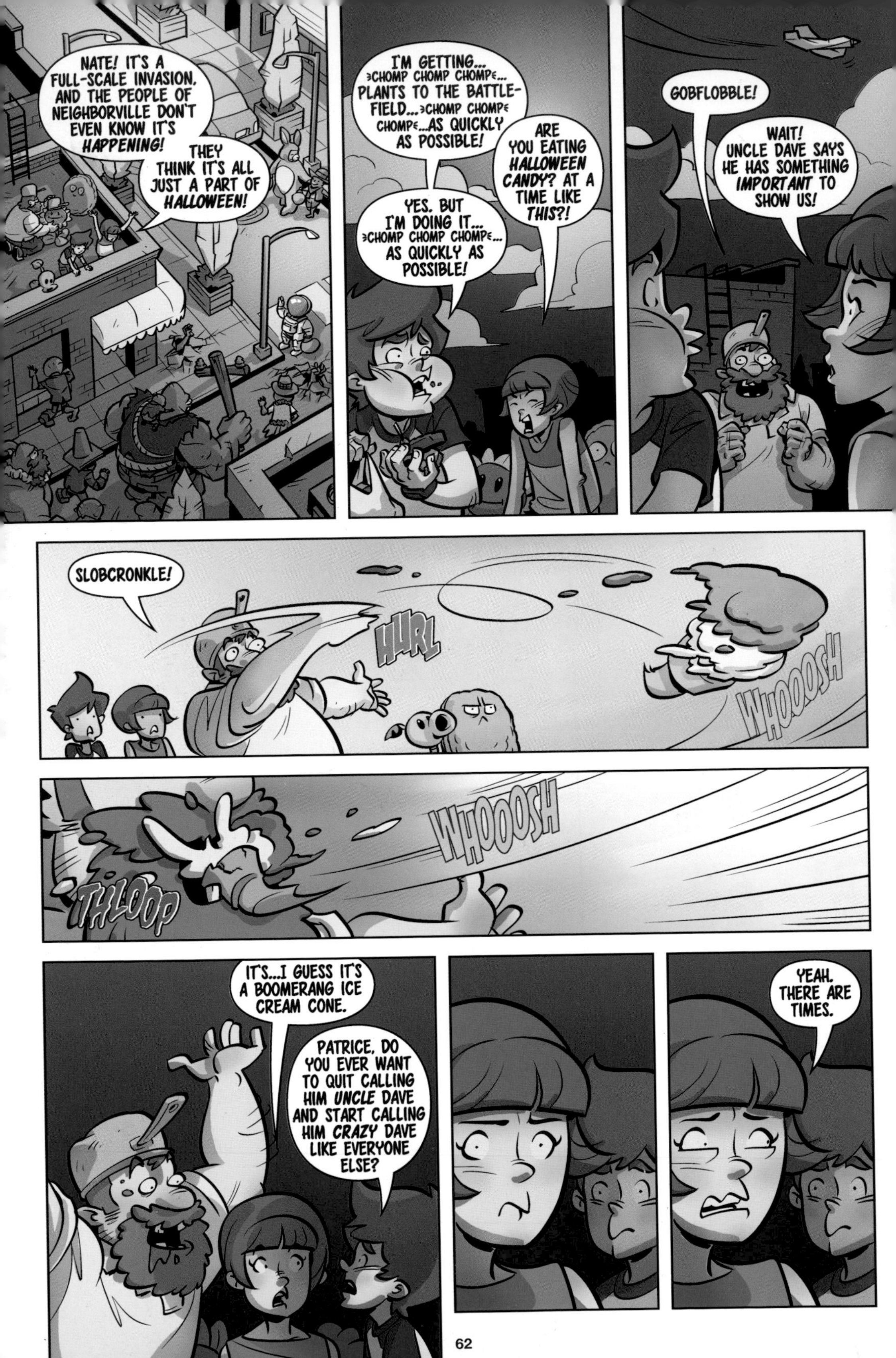

NATE! IT'S A FULL-SCALE INVASION, AND THE PEOPLE OF NEIGHBORVILLE DON'T EVEN KNOW IT'S *HAPPENING!*
THEY THINK IT'S ALL JUST A PART OF *HALLOWEEN!*
I'M GETTING... ∋CHOMP CHOMP CHOMP∈... PLANTS TO THE BATTLE-FIELD... ∋CHOMP CHOMP∈ CHOMP∈...AS QUICKLY AS POSSIBLE!
ARE YOU EATING *HALLOWEEN CANDY?* AT A TIME LIKE *THIS?!*
YES. BUT I'M DOING IT... ∋CHOMP CHOMP CHOMP∈... AS QUICKLY AS POSSIBLE!
GOBFLOBBLE!
WAIT! UNCLE DAVE SAYS HE HAS SOMETHING *IMPORTANT* TO SHOW US!
SLOBCRONKLE!
HURL
WHOOOSH
WHOOOSH
THLOOP
IT'S...I GUESS IT'S A BOOMERANG ICE CREAM CONE.
PATRICE, DO YOU EVER WANT TO QUIT CALLING HIM *UNCLE* DAVE AND START CALLING HIM *CRAZY* DAVE LIKE EVERYONE ELSE?
YEAH. THERE ARE TIMES.

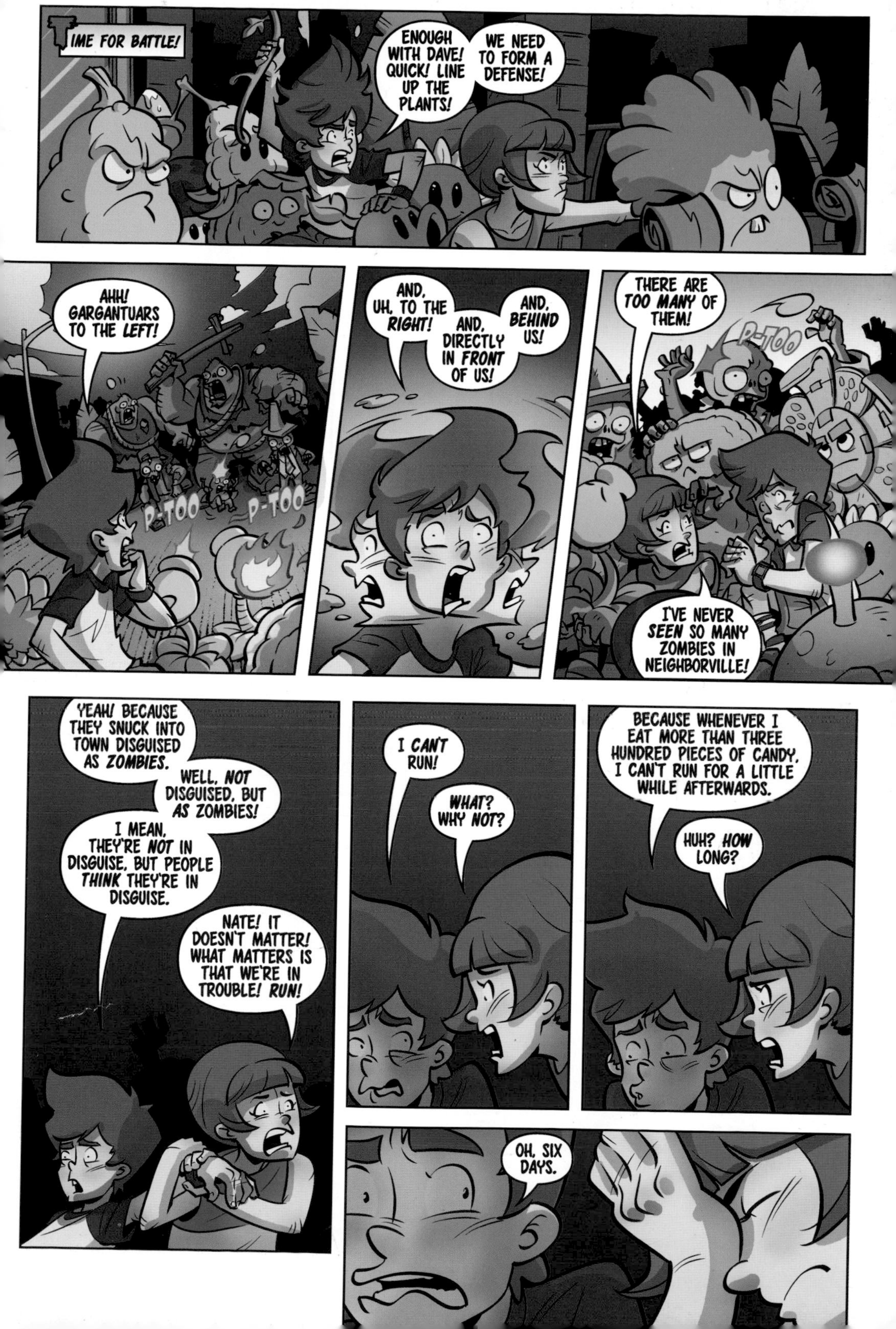
TIME FOR BATTLE!
ENOUGH WITH DAVE! QUICK! LINE UP THE PLANTS!
WE NEED TO FORM A DEFENSE!
AHH! GARGANTUARS TO THE LEFT!
P-TOO
P-TOO
AND, UH, TO THE RIGHT!
AND, DIRECTLY IN FRONT OF US!
AND, BEHIND US!
THERE ARE TOO MANY OF THEM!
P-TOO
I'VE NEVER SEEN SO MANY ZOMBIES IN NEIGHBORVILLE!
YEAH! BECAUSE THEY SNUCK INTO TOWN DISGUISED AS ZOMBIES.
WELL, NOT DISGUISED, BUT AS ZOMBIES!
I MEAN, THEY'RE NOT IN DISGUISE, BUT PEOPLE THINK THEY'RE IN DISGUISE.
NATE! IT DOESN'T MATTER! WHAT MATTERS IS THAT WE'RE IN TROUBLE! RUN!
I CAN'T RUN!
WHAT? WHY NOT?
BECAUSE WHENEVER I EAT MORE THAN THREE HUNDRED PIECES OF CANDY, I CAN'T RUN FOR A LITTLE WHILE AFTERWARDS.
HUH? HOW LONG?
OH, SIX DAYS.

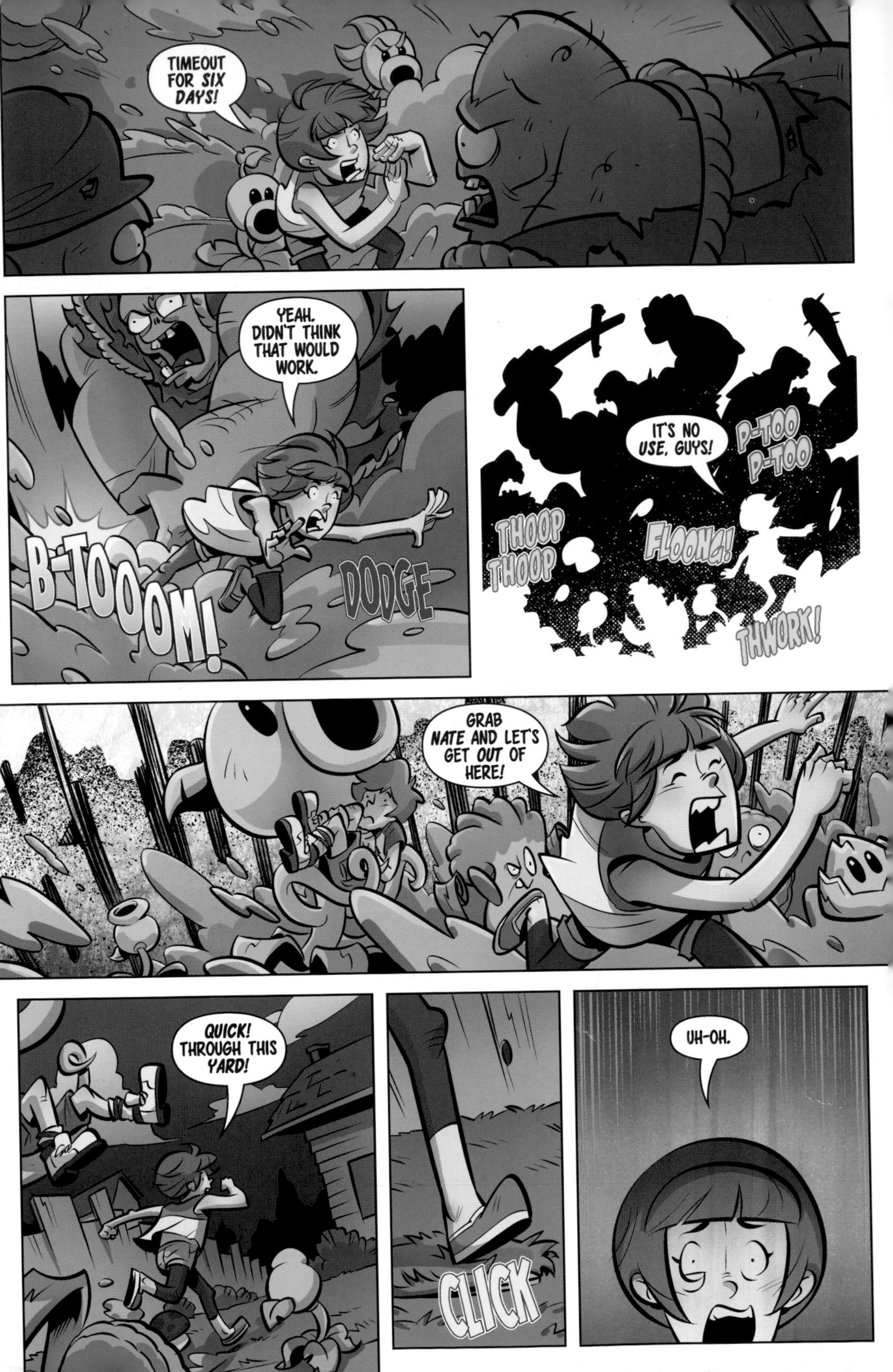
TIMEOUT FOR SIX DAYS!
YEAH. DIDN'T THINK THAT WOULD WORK.
B-TOOOOM!
DODGE
IT'S NO USE, GUYS!
P-TOO P-TOO
THOOP THOOP
FLOONG!
THWORK!
GRAB NATE AND LET'S GET OUT OF HERE!
QUICK! THROUGH THIS YARD!
CLICK
UH-OH.

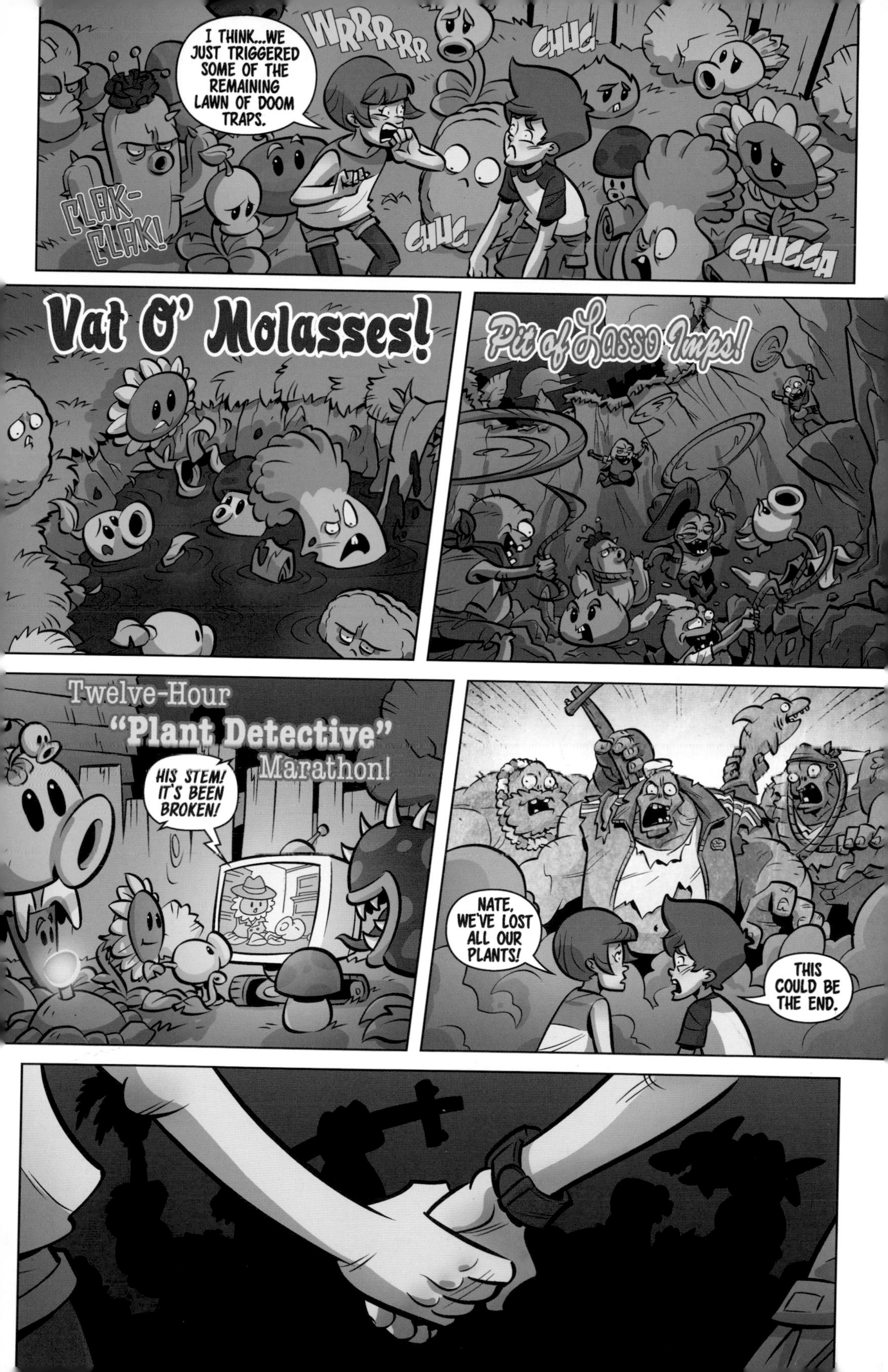

I THINK...WE JUST TRIGGERED SOME OF THE REMAINING LAWN OF DOOM TRAPS.
WRRRRRR
CHUG
CLAK-CLAK!
CHUG
CHUGGA
Vat O' Molasses!
Pit of Lasso Imps!
Twelve-Hour "Plant Detective" Marathon!
HIS STEM! IT'S BEEN BROKEN!
NATE, WE'VE LOST ALL OUR PLANTS!
THIS COULD BE THE END.

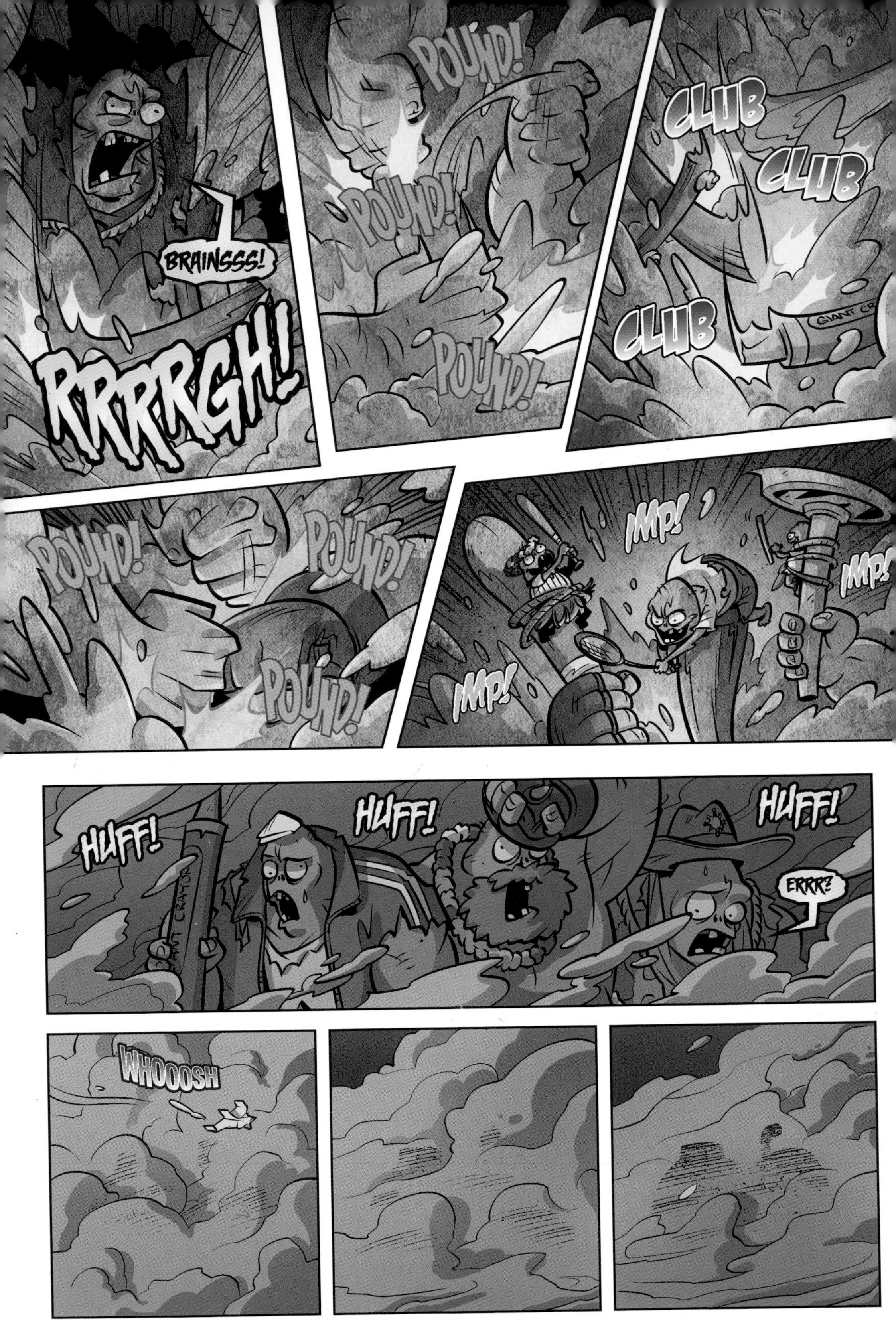
BRAINSSS!
RRRRGH!
POUND!
POUND!
POUND!
CLUB
CLUB
CLUB
GIANT CR
POUND!
POUND!
POUND!
IMP!
IMP!
IMP!
HUFF!
HUFF!
HUFF!
GIANT CRAYON
ERRR?
WHOOOSH

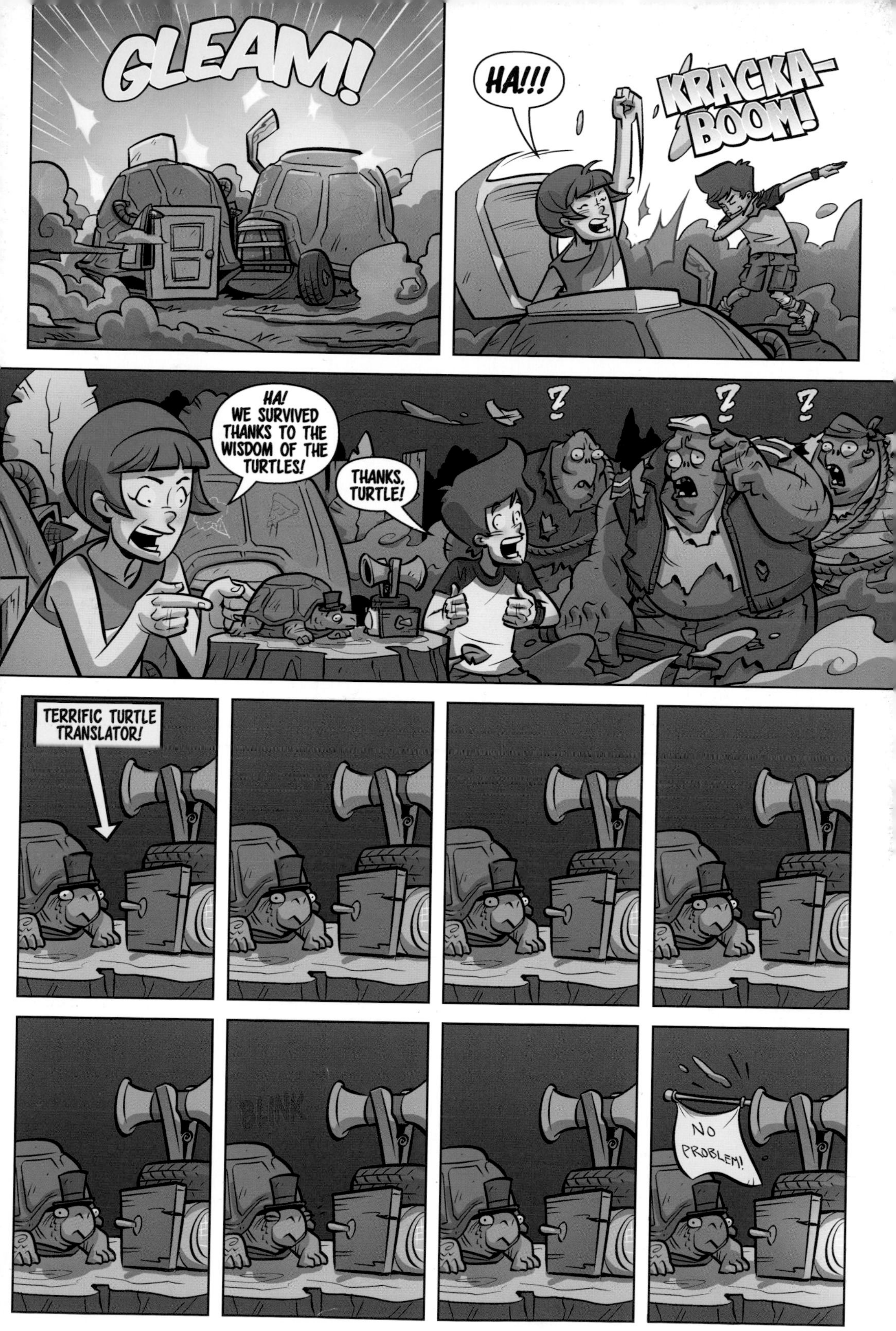
GLEAM!
HA!!!
KRACKA-BOOM!
HA! WE SURVIVED THANKS TO THE WISDOM OF THE TURTLES!
THANKS, TURTLE!
TERRIFIC TURTLE TRANSLATOR!
BLINK
NO PROBLEM!

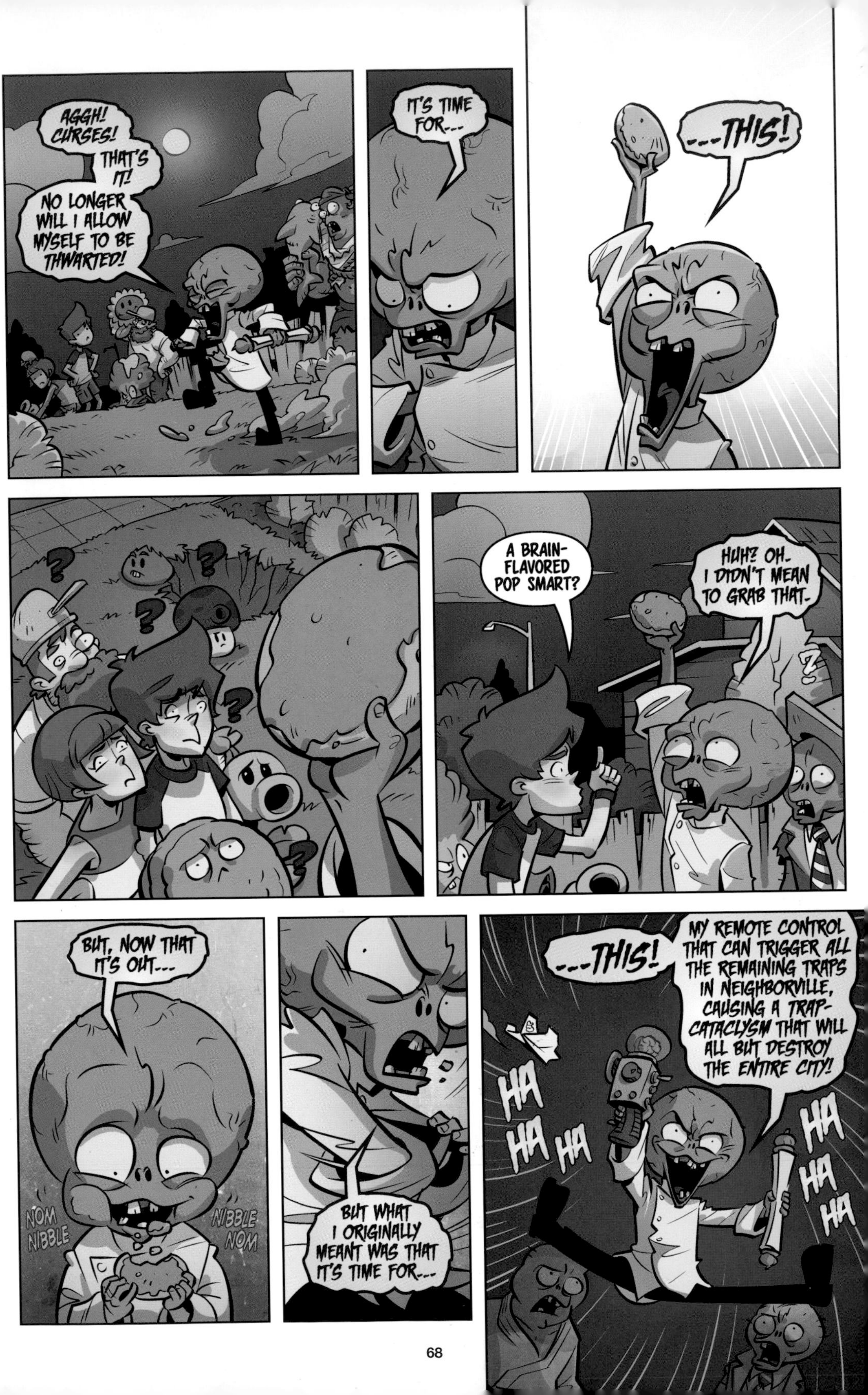

AGGH! CURSES!
THAT'S IT!
NO LONGER WILL I ALLOW MYSELF TO BE THWARTED!
IT'S TIME FOR...
...THIS!
A BRAIN-FLAVORED POP SMART?
HUH? OH. I DIDN'T MEAN TO GRAB THAT.
BUT, NOW THAT IT'S OUT...
NOM NIBBLE
NIBBLE NOM
BUT WHAT I ORIGINALLY MEANT WAS THAT IT'S TIME FOR...
...THIS!
MY REMOTE CONTROL THAT CAN TRIGGER ALL THE REMAINING TRAPS IN NEIGHBORVILLE, CAUSING A TRAP-CATACLYSM THAT WILL ALL BUT DESTROY THE ENTIRE CITY!
HA HA HA
HA HA HA HA

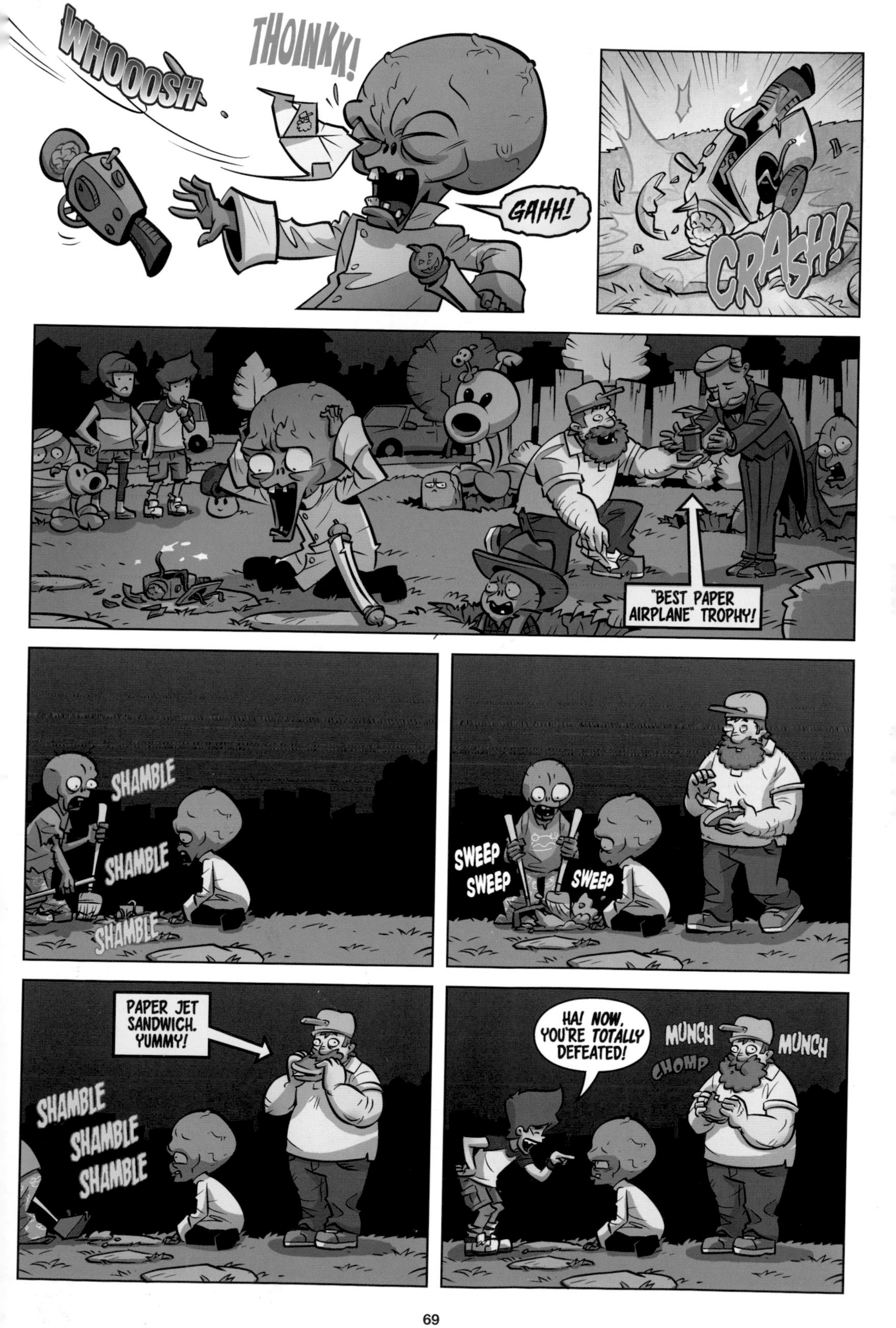
WHOOOOSH
THOINKK!
GAHH!
CRASH!
"BEST PAPER AIRPLANE" TROPHY!
SHAMBLE
SHAMBLE
SHAMBLE
SWEEP
SWEEP
SWEEP
PAPER JET SANDWICH. YUMMY!
SHAMBLE
SHAMBLE
SHAMBLE
HA! NOW, YOU'RE TOTALLY DEFEATED!
MUNCH
CHOMP
MUNCH

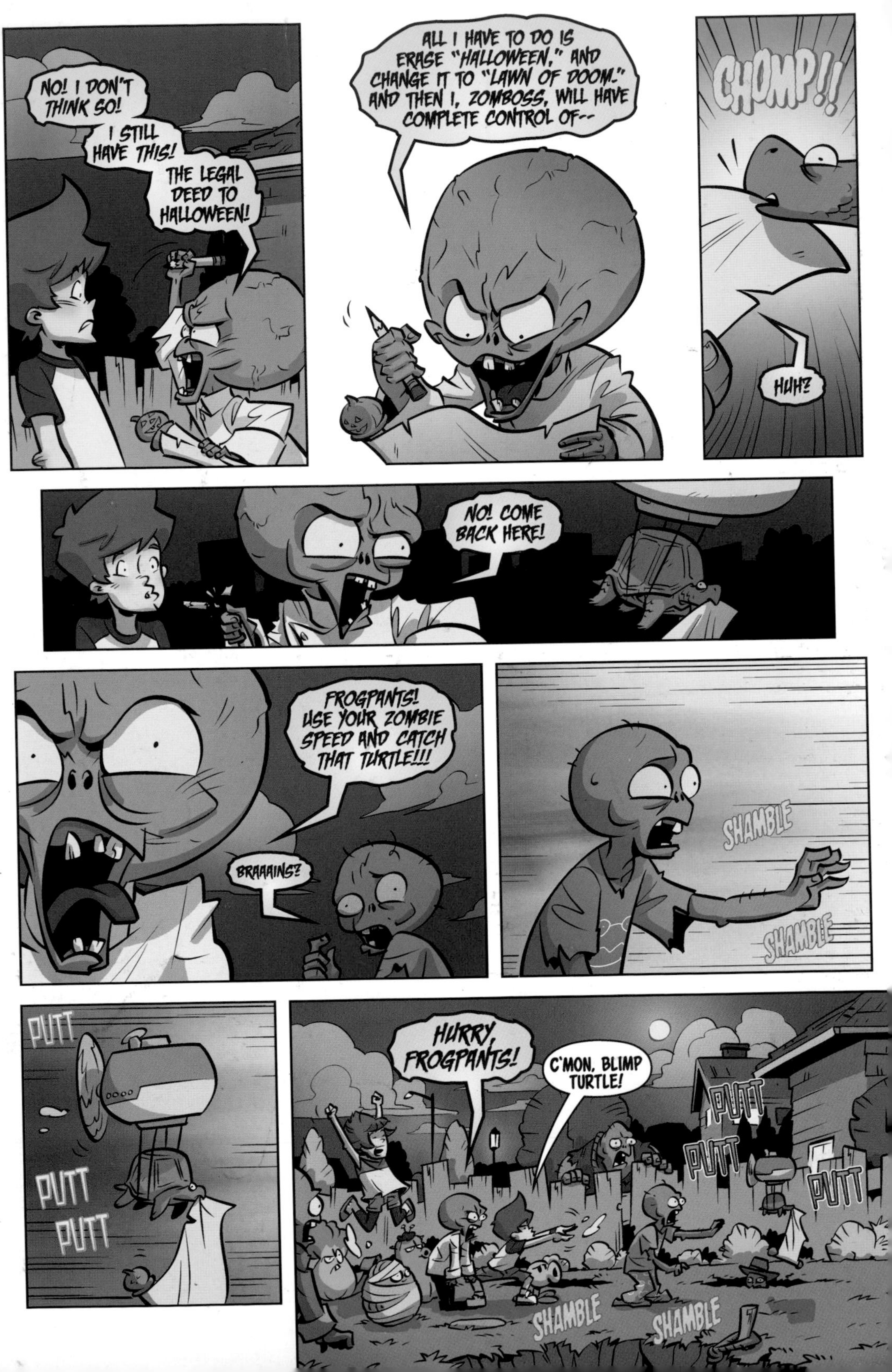
NO! I DON'T THINK SO!
I STILL HAVE THIS!
THE LEGAL DEED TO HALLOWEEN!
ALL I HAVE TO DO IS ERASE "HALLOWEEN," AND CHANGE IT TO "LAWN OF DOOM." AND THEN I, ZOMBOSS, WILL HAVE COMPLETE CONTROL OF--
CHOMP!!
HUH?
NO! COME BACK HERE!
FROGPANTS! USE YOUR ZOMBIE SPEED AND CATCH THAT TURTLE!!!
BRAAAINS?
SHAMBLE
SHAMBLE
PUTT
PUTT
PUTT
HURRY, FROGPANTS!
C'MON, BLIMP TURTLE!
PUTT
PUTT
PUTT
SHAMBLE
SHAMBLE

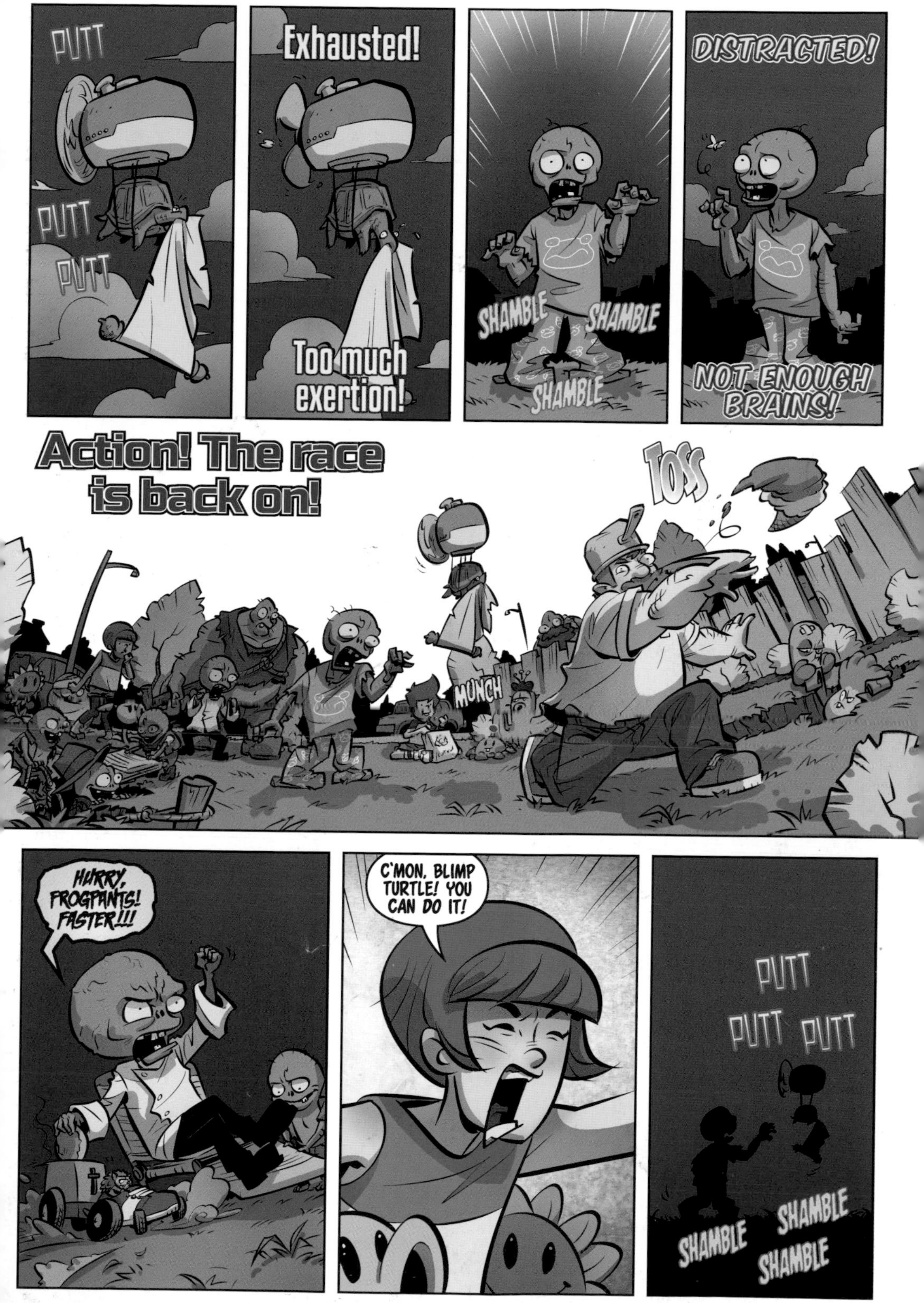
PUTT
PUTT
PUTT
Exhausted!
Too much exertion!
SHAMBLE
SHAMBLE
SHAMBLE
DISTRACTED!
NOT ENOUGH BRAINS!
Action! The race is back on!
TOSS
MUNCH
HURRY, FROGPANTS! FASTER!!!
C'MON, BLIMP TURTLE! YOU CAN DO IT!
PUTT
PUTT PUTT
SHAMBLE
SHAMBLE
SHAMBLE

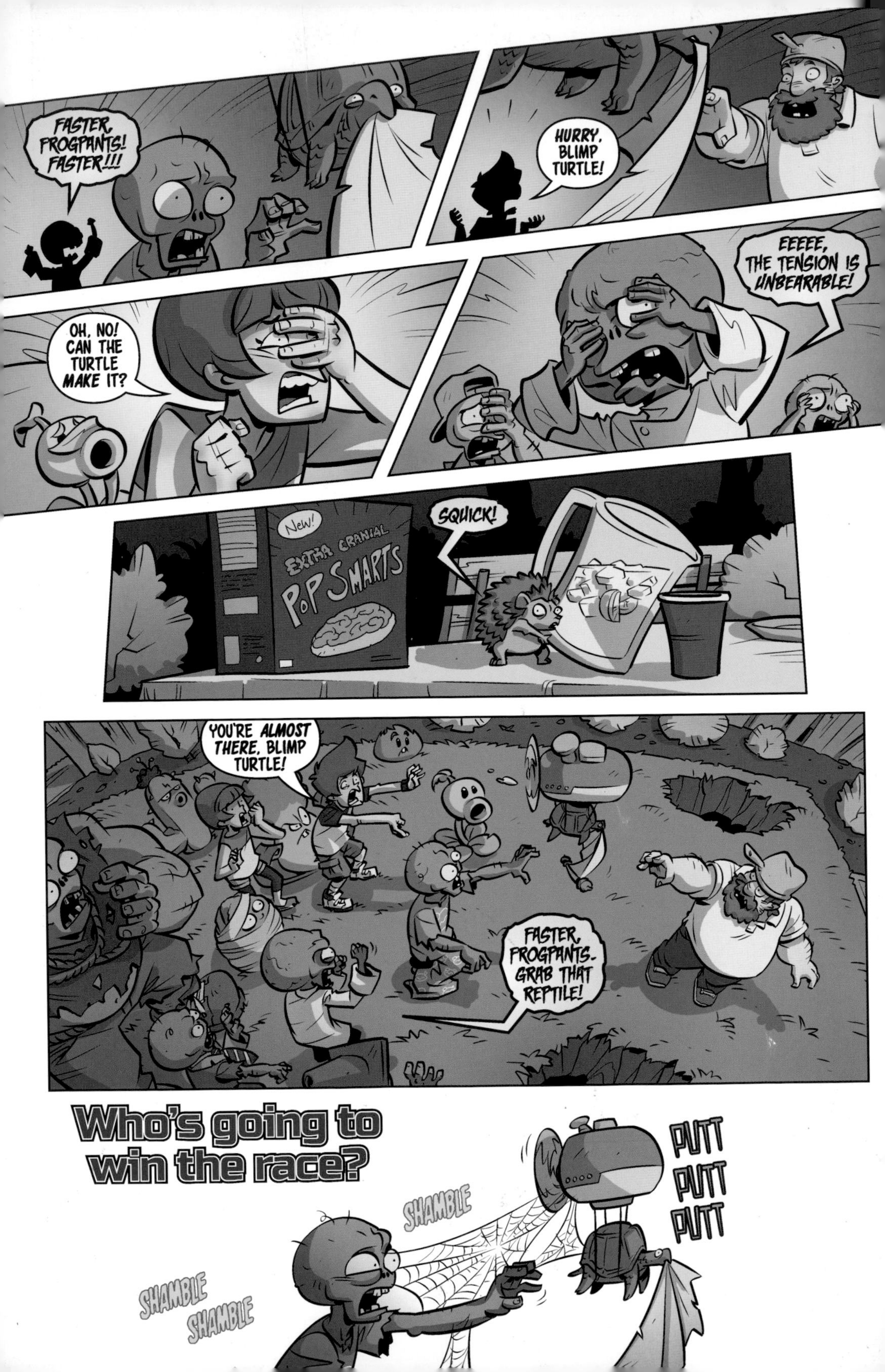

FASTER, FROGPANTS! FASTER!!!
HURRY, BLIMP TURTLE!
OH, NO! CAN THE TURTLE MAKE IT?
EEEEE, THE TENSION IS UNBEARABLE!
New!
EXTRA CRANIAL
POP SMARTS
SQUICK!
YOU'RE ALMOST THERE, BLIMP TURTLE!
FASTER, FROGPANTS- GRAB THAT REPTILE!
Who's going to win the race?
PUTT PUTT PUTT
SHAMBLE
SHAMBLE SHAMBLE

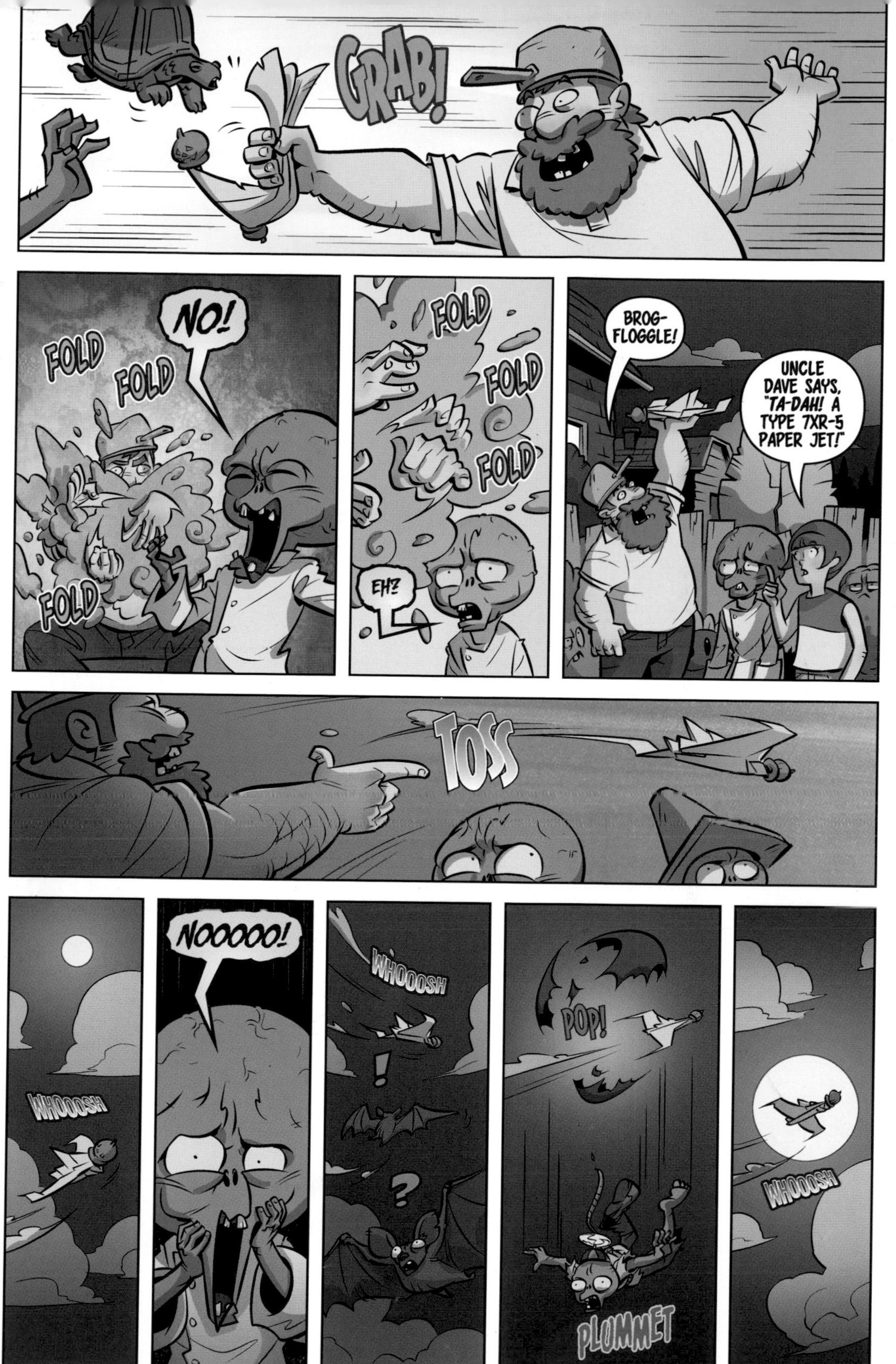
GRAB!
NO!
FOLD
FOLD
FOLD
FOLD
FOLD
FOLD
EH?
BROG-FLOGGLE!
UNCLE DAVE SAYS, "TA-DAH! A TYPE 7XR-5 PAPER JET!"
TOSS
WHOOOSH
NOOOOO!
WHOOOSH
!
?
POP!
PLUMMET
WHOOOSH

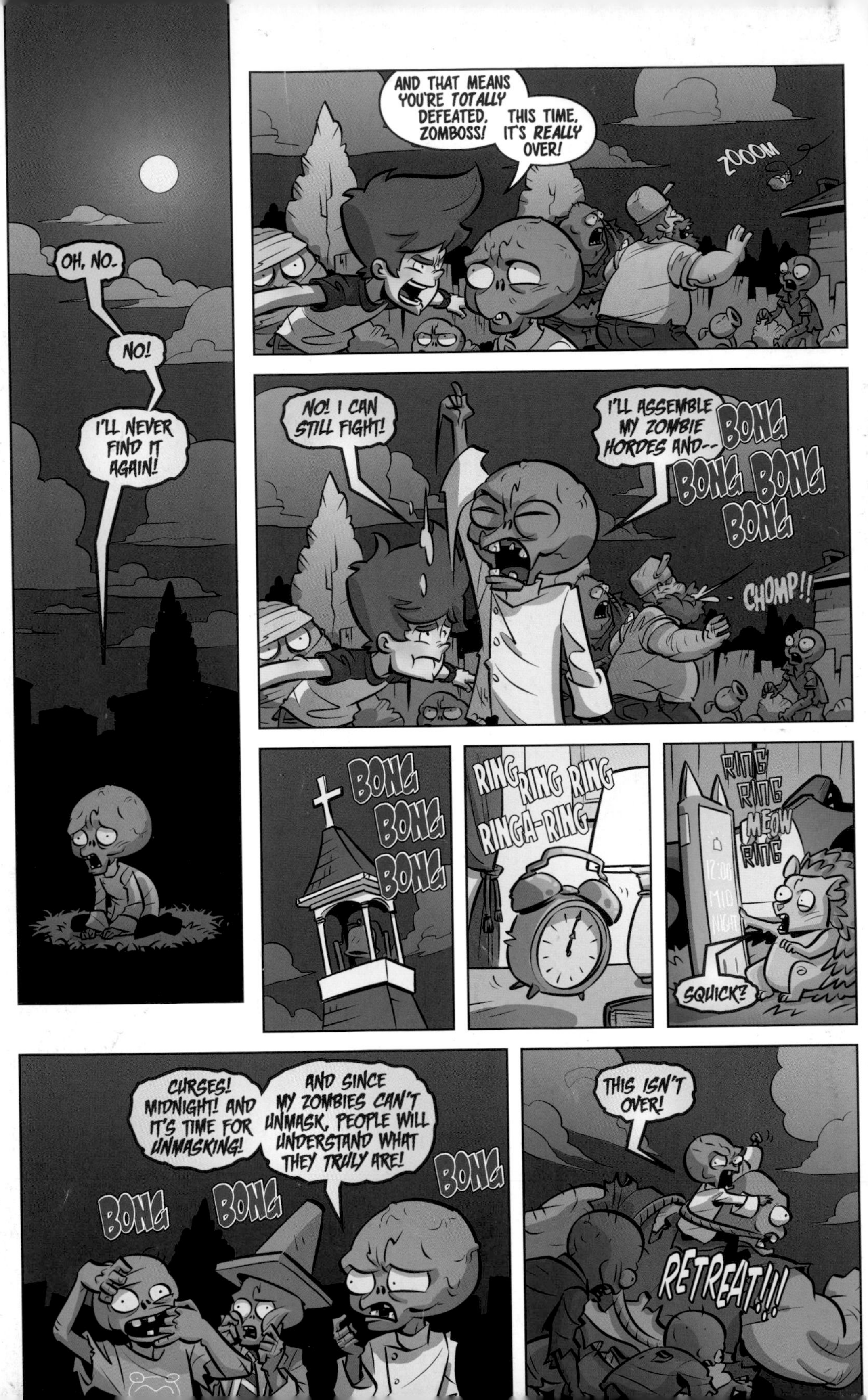
OH, NO.
NO!
I'LL NEVER FIND IT AGAIN!
AND THAT MEANS YOU'RE TOTALLY DEFEATED, ZOMBOSS!
THIS TIME, IT'S REALLY OVER!
ZOOOM
NO! I CAN STILL FIGHT!
I'LL ASSEMBLE MY ZOMBIE HORDES AND--
BONG
BONG BONG
BONG
CHOMP!!
BONG
BONG
BONG
RING RING RING
RINGA-RING
RING
RING
MEOW
RING
12:00
MID
NIGHT
SQUICK?
CURSES! MIDNIGHT! AND IT'S TIME FOR UNMASKING!
AND SINCE MY ZOMBIES CAN'T UNMASK, PEOPLE WILL UNDERSTAND WHAT THEY TRULY ARE!
BONG
BONG
BONG
THIS ISN'T OVER!
RETREAT!!!

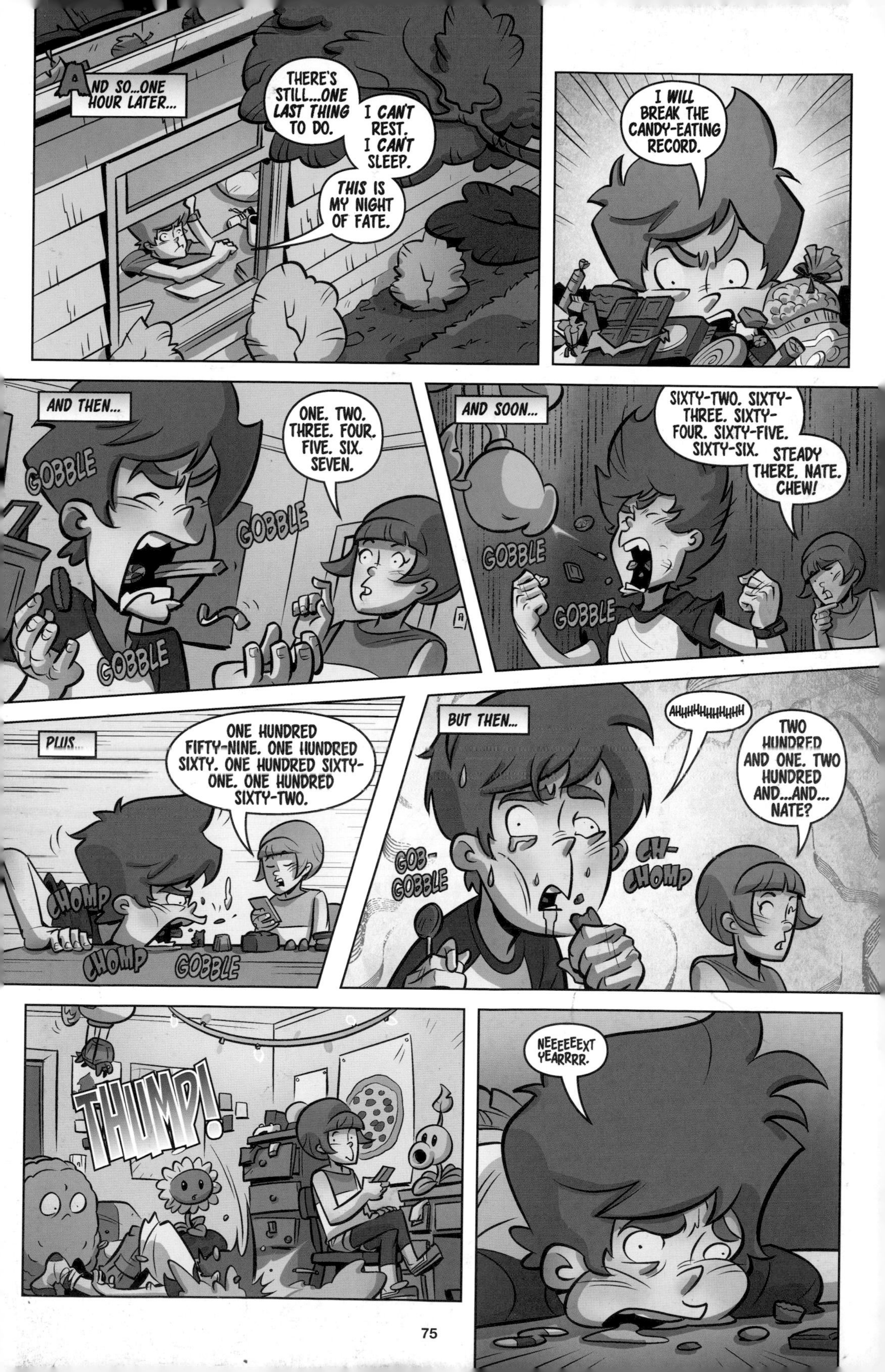
AND SO...ONE HOUR LATER...
THERE'S STILL...ONE LAST THING TO DO.
I CAN'T REST. I CAN'T SLEEP.
THIS IS MY NIGHT OF FATE.
I WILL BREAK THE CANDY-EATING RECORD.
AND THEN...
ONE. TWO. THREE. FOUR. FIVE. SIX. SEVEN.
GOBBLE
GOBBLE
GOBBLE
AND SOON...
SIXTY-TWO. SIXTY-THREE. SIXTY-FOUR. SIXTY-FIVE. SIXTY-SIX.
STEADY THERE, NATE. CHEW!
GOBBLE
GOBBLE
PLUS...
ONE HUNDRED FIFTY-NINE. ONE HUNDRED SIXTY. ONE HUNDRED SIXTY-ONE. ONE HUNDRED SIXTY-TWO.
CHOMP
CHOMP
GOBBLE
BUT THEN...
AHHHHHHHHHHH
TWO HUNDRED AND ONE. TWO HUNDRED AND...AND... NATE?
GOB-GOBBLE
CH-CHOMP
THUMP!
NEEEEEEXT YEARRRR.

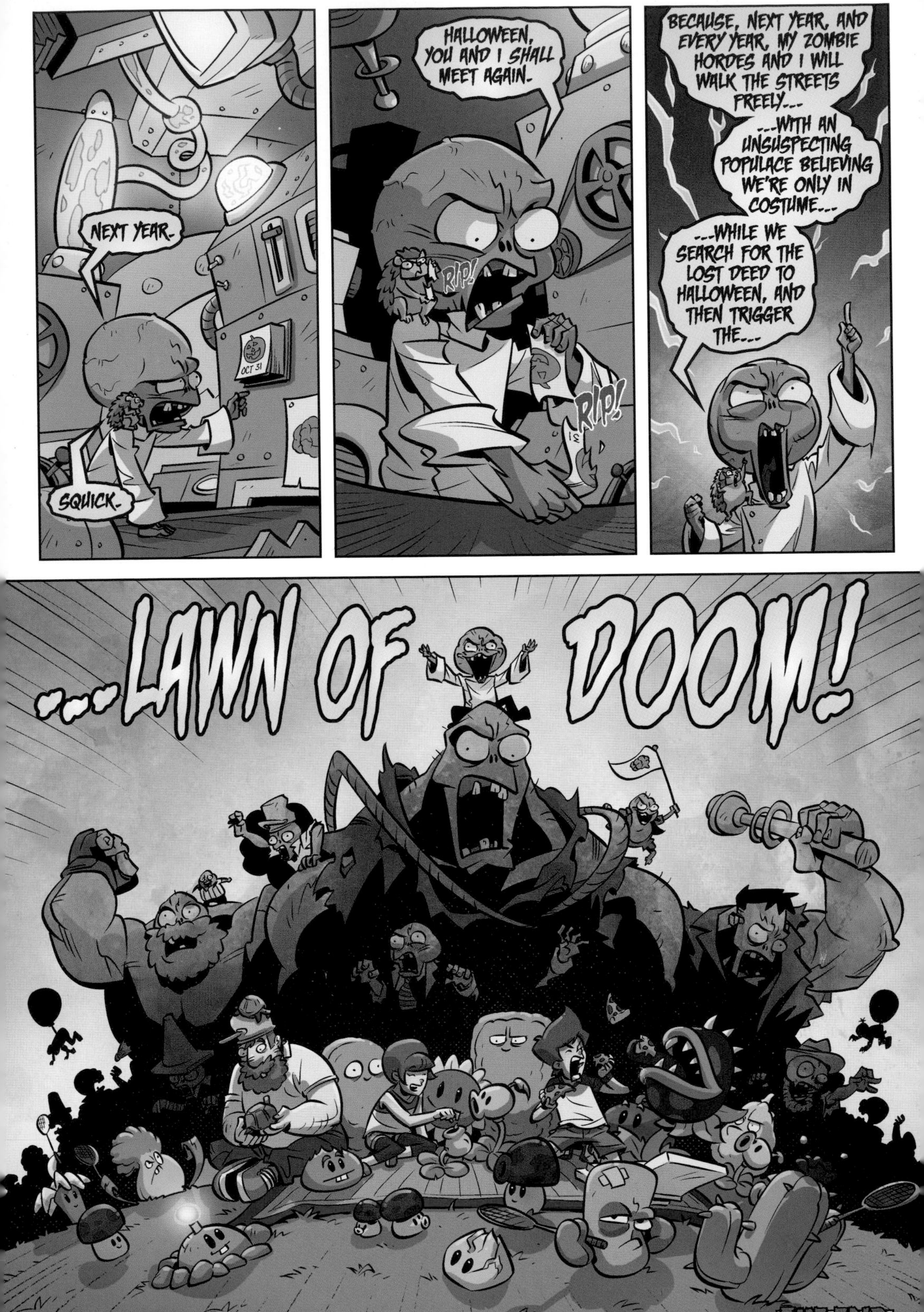
NEXT YEAR.
SQUICK.
OCT 31
HALLOWEEN, YOU AND I SHALL MEET AGAIN.
RIP!
RIP!
BECAUSE, NEXT YEAR, AND EVERY YEAR, MY ZOMBIE HORDES AND I WILL WALK THE STREETS FREELY...
...WITH AN UNSUSPECTING POPULACE BELIEVING WE'RE ONLY IN COSTUME...
...WHILE WE SEARCH FOR THE LOST DEED TO HALLOWEEN, AND THEN TRIGGER THE...
...LAWN OF DOOM!
THE END

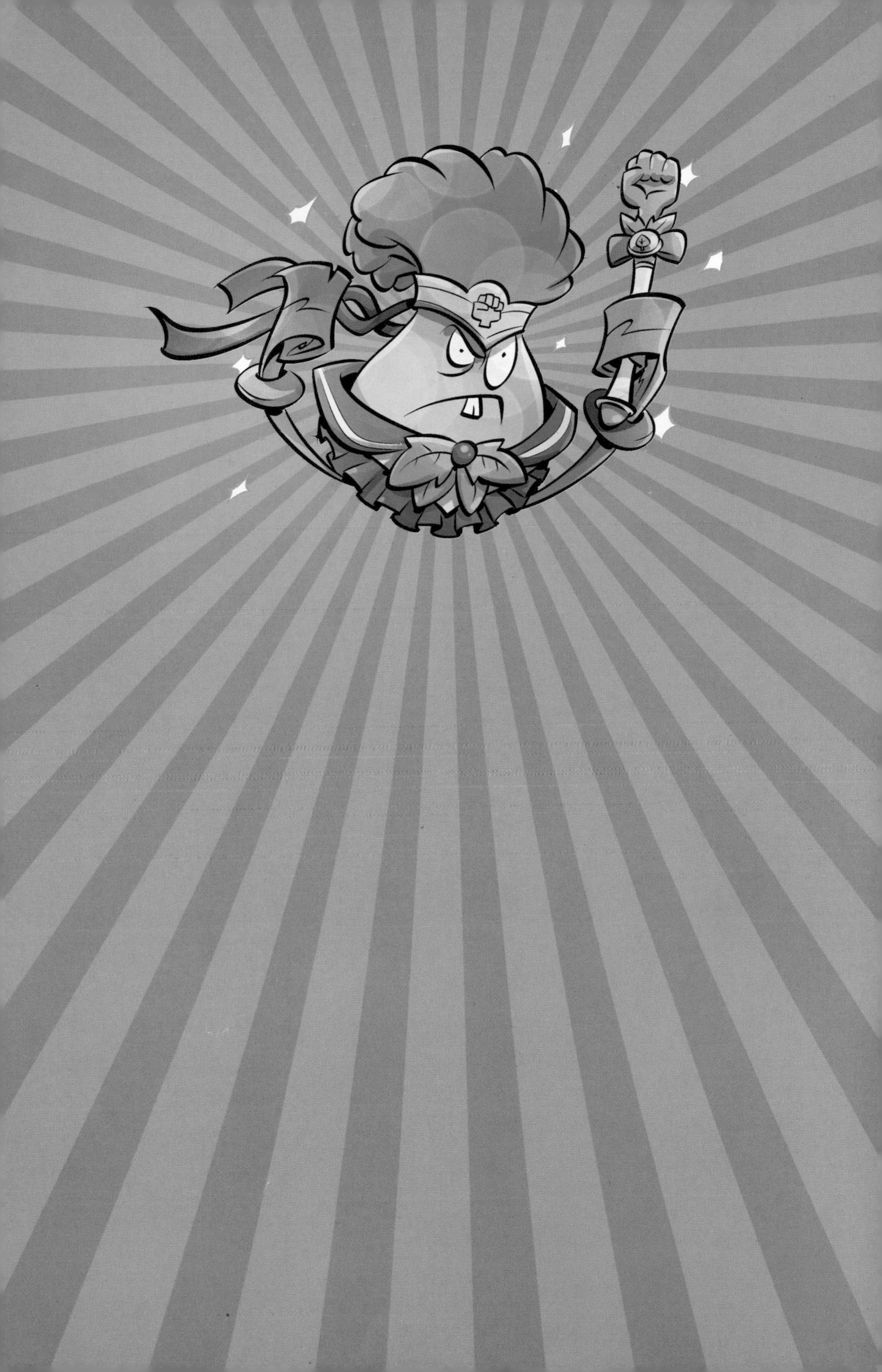

PLANTS VS. ZOMBIES: LAWN OF DOOM
cover pencils by RON CHAN

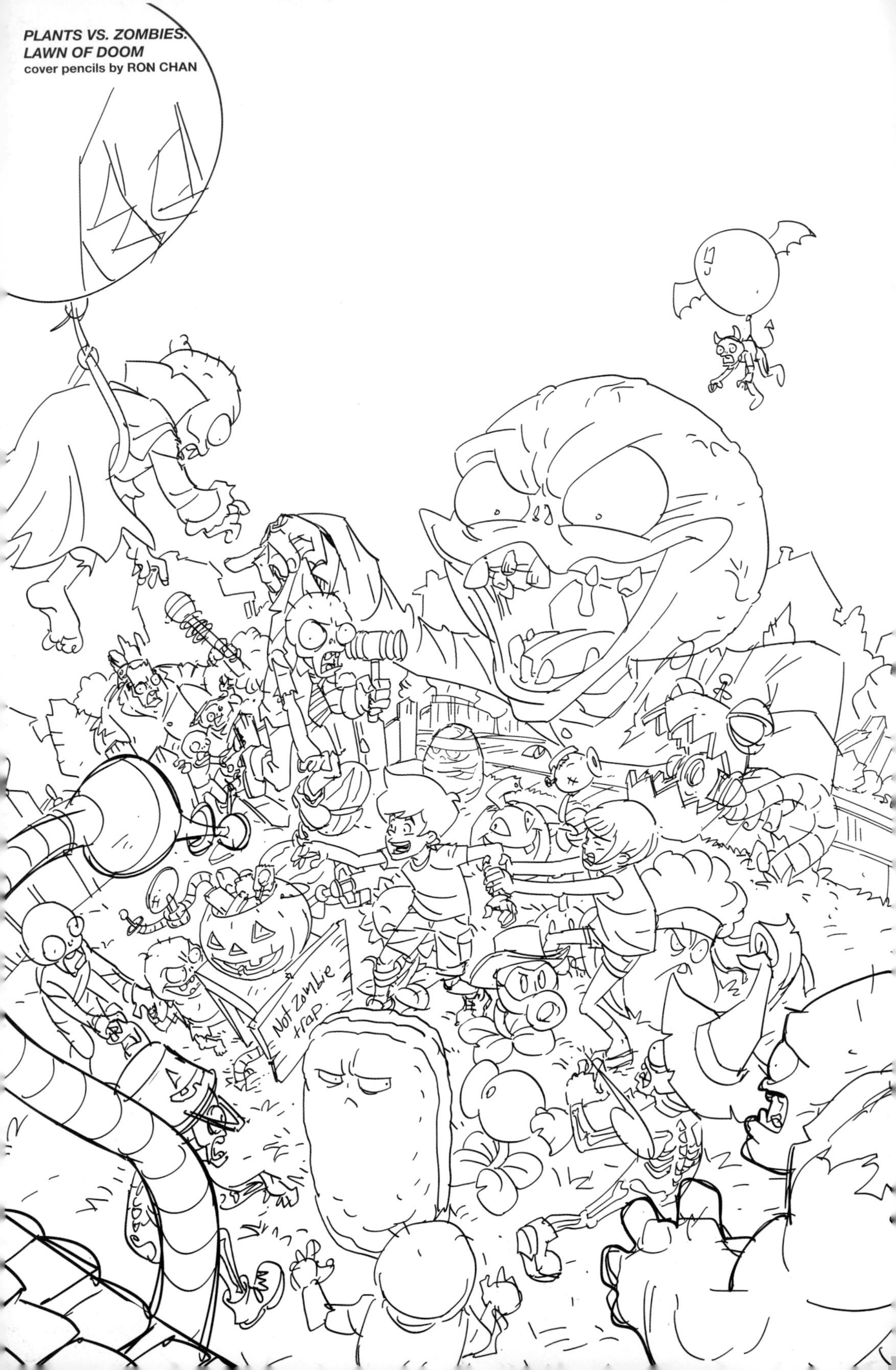
Not Zombie trap.

PLANTS VS. ZOMBIES: LAWN OF DOOM
cover inks by RON CHAN

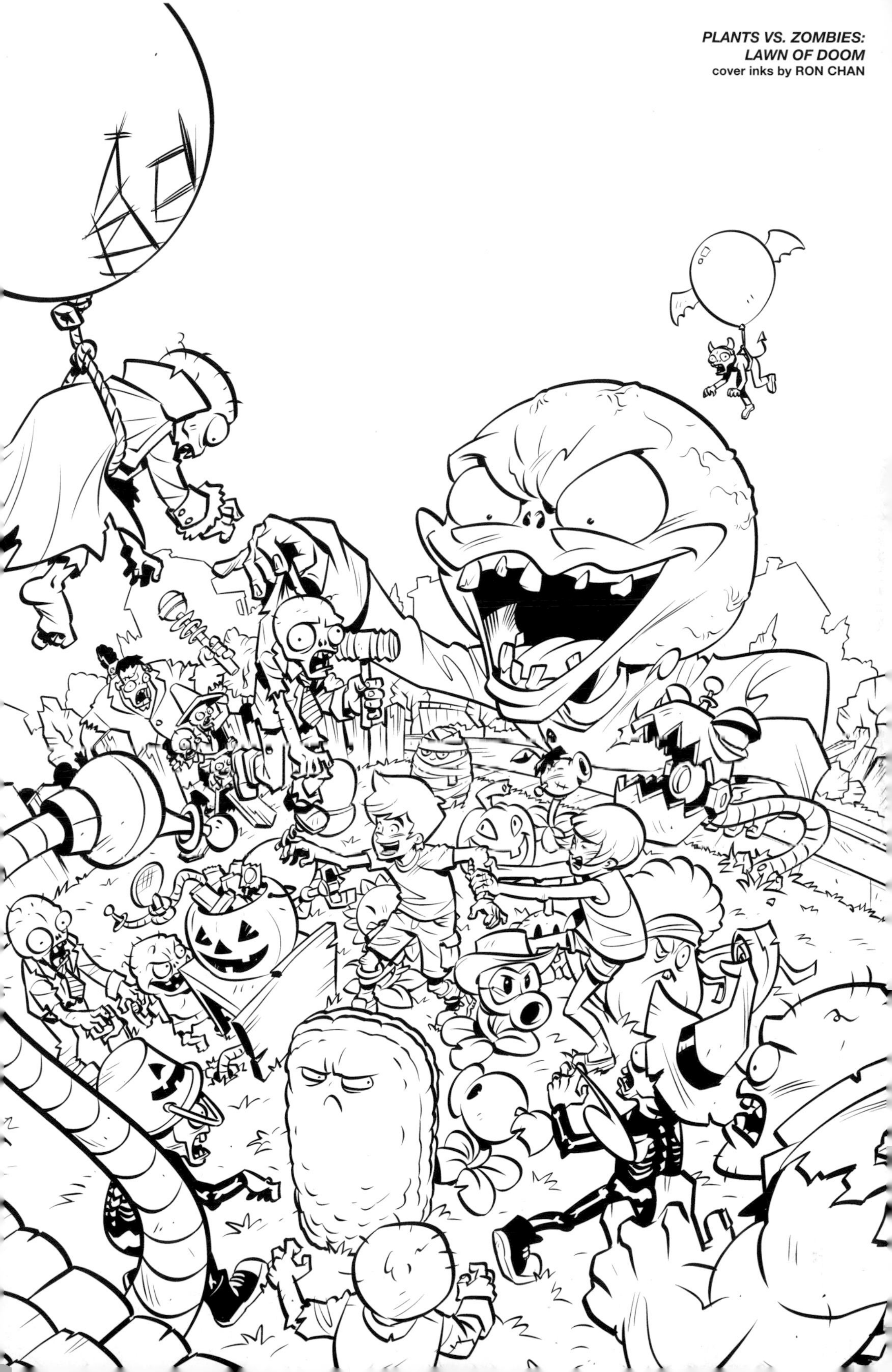

PENCIL ART FROM *LAWN OF DOOM* PAGES 38–41 BY RON CHAN!

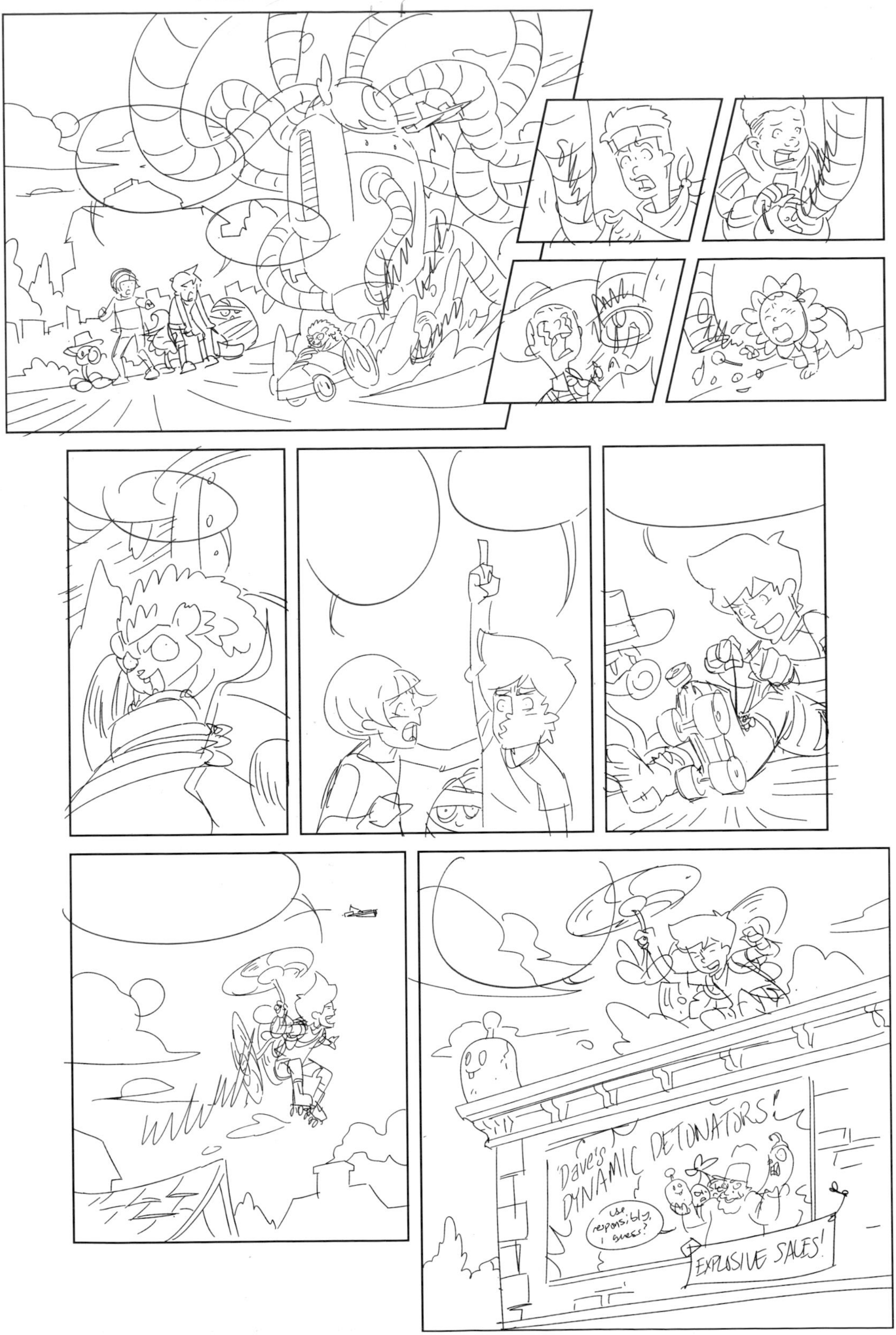
'Dave's DYNAMIC DETONATORS!
use responsibly, I guess?
EXPLOSIVE SALES!

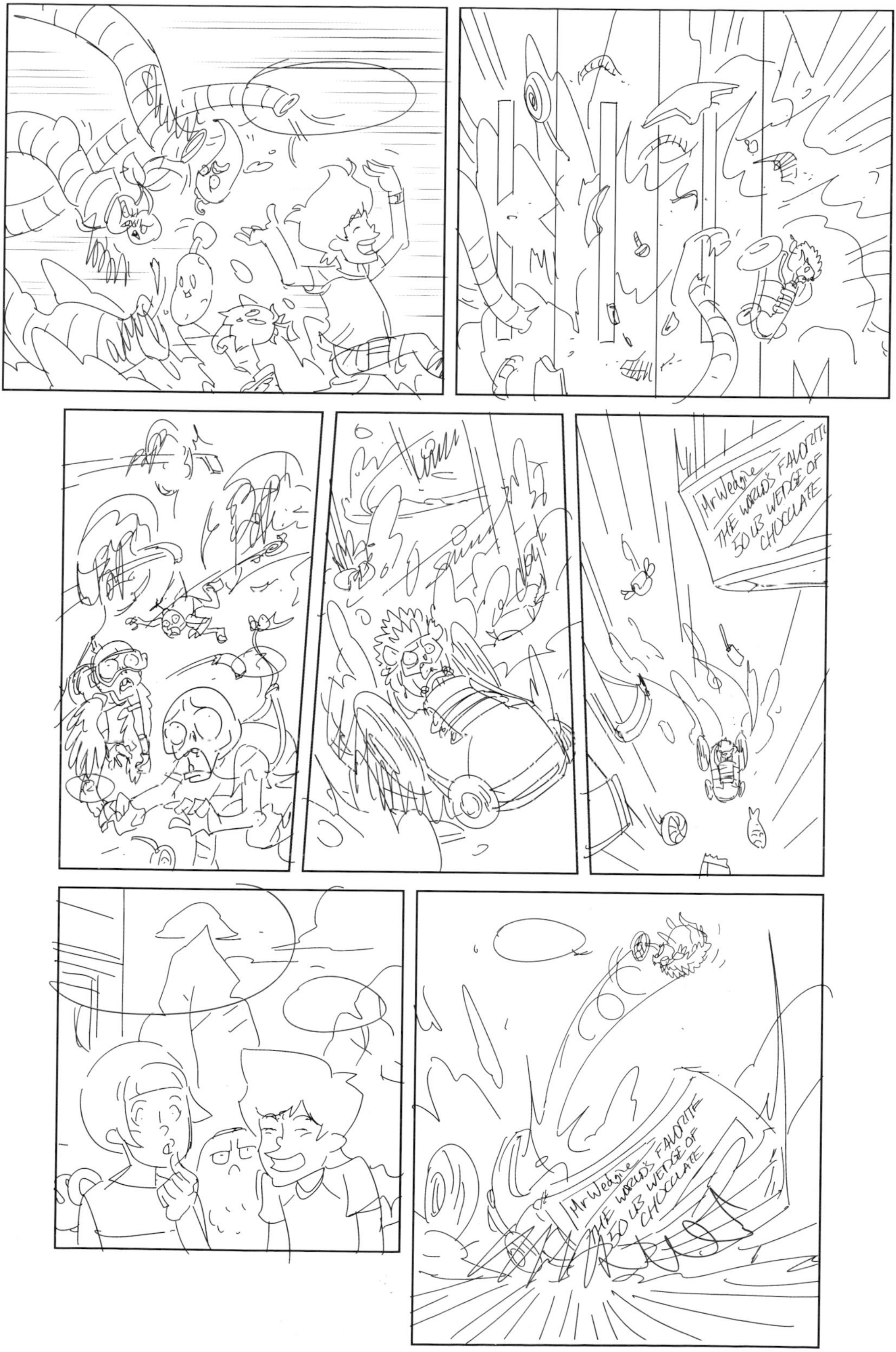
Mr Wedgie
THE WORLD'S FAVORITE
50 LB WEDGE OF
CHOCOLATE
Mr Wedgie
THE WORLD'S FAVORITE
50 LB WEDGE OF
CHOCOLATE

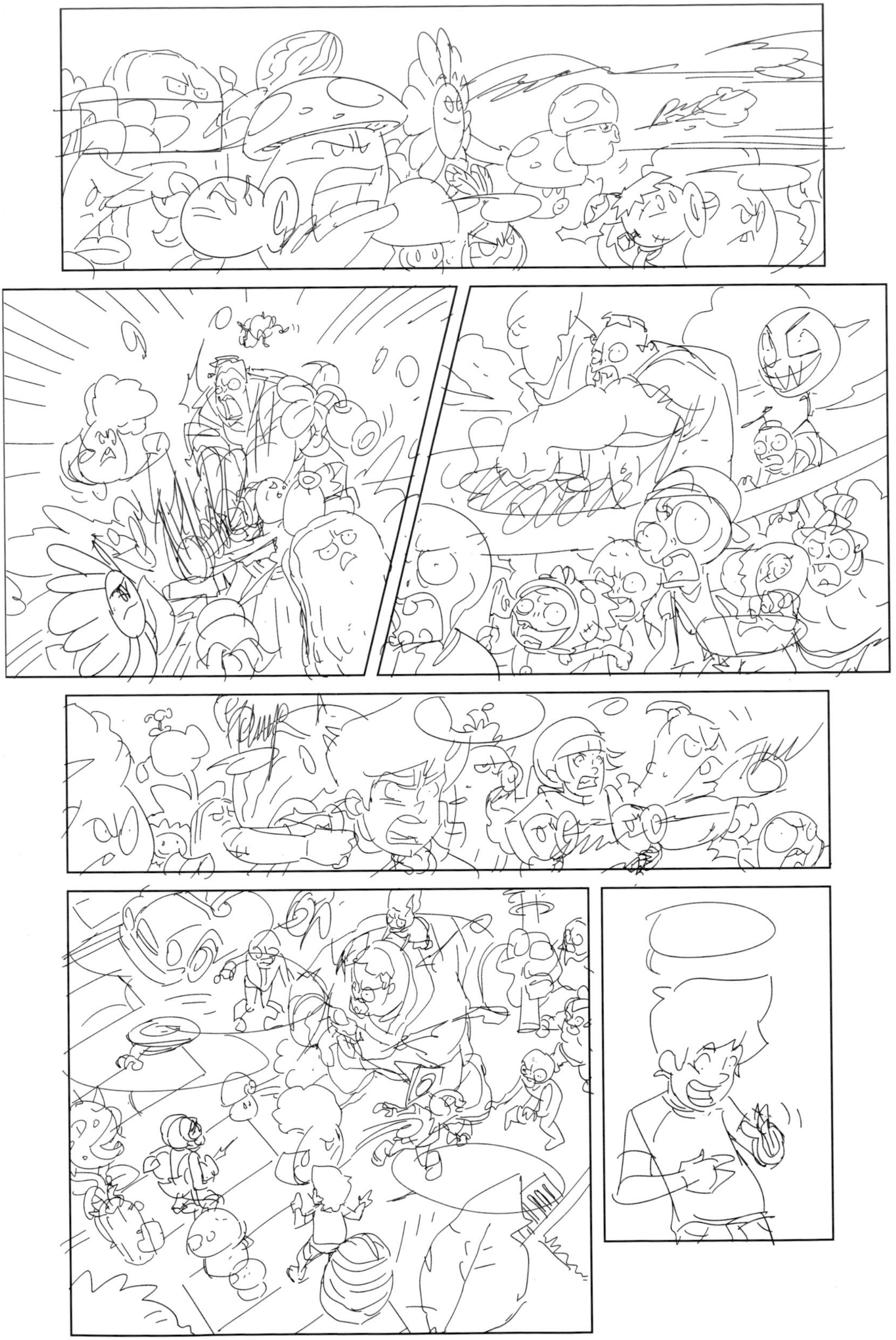

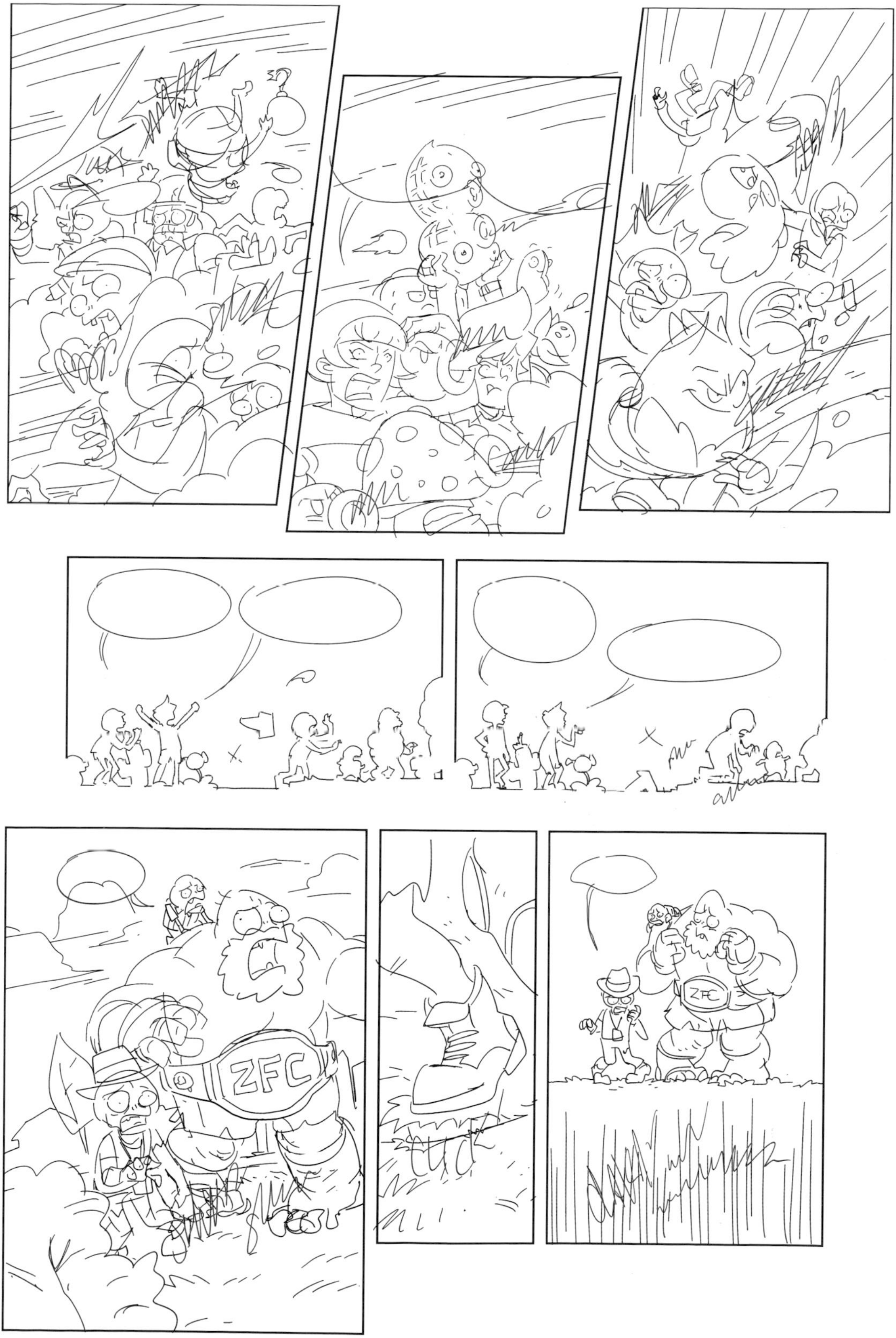
ZFC
ZFC

CREATOR BIOS

Paul Tobin

Ron Chan

PAUL TOBIN enjoys that his author photo makes him look insane, and he once accidentally cut his ear with a potato chip. He doesn't know how it happened, either. Life is so full of mystery. If you ask him about the Potato Chip Incident, he'll just make up a story. That's what he does. He's written hundreds of stories for Marvel, DC, Dark Horse, and many others, including such creator-owned titles as *Colder* and *Bandette*, as well as *Prepare to Die!*—his debut novel. His *Genius Factor* series of novels about a fifth-grade genius and his war against the Red Death Tea Society debuted in March 2016 with *How to Capture an Invisible Cat*, from Bloomsbury Publishing, and continued in early 2017 with *How to Outsmart a Billion Robot Bees*. Paul has won some Very Important Awards for his writing but so far none for his karaoke skills.

RON CHAN is a comic book and storyboard artist, video game fan, and occasional jujitsu practitioner. He was born and raised in Portland, Oregon, where he still lives and works as a member of the local artist collective Helioscope. His comics work has been published by Dark Horse, Marvel, and Image Comics, and his storyboarding work includes boards for 3D animation, gaming, user-experience design, and advertising for clients such as Microsoft, Amazon Kindle, Nike, and Sega. He really likes drawing Bonk Choys. (He also enjoys eating actual bok choy in real life.)

Matt J. Rainwater

Steve Dutro

Residing in the cool, damp forests of Portland, Oregon, **MATT J. RAINWATER** is a freelance illustrator whose work has been featured in advertising, web design, and independent video games. On top of this, he also self-publishes several comic books, including *Trailer Park Warlock*, *Garage Raja*, and *The Feeling Is Multiplied*—all of which can be found at MattJRainwater.com. His favorite zombie-bashing strategy utilizes a line of Bonk Choys with a Wall-nut front guard and Threepeater covering fire.

STEVE DUTRO is an Eisner Award-nominated comic-book letterer from Redding, California, who can also drive a tractor. He graduated from the Kubert School and has been lettering comics since the days when foil-embossed covers were cool, working for Dark Horse (*The Fifth Beatle*, *I Am a Hero*, *Planet of the Apes*, *Star Wars*), Viz, Marvel, and DC. He has submitted a request to the Department of Homeland Security that in the event of a zombie apocalypse he be put in charge of all digital freeway signs so citizens can be alerted to avoid nearby brain-eatings and the like. He finds the *Plants vs. Zombies* game to be a real stress-fest, but highly recommends the *Plants vs. Zombies* table on *Pinball FX2* for game-room hipsters.

ALSO AVAILABLE FROM DARK HORSE!

THE HIT VIDEO GAME CONTINUES ITS COMIC BOOK INVASION!

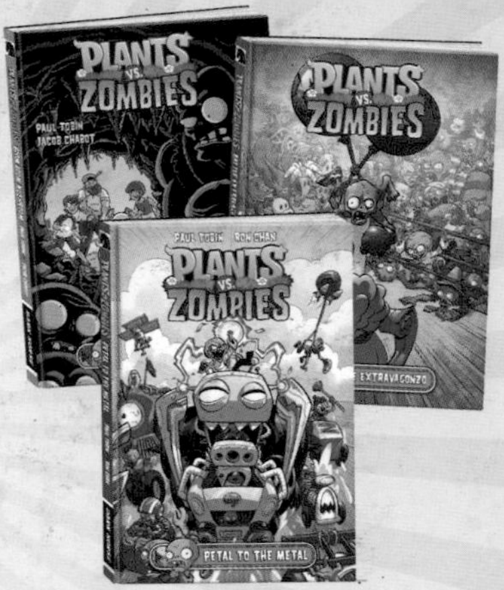
PLANTS vs. ZOMBIES
PAUL TOBIN
JACOB CHABOT
PLANTS vs. ZOMBIES
EXTRAVAGONZO
PAUL TOBIN
RON CHAN
PLANTS vs. ZOMBIES
PETAL TO THE METAL

PLANTS VS. ZOMBIES: LAWNMAGEDDON
Crazy Dave—the babbling-yet-brilliant inventor and top-notch neighborhood defender—helps young adventurer Nate fend off a zombie invasion that threatens to overrun the peaceful town of Neighborville in *Plants vs. Zombies: Lawnmageddon*! Their only hope is a brave army of chomping, squashing, and pea-shooting plants! A wacky adventure for zombie zappers young and old!
ISBN 978-1-61655-192-6 | $9.99

THE ART OF PLANTS VS. ZOMBIES
Part zombie memoir, part celebration of zombie triumphs, and part anti-plant screed, *The Art of Plants vs. Zombies* is a treasure trove of never-before-seen concept art, character sketches, and surprises from PopCap's popular Plants vs. Zombies games!
ISBN 978-1-61655-331-9 | $9.99

PLANTS VS. ZOMBIES: TIMEPOCALYPSE
Crazy Dave helps Patrice and Nate Timely fend off Zomboss's latest attack in *Plants vs. Zombies: Timepocalypse*! This new standalone tale will tickle your funny bones and thrill your brains through any timeline!
ISBN 978-1-61655-621-1 | $9.99

PLANTS VS. ZOMBIES: BULLY FOR YOU
Patrice and Nate are ready to investigate a strange college campus to keep the streets safe from zombies!
ISBN 978-1-61655-889-5 | $9.99

PLANTS VS. ZOMBIES: GARDEN WARFARE
Based on the hit video game, this comic tells the story leading up to the events in *Plants vs. Zombies: Garden Warfare 2*!
ISBN 978-1-61655-946-5 | $9.99

PLANTS VS. ZOMBIES: GROWN SWEET HOME
With newfound knowledge of humanity, Dr. Zomboss strikes at the heart of Neighborville . . . sparking a series of plant-versus-zombie brawls!
ISBN 978-1-61655-971-7 | $9.99

PLANTS VS. ZOMBIES: PETAL TO THE METAL
Crazy Dave takes on the tough *Don't Blink* video game—and challenges Dr. Zomboss to a race to determine the future of Neighborville!
ISBN 978-1-61655-999-1 | $9.99

PLANTS VS. ZOMBIES: BOOM BOOM MUSHROOM
The gang discover Zomboss' secret plan for swallowing the city of Neighborville whole! A rare mushroom must be found in order to save the humans aboveground!
ISBN 978-1-50670-037-3 | $9.99

PLANTS VS. ZOMBIES: BATTLE EXTRAVAGONZO
Zomboss is back, hoping to buy the same factory that Crazy Dave is eyeing! Will Crazy Dave and his intelligent plants beat Zomboss and his zombie army to the punch?
ISBN 978-1-50670-189-9 | $9.99

PLANTS VS. ZOMBIES: LAWN OF DOOM
With Zomboss filling everyone's yards with traps and special soldiers, will he and his zombie army turn Halloween into their scarier Lawn of Doom celebration?!
ISBN 978-1-50670-204-9 | $9.99

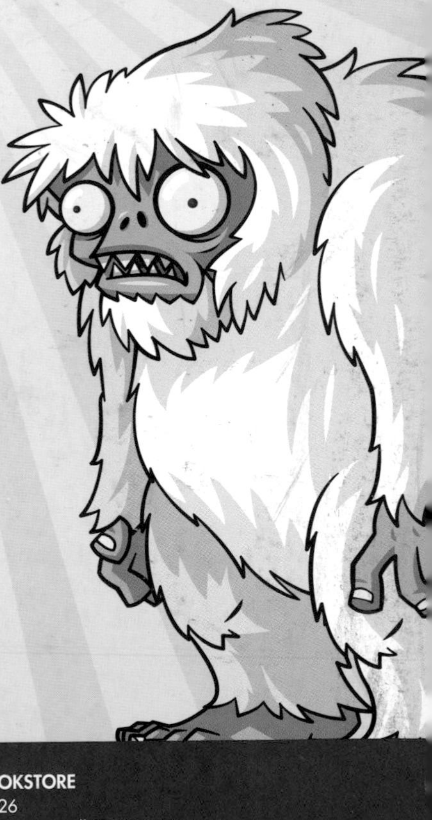

DARK HORSE BOOKS
EA
PopCap

AVAILABLE AT YOUR LOCAL COMICS SHOP OR BOOKSTORE
To find a comics shop in your area, call 1-888-266-4226
For more information or to order direct visit **DarkHorse.com** or call 1-800-862-0052

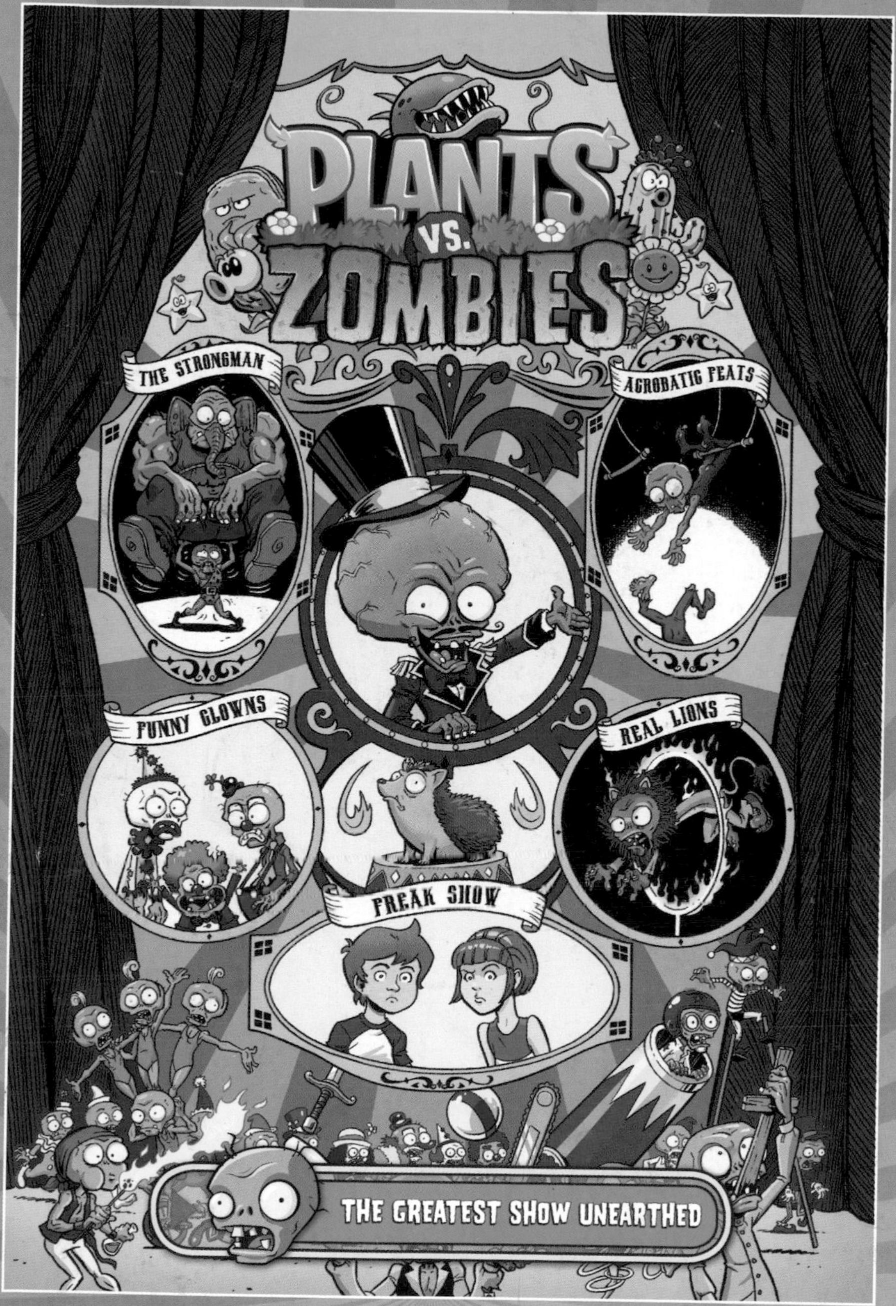
PLANTS VS. ZOMBIES
THE STRONGMAN
ACROBATIC FEATS
FUNNY CLOWNS
REAL LIONS
FREAK SHOW
THE GREATEST SHOW UNEARTHED

PLANTS VS. ZOMBIES: THE GREATEST SHOW UNEARTHED
COMING TO TOWN FEBRUARY 2018!

Dr. Zomboss thinks that all humans hold a secret desire to run away and join the circus, so he aims to use his newly created Big Z's Adequately Amazing Flytrap Circus to lure Neighborville's citizens to their doom! Once plant-friendly neighborhood defenders Nate and Patrice infiltrate his show, though, Ringmaster Zomboss and his hapless zombies are in for a garden-ful of trouble!

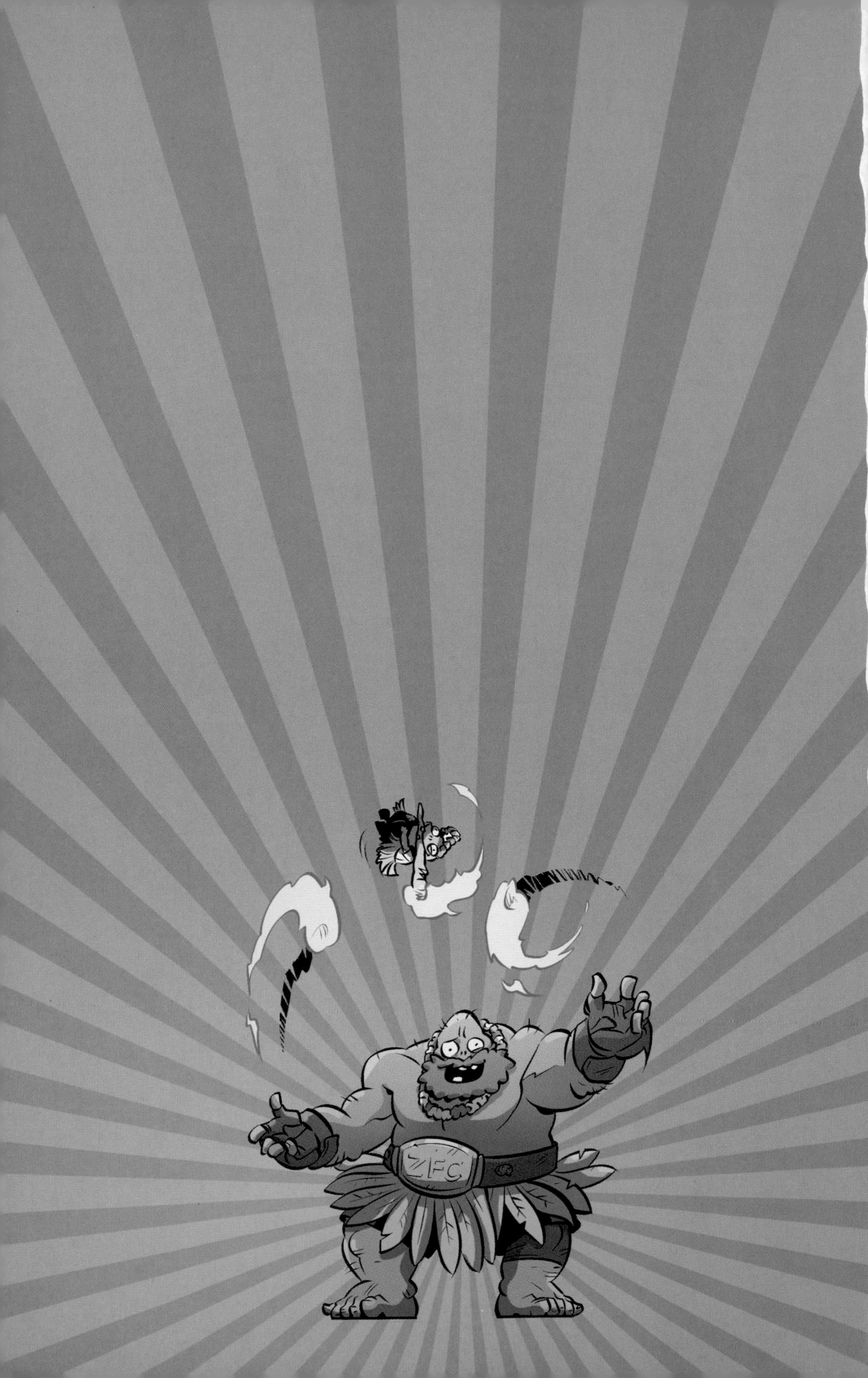
ZLFC